Julie Shackman is a feel-good journalist.

She lives in Scotland with her l̲   ̲a̲n̲d̲ ̲t̲h̲e̲i̲r̲ little Romanian rescue pup, Cooper.

julieshackman.co.uk

x.com/G13Julie
instagram.com/juliegeorginashackman
facebook.com/julie.shackman
bookbub.com/authors/julie-shackman

Also by Julie Shackman

A Secret Scottish Escape

A Scottish Highland Surprise

The Cottage in the Highlands

A Scottish Country Escape

The Highland Lodge Getaway

The Bookshop by the Loch

A Scottish Island Hideaway

A Scottish Island Summer

A SCOTTISH LIGHTHOUSE ESCAPE

Scottish Escapes

JULIE SHACKMAN

ONE MORE CHAPTER

One More Chapter
a division of HarperCollins*Publishers* Ltd
1 London Bridge Street
London SE1 9GF
www.harpercollins.co.uk
HarperCollins*Publishers*
Macken House, 39/40 Mayor Street Upper,
Dublin 1, D01 C9W8, Ireland

This paperback edition 2025

1

First published in Great Britain in ebook format
by HarperCollins*Publishers* 2025

A catalogue record of this book is available from the British Library
ISBN: 978-0-00-861437-9

Printed and bound in the UK using 100% Renewable Electricity
by CPI Group (UK) Ltd

*For the lighthouse keepers, old sea dogs
and members of the RNLI*

Chapter One

I plucked my ringing mobile out of my bag which was next to me on the back seat of the silver Mercedes my publishers had kindly sent to pick me up.

We were easing up to a set of traffic lights in London's South Kensington and the pavements and shop windows were awash with gilded, first-of-July sunshine.

My husband Joe's infectious smile shone up at me from the screen. 'Hey, Rosebud. Sorry, but I've been held up at the office. I'll be there as soon as I can, okay?'

I rolled my eyes and laughed. Joe's habit of arriving late to everything from dental appointments to my book launches was a running joke between us and even his work colleagues. 'I'm getting a T-shirt made up with the caption, *"Sorry, Rosebud, but I'm running late"* printed up for you.'

His laughter rumbled down the line. 'Blame that new cosy crime writer who's arguing over his contract. Love you.'

'Love you too.'

I dropped my phone back into my bag and appreciated the brilliant white buildings as we headed towards the Victoria and Albert Museum.

That was where the launch of my new festive, feel-good romance, *Snow, I'll Always Love You*, was taking place tonight and I was brimming with excitement. Even though it was still summer, my publishers were keen to drum up some pre-Christmas razzamatazz. That's why my launch was taking place today, so that we could squeeze in every last bit of promo and marketing in the run-up to the festive season!

Not only had I been able to go crazy with its Christmas content, but it featured two of my favourite characters so far; my witty, bubbly, struggling drama student Bex and my grumpy, sexy theatre critic Nathan, who find themselves snowed in, together with several other guests, at a stately home, where Bex is making ends meet by working in hospitality.

Writing about my favourite time of the year hadn't been a hardship.

I loved the festive season and I was determined to make this Christmas even more special for Joe and me. We'd both been working flat out, so I'd booked a gorgeous, secluded cottage in the Peak District for the three of us as a surprise, from the twenty-third to the twenty-eighth of December. When I say the three of us, I meant me, Joe and our three-year-old Labradoodle, Bronte. The property came complete with its own outdoor jacuzzi, so we could sip something chilled and gaze across at the moody, lavender and jade hills as they became swaddled in snow. Hopefully.

I nestled back against the dark-chocolate leather seats as the chauffeur, Darren, weaved us past bijoux restaurants with rippling awnings and bespoke designer kitchens made from Italian marble. The early evening summer sky was beginning to morph into delicious shades of tangerine and raspberry, as Darren eased us effortlessly into the kerb.

Gazing out and upwards through the window, I contemplated the stunning, buttery stone-arched entrance to the Victoria and Albert Museum.

Darren got out, strode round to my side and eased open the car door. 'Have a wonderful book launch, madam.'

I eased my bag over my shoulder and clipped onto the pavement in my magenta kitten heels.

'Thanks, Darren. I'll try.' I slipped my hand into my bag, located my purse and plucked a twenty-pound note from it. Darren began to protest but I shook my head. 'Please,' I insisted. 'That should hopefully treat you to a couple of pints, although going by the prices around here, maybe not.'

He grinned and reluctantly took the money. 'Thank you, madam. That's very kind of you.'

I watched Darren clamber back into the car, looking dapper in his dark, satin waistcoat as he began to glide back into the traffic.

Then I glanced over my shoulder, hoping that Joe might be barrelling up the pavement towards me.

'Ready for another book launch then, Rosie?'

My beaming literary agent Mia Covington materialised beside me, having stepped out of a nearby taxi.

'Of course, she is,' trilled Lola Sykes, my editor at Jarred Roberts Publishing, who came dashing up.

The three of us exchanged kisses and hugs. I let out an excited rush of air, as the three of us approached the museum steps. 'I know this is my sixth novel, but I never get tired or bored of seeing my new book baby.'

Mia, her ghost grey eyes glistening, squeezed my arm with one jewelled hand. 'That's the way it should be.'

We negotiated the heavy steps towards the golden-illuminated interior of the V&A, our heels clacking in unison.

I tried to calm the butterflies tumbling in my stomach at the sight of the glittering Christmas lights and wreaths festooned everywhere. The publicity team at my publishers had done a wonderful job, turning the interior of the museum into a sparkling, festive cornucopia to complement my book. We were greeted by a sharply-dressed young man from the marketing team, who checked off our names and presented us with fancy name badges made out of sumptuous purple velvet.

We were then directed over to the cloakroom, where a girl with pink, highlighted hair proffered a wide smile and took our coats.

I adjusted the strap of my bag over my shoulder and gazed up at the spiralling crenelations that looked like whipped cream, soaring upwards into the sky.

Mia, with her shoulder-length, dark curls, and Lola, sporting her pale blond hair in a chignon, disappeared for a moment and came sashaying back with champagne flutes and handed me one. I pushed my riot of long, red curls back behind my ears and took a grateful gulp. 'We're like a modified version of the Spice Girls,' Lola joked.

'I'm bloody well not volunteering to be old spice,' tutted Mia, who was only in her early forties.

I continued to take in the endless and illuminated surroundings of the V&A. At every turn, there were glittering exhibition cases housing Roman artefacts, pieces of Venetian architecture and sumptuous waterfalls of embroidered fabrics from the Renaissance.

Even though I was London born and bred, I'd never been inside the V&A until now and was rather ashamed of that admission. I surmised I probably wasn't the only Londoner though to carry that secret. I'd often hurried past its grand, imposing features and promised myself I'd venture inside when I had a few spare moments, but that time never seemed to arrive.

The main hall, with its impressive, cream archways running all the way along and down towards the rear gardens, stretched upwards as if trying to touch the tantalising swirls of the pink-tinged clouds.

More Christmas themed decorations dripped from the pillars. Swathes of holly, ivy and berries were wrapped around the columns and furnished the top of the great hall's numerous arches.

Silver lights like sparkling snowflakes were strung around the centre piece of what looked like an inverted Christmas tree consisting of various shades of green foliage.

And just a little further down the space and suspended from the ceiling was the biggest, glossiest print of my book cover, depicting a coloured illustration of a loved-up couple, kissing in a snow globe.

'Couldn't you have got that made any bigger?' I grinned at Lola.

She angled her chignon to one side. 'Stop being so coy, Winters. You know you love it.'

Mia's knee-length, cranberry fitted silk suit shimmered as she moved. 'Wait till you see the other one.'

'What? Other one of what?'

Mia arched one plucked, dark brow at me and gestured over my shoulder.

'Oh God,' I groaned, at the sight greeting me.

Also suspended from the ceiling was a huge head and shoulders colour shot of me.

My fiery hair was exploding in its natural ringlets down my back and I was staring down the camera, with a teasing glint in my eye. I'd have to take a screenshot of it. Wait till Joe arrived and saw that! I glanced down at my watch. It would soon be seven o'clock. My heart gave a little excited judder at the thought of my husband. I scanned the guests, but there was still no sign of him. He was often too conscientious for his own good. Oh well, I was sure he'd arrive soon. No doubt dealing with last minute legal emails.

'Well, what do you think?' grinned Lola, pointing up at

my author photo, as though I hadn't seen it. The Space Station would be able to see that thing.

I swung round to Lola and Mia, my face burning. 'Jesus. I look like Merida out of Disney's *Brave*!'

'Nothing wrong with that,' brushed off Lola, giving the hem of her electric blue, wraparound dress a swish.

I thought of my late Mum and what she would have made of all of this. I could see her smiling. 'I'll say. I'm so proud of you. Don't hide your light under a bushel, sweetheart,' she would say, taking an appreciative gulp of her champagne. I suspected she would've worn something swirly in burgundy, to highlight the matching shade in her flicky bob.

Around us, press photographers had arrived and were taking snaps of the assembled guests. I recognised a lot of them from the publishing and writing world, but there were a few others I didn't know from TV reality shows and a sprinkling of soap actors, until Mia and Lola pointed them out to me and named names.

I realised I'd been so preoccupied with the giant posters of my cover and my looming face that I hadn't drunk much of my champagne yet.

Writerly doubt crept into my head while I took a few more grateful gulps of the pale gold fizz. It hit the back of my throat. 'I just hope my readers love this one as much as my other books,' I murmured to Lola.

'Will you stop worrying? Your readers are crazy about every novel you write. You wouldn't be consistently hitting the top five if they didn't.'

'It's imposter syndrome,' said Mia out of the corner of her mouth. Her manicured hand flashed. 'Nothing wrong with it though, in my humble opinion. Shows you care. Means you want to get better with every book you write.' She took a measured sip of her glass and waggled it. 'I wish a lot of my other authors were more like you, sweetheart. Big-headed tossers some of them.'

Lola laughed.

'It's true!' protested Mia. 'I seem to spend half my time soothing their egos or being an agony aunt.' She waggled her glass. 'I mean, don't get me wrong. I love being an agent. But sometimes, it would make life a little easier if they were more like my favourite redhead here.'

I shook my head and laughed. 'You're only saying I'm your favourite because you're getting pissed.'

'Nope. I know exactly what I'm saying.' She reached out a hand and clasped mine with affection. 'You're a delight to work with, honey.'

Lola eyed me with a soft smile. 'I agree with Mia. You deserve your success, Rosie. You've worked damned hard to get where you are. You enjoy it.'

I admired the huge, suspended version of my latest book cover as it dangled from the museum ceiling. Those years of writing and submitting to publishers and agents. The knock-backs or the stony silences when I didn't receive a response at all. The feeling of despondency whenever I did receive a polite 'no'. I could've decorated my bathroom with the rejection letters I'd received. I gazed up again at the giant, bright cover of *Snow, I'll Always Love You*. 'My first few books hardly hit the big time,' I cringed at the recollection. 'Things didn't start happening for me until a couple of years ago.'

'Yes, well, you've grown as a writer since then,' said Lola. 'And how's that gorgeous husband of yours? No sign of him yet?'

My mouth melted into a soppy grin. 'He's great thanks. I'm sure he'll be along soon.' I glanced down at my watch again. 'No doubt finishing something off at work.'

Joe.

My muse.

My heart performed a little skip of happiness. It didn't seem like five whole years since we got married.

I met Joe Hutton six years ago, just after my twenty-sixth birthday. I'd signed my publishing deal for my first novel, *You Make Lovin' Fun*. Joe had been and still was in the legal department at Jarred Roberts, and I remember feeling that electric shock the first time I saw him.

Blond, blue-eyed and looking more like a Californian surfer than a legal eagle, he'd chased after me from the off, and I'd made no moves whatsoever to run away.

It'd felt right from the first time we grinned at one another. Joe had captivated me with his drive, intelligence, sense of humour and blond, good looks.

I took another, considered mouthful of champagne. From working as a librarian in Ealing, where I was born and grew up, to becoming a writer of best-selling, feel-good romance, marrying someone with a passing resemblance to Matthew McConaughey and living in the buzzy central

London area of Hampstead, none of what had happened in my life felt as if it had happened to me. It was like I'd watched all these wonderful things unfold and blossom for someone else. Imposter syndrome was alive and well and living in my head a lot of the time. Even now, frissons of disbelief shot through me.

'You promised you'd let me know if Joe discovered he's got an older brother,' joked Mia over the top of her glass.

'And I'll keep my promise,' I smiled. 'You know he's an only child like me, but he always says he'd love to investigate his family tree, if he wasn't so busy with work.'

'Well, you tell him to stop being such a sodding workaholic, Winters, and get cracking with that family tree research. I'm not getting any younger.'

'You're only forty-two!' I laughed, incredulous. 'And you're stunning! You go on as though you were Methuselah.'

'Sssh!' hissed a horrified Mia. 'It's alright for you and Blondie here. You're both ten years younger than me.'

'Doesn't matter what age you are,' replied Lola into her glass. 'Looking for The One at any age is a pain in the arse.' She pulled a face. 'I've deleted those dating apps. I'm fed up with meeting guys who never look like their photo, never ask me about myself or spend all evening mooning after their ex-wife.' She slid me a smile. 'You and Joe keep me optimistic, though.'

'None of those idiots were good enough for you, Lola.'

She laughed. 'You never met any of them.'

'Trust me. They weren't.'

Mia wrinkled her nose, as the chatter and clinking glasses swirled around us. 'Your mum, God bless her, had the right attitude. She had them all sized up in no time.'

I buried a smile as I thought about my mum, Tessa, again. My dad, Jack, had passed away suddenly from a heart attack when I was ten, and she'd been the most amazing single parent for the last twenty-two years, giving me all the love, care, support and encouragement that I should've had from two parents. They'd been married for eleven years when Dad died. Eleven years of married life together. Not long at all, in the scheme of things. God, I missed them both so much but Mum especially. She'd seen my first few books being published, but had passed away suddenly two years ago, at the age of just fifty-eight, just as my novels were about to start making an impact. I inherited my love of reading from her. She'd been an enthusiastic and passionate secondary school English teacher.

My late maternal grandparents had shared a happy and fulfilling life together too. Guilt nibbled at me, as I thought about them. I'd been so busy I hadn't been able to head up to Rowan Bay in the Scottish Highlands and make plans to sell their cottage.

My late Grandfather Howard had passed away five years ago, but I only lost my Grandma Tilda four months ago, in March. I'd always loved her maiden name of Winters and had adopted that as my pen name, and then in everyday life, rather than using my real surname of Ward.

Mum once confided in me that she thought Rosie

Winters had a much prettier and more romantic ring to it as well!

Once the circus for this book release was over, I'd suggest to Joe that we take a break up there. We could maybe spend a romantic Hogmanay up in Scotland and then begin sorting things out, so we could put the property on the market.

The last time I'd been up there was in March for Grandma's funeral. She'd been a very talented artist, and my mum always used to say she was convinced that was who I inherited my creative prowess from.

I used to love spending my school holidays with my grandparents up there, picking up shells that were studded into the sand down by the bay and hoping to catch glimpses of puffins, dolphins and seals.

I still swapped phone calls and letters with the charming old lighthouse keeper, Barclay Hogan, though. The lighthouse was situated close to my late grandparents' cottage, just up on the opposite cliffside, so Barclay had kept me entertained with his seafaring stories. He always used to call me 'Red', and the name stuck.

Come to think of it, I hadn't heard from Barclay for a couple of weeks. Joe and I could see him too, if we went to the cottage for New Year. We could drop by for a surprise visit.

I looked around for any sign of Joe and experienced another niggle of disappointment; I'd hoped he'd be by my side when I laid eyes on the book launch decorations. Oh well. I knew he was crazy busy at work. His schedule had become even more hectic over the past few months. Nevertheless, my stomach wriggled at the thought of him arriving soon, to share this special evening with me.

All around me, people were nodding, smiling, chatting and congratulating me. Champagne flutes winked under the lights and peals of laughter rang into the air. I was asked about my book from journalists; are Bex and Nathan based on any real people? Where did I get the inspiration for my latest plot? What are the key themes? Who would play Nathan Dallas if my book were to be turned into a movie? Was it true that my main male protagonists were based in some way on Joe?

I felt myself pink up. 'Yes, it's true. My husband does act as the inspiration for my heroes.' My latest protagonist, the steely, sexy critic Nathan, was no exception.

The books I'd written before I met Joe hadn't carried the same vivacious joy and vivid heroes. They'd sold well, but it was only after falling in love with him, that my writing had become infused with real energy. Even then, it'd taken a few more years before my career as an author really took off, my sales went into the stratosphere and I found my books swooping into the top five.

I never took for granted how fortunate I was.

A sumptuous array of festive-inspired finger foods appeared next and were circulated on shiny platters among the guests. There were reindeer mince pies with twiglet antlers, mini-Christmas crackers stuffed with goats' cheese, Christmas devilled eggs with fresh herbs, mincemeat Christmas trees, snowmen cheese balls, and lemon, garlic and herb baubles. It was Christmas kitsch at its best and I loved it!

While we were taking great delight in savouring the cuisine, a trio of musicians appeared and set up in the far-right corner. Armed with a violin, cello and harp, they struck up classy renditions of traditional Christmas carols and even threw in some Mariah Carey.

If anybody here didn't feel Christmassy by now, even though it was twenty-one degrees outside and the middle of summer, there was no hope for them! I could feel my face breaking into a huge smile, as I tapped my foot along to their version of Sir Elton John's 'Step into Christmas'.

My heart lifted in my chest.

I never realised I could feel this happy and content. Not after losing Mum. But with my next book eagerly anticipated, a brand new, two-book deal rumoured to be on the way and Joe by my side, the future was taking on a much rosier hue.

While Mia and Lola chatted to me, bringing famous and not-so-famous faces up to talk to me, my mind kept wandering to the book I'd just started writing. I liked to have my book delivery deadlines in my diary, so I had a date to work towards.

This one was about a grumpy, widowed romance writer who has to recruit a PA when he's left to bring up his orphan nephew on his own. A ripple of satisfaction took over. I'd been so lucky. I was doing what I loved most in the world. Writing romance. People wanted to read my books and I never got tired of it.

Our gorgeous apartment in Hampstead, with its polished, tiled floors, panoramic windows, wet room and balconies, was Joe's and my haven. Never in a million years did I think that I, Rosie Ellenor Ward, from a single-parent family council house in Ealing, would end up where I was: bestselling author Rosie Winters.

I plucked a second glass of champagne from a passing waitress. The warmth hit me, making me feel fuzzy and comfortable. Joe would be here soon, I was sure, and then I could show him the massive photograph of my big, red, curly head. I let out a small laugh into my champagne flute.

The John Madejski Gardens outside the V&A at the rear of the museum shone out from under the amber architecture. The large, oval pond shimmered under the evening sunshine.

I glanced down at my watch again. Where was Joe, I thought with a stab of irritation. This was getting ridiculous now.

I drained the rest of my champagne and set the empty glass on a passing waiter's tray, before fetching my mobile out of my bag again.

I pulled up his number and after a few rings, I heard his breathless voice rasp down the line. 'I'm so sorry, darling. I'm just across the road. Honestly.'

I could just about hear his voice over a cacophony of parping horns, voices and the buzz of traffic.

'I got caught by Charles while heading out the door.'

I could feel frustration tugging at my insides. 'Joe, I appreciate you're busy, but you know what these events mean to me and having you by my side. Can you please hurry up?'

Maybe it was a godsend that at that moment, Mia beckoned me over to speak to a magazine book reviewer.

It meant I didn't hear a sudden, sharp screech of brakes and horrified screams.

Chapter Two

My head was constantly rattling like a box of tools.

I'd been hollowed out; my heart smashed into a million jagged pieces that I had no inclination to gather up and try to piece back together again.

In his rush to get to my book launch, Joe had made a dash for it across the busy road and not seen the lorry bearing down towards him. The driver had slammed on his brakes but it was too late.

Joe was killed instantly.

The poor lorry driver, a fifty-something father of three from the North of England, had been riddled with guilt and sought counselling after the accident. He'd written to me, the tumultuous state he was in evident in his erratic, emotional handwriting.

I'd gripped the lined writing paper, scanning the words but not allowing my brain to process them.

I didn't blame him. It hadn't been his fault: Joe was

dashing across that road, still gripping his mobile as he hurried to get to me. That had been all my doing.

I'd been nagging him, only thinking of myself, hassling him to get to the museum. To get to me.

Meanwhile, I had morphed into a lifeless dummy after Joe's death. My head whirled like a carousel. This must be some sick joke. He wasn't gone.

I'd blundered through his funeral in his hometown of Chorleywood in Hertfordshire just over a week later, supported physically and mentally by Mia and Lola, and with Joe's devastated parents, Nancy and Jeremy, trying and failing to be brave.

They were buttoning up their emotions and caging them inside, ready for the tsunami of grief to release itself when they least expected it.

My dead eyes hadn't appreciated the rainbow of flowers at the crematorium. Not even the wonderful floral depiction of a pair of running shoes, from his buddies on his regular park runs, or the floral football in Joe's beloved Aston Villa's colours of blue and claret, kindly sent by my friend Barclay, the lighthouse keeper.

Joe had loved eighties rock music, especially Def Leppard, and as his casket had slid behind the curtain to the sounds of his favourite track of theirs, 'Love Bites', I knew every ounce of optimism for our future together had died with him.

There was still all this love and longing for him thrashing around inside of me and yet Joe wasn't here to receive it. There was nowhere for it to go; it just kept reverberating around.

Often, I'd hear a series of desperate, ragged gasps that would make me jump. Then I'd realise the sound was coming from me.

I'd rung Barclay up in Rowan Bay a few days after Joe's death and somehow managed to tell him about what had happened and given him the funeral arrangement details.

Barclay's normally raspy, mischievous voice had sunk into despair at the news. 'My heart isn't what it was,' he'd apologised. 'I probably won't make Joe's funeral.'

'Don't worry, Barclay. I understand, and so would Joe.'

I hadn't wanted to see anyone since it happened, except for Mia, who insisted on having the spare key to the apartment. I'd tried to cocoon myself away with Bronte in our home, which was located on the top floor of the building, overlooking the stunning, frilly-green landscape of Hampstead Heath.

Whenever the entry buzzer rang out, Mia would deal with callers, answer my phone and field contact from the press.

For the first few days after Joe had died, Mia stayed over. She tidied up, made me snacks and persuaded me to eat something, even though I wasn't hungry. I was so grateful to her. The prospect of having to pretend I was coping, made me feel even more exhausted. Even the idea of speaking to Joe's parents was one I couldn't contemplate. He had his dad's smile and his Mum's animated, blue eyes. They inadvertently carried Joe with them, in echoes of their mannerisms and I couldn't handle it. The realisation made me ashamed. They'd lost their only son and were going through torment too.

The only time I managed to leave the flat was to take Bronte for a walk a few times a day, and even that was a struggle. I couldn't look at the glossy, sun-stroked trees, hear kids bursting into fits of giggles or listen to people complaining about the rising cost of a pint of milk. Every snapshot of life or joy emanating from others was like a knife wound to my chest. Didn't they know Joe was gone? Didn't they understand what loss and pain felt like? What burning guilt was? If I hadn't been such a bossy cow...

It was the beginning of September now and two long, heart-breaking months since Joe's death.

Mia had dropped by after completing another grocery shop for me, and I was sitting on the sofa, with Bronte at my feet, clutching a cold mug of tea and staring into space.

She'd been packing the items in my fridge. Usually, she'd try to fill the air with chatter, but not today. 'You, okay?' I asked her turned back. 'You seem a bit preoccupied.'

Mia turned round. She was clutching a jar of apricot jam. She set it down on the breakfast bar and reached for her bag. She pulled out a letter. 'This arrived for you at the agency.'

She came over and handed it to me, before sinking down

beside me on the sofa. Her silky, beige trousers whispered as she moved.

I set my cold mug of tea down on the coaster on the glass coffee table in front of me. 'What is it? Who's it from?'

I turned over the white envelope. It was addressed to me, c/o Mia. I didn't recognise the handwriting. It was small and neat, controlled.

I slipped my hand inside and pulled out the letter. What came with it was three glossy photographs of Joe with another woman. I stared down at the images. She was tall and athletic-looking, about my age, with feline, jade-coloured eyes and long, straight, dark hair.

In the first photograph, they were in some posh restaurant, snuggled up together and raising glasses at the camera. In the second, they were wrapped around each other, on what looked like a white sanded beach. He was in long swimming shorts and she was sporting a black and white bikini.

The third photograph was a selfie. They were gazing into each other's eyes, on the verge of kissing.

My head was reeling. My attention snapped from the pictures and back up to Mia, over and over. 'What are these? What's going on?'

'Read the letter.' She rested one concerned hand on my knee.

I turned my confused attention to what it said.

Ms Winters,

I'm so sorry for your loss, but I had to contact you.

I'm not doing this out of any sense of spite or revenge. I'm doing it because you have a right to know what Joe was really like; how he used both of us and how he lied to get what he wanted.

My name is Greta Vincent and for the past three years, Joe and I were in a relationship.

The words shifted and swirled in front of my eyes. I jerked my head up to look at Mia. 'Is this some sort of joke?' My voice was cracking.

Mia's face was etched with sympathy. 'Sweetheart, you need to read this. I'm so sorry.'

My heart bounced harder and faster against my chest. I couldn't comprehend what was going on. There must be some mistake.

Trying to steady my breathing, I turned back to the contents of the letter.

We met in a bar in Marylebone at Christmas time. We were both there attending leaving parties for our respective companies. We got talking and he told me that he was in an unhappy marriage. I fell for him quickly and he said he wanted to leave you and start over with me.

But every time I broached the subject, he said he would tell you everything when the time was right – but that time never came.

I spent three years of my life waiting for him, foolishly believing his lies and convincing myself that you were some sort of evil ogre who wouldn't give him his freedom. But after Joe died, I found out the truth. I read about your happy marriage and how much you loved him.

He played us both.

Do you know he was late for your book launch because we'd been together that afternoon? And he even lied to me about that. When I asked him why he was in such a rush to leave, he said he'd received an email from an upset author and had to go and discuss some urgent legal issue that had arisen.

Joe was incapable of telling the truth.

My hands shook as I held the crisp, vanilla notepaper. Her address and phone number in the top right corner melted in front of my eyes. Where did she live? Was that Fulham?

I struggled to comprehend what was playing out in front of me. I'd been blaming myself. I'd been carrying around this guilt, like a chain around my neck since the moment he'd died, thinking I'd been the reason Joe was killed. It turned out he'd been in bed with his mistress right before he was knocked over.

Realisation hit me like an express train. All the times he'd been late home or had to go on business trips; the meetings that dragged on well into the evening. It had been lies. He'd been with her. Living another life.

And to think Joe had been my writing inspiration for my sweeping romances. I'd been infused with happiness and creativity because of him. And yet, it turned out, all I'd been writing was a tissue of lies. I'd been deceiving my readers.

My life was crumbling all around me again. For a second time. My marriage and my career had turned out to be untruths.

Mia removed the letter from my vicelike grip. 'I'll deal with this.' She snatched up the photographs scattered over my lap and stuffed them and the letter back in the envelope. 'This is between you and me. No one else will ever know about this. You have my word.'

She dumped the letter on the arm of the sofa and moved to bundle me into her arms, but I sprung from the sofa, as though thousands of volts had charged through me. I folded my arms. Everything had been a lie. I'd imagined it all. My happy marriage to the man I loved and my successful romance novels.

Faintly through the fog, I heard Mia's voice. 'You will get through this. You have so much to live for – your family, your writing…'

A dark cloud of decision took hold. I couldn't do anything about Joe's infidelity, but my career and what I did in the future were something I was in control of, it was something that I could make or break, unlike my marriage. Joe had done that all by himself. My jaw wobbled. The thought of writing again made nausea lodge in my throat. No, that was done. Over. No more of Rosie Winters, the romance author. 'I'm never writing again, Mia. My heart isn't in it anymore, especially after that.' I jabbed one shaking finger at the letter beside her.

'You've had the most awful shock. The last couple of months have been a nightmare for you and then this sodding letter arrives.' She shook her dark hair. 'You need to give yourself time. There's no pressure, sweetheart. There's no rush to sign any new contracts.'

My eyes flashed with a combination of hurt and fury at her. 'I'm not signing any more contracts. How can I write any more romances after this?'

In one swift move, Mia was beside me and taking me in her arms. Bronte was studying both of us from where she was still curled up on the rug. 'I'm not making you do anything you don't want to do. Your heart is broken. You have to mend.'

'What? After finding out my dead husband has been cheating on me for three years?'

I inhaled the scent of her lemon perfume. Her bouncy, dark hair tickled my nose. And I clung to her for what seemed like an eternity, with racking sobs escaping from my chest.

Chapter Three

Mia had volunteered to stay, but I'd insisted I would be fine alone.

Travelling up in the glass and chrome lift with Bronte on her lead after her afternoon walk, I fought not to look at my reflection. My navy-blue eyes were red-rimmed and my hair was spilling past my shoulders in a static, unwashed bush. Was I asleep? Was this one of those horrendous nightmares where, when you wake up, the bedsheets are all tangled around you and you're gulping with relief that it wasn't real? My eyes forced themselves to look back at my reflection again. I felt consumed by everything that was happening.

My head echoed with the contents of Greta Vincent's letter.

I remembered I still had Joe's gold St Christopher glistening around my neck.

I reached up a hand to hold it in my palm. He never

used to take it off. His grandparents had bought it for him when he was seventeen and about to set off interrailing with a couple of friends for a few months around Europe before starting his law degree at Durham University.

As I stood there, eyeing my image staring back at me, I recalled slipping it around my neck days after he'd died, feeling the coolness of it nestling against my skin. It was as though I was still clinging to a tiny, physical part of him.

I fiddled with the chain and with one shaky hand, unclipped the St Christopher. I stuffed it in my jeans pocket. The thought of keeping it on a moment longer deadened my heart.

Bronte gazed up, her amber eyes wide and imploring. The lift eased to a halt with both of us inside. I stepped out and clung to her pink leather lead, as though it were my security blanket. We were in the fragranced, carpeted hallway.

Part of me wanted to turn tail and run, to flee and never look back, squeeze myself into a black hole and close the lid.

I hesitated at our apartment door, a polished, cherry wood affair with the number twelve in gold digits and the obligatory spy hole.

My hand thrashed around inside my back jeans pocket to locate my door key. My head and stomach were spinning. I was going back in there with Bronte, to surround myself with the ghost of Joe. The cheating, lying one.

I crouched down and buried my face in her fuzzy coat. She lashed me with frantic licks of her tongue.

I wanted to howl like she sometimes did. I wanted to let it all out and make everyone realise that the spectacular husband Joe had been was just a cheap façade. His death had opened up the truth and it was ugly.

I slowly rose up from the floor and kept my coat on. I felt wrung out and spent.

With dread gripping me, I unlocked the door, unclipped Bronte's lead and watched her gaze around herself for a few moments. She was looking for him. Her tail dropped and after another few seconds of confusion, she trotted off into the sitting room to play with her squeaky ball.

I recoiled from the familiar sight of the oval, gilt-edged hallway mirror and of the lavish, red and yellow rug we'd bought in Mexico on our honeymoon. I wrapped my arms around myself, like a protective shield.

I couldn't contain the heartbreak and resentment that were erupting out of me like hot lava. I didn't want to be like this or sound like this. My usually soft London accent had twisted into something unrecognisable and bitter. I could hear myself biting and snapping when I had to speak to someone like the bank, to have Joe's name removed from our joint account.

The apartment spotlights were like dimmed eyes peering down at me.

My breath came out in a series of desperate, ragged gasps.

My attention fell on the polished, blond wood hallway floorboards and on the painting my grandmother had given me, her depiction of a tangerine-and-hot-pink Rowan Bay sunset.

How much longer could I stay here, not venturing out? Ever since he'd died, I had been trying not to look for traces of Joe. His fingerprints on the TV remote, the scent of Sauvage, his favourite cologne, on his work shirts, the trace of his cedar-smelling shampoo on his pillow.

My eyes settled on our stone-coloured, vintage Mario Bellini sofa in the sitting room. I was hugging myself even tighter now, so tight, it was almost as if I were being embraced by a boa constrictor. I took in a long, low breath.

I had realised why Joe hadn't left me for Greta. He had been a solicitor. He knew what he would lose financially, if we'd divorced. He had wanted the best of both worlds; one foot in each and hopping from one to the other whenever it suited him.

Bronte, on hearing my raised breathing, poked her head round the sitting room door. She waggled her tail at me. That small gesture of love made me want to crumple again.

My life was tumbling down around me like a stack of playing cards.

This apartment. Our holiday photos dotted around. The beautiful memories we'd made together. The accessories and furniture we'd chosen. My books. My feel-good romances. Everything we'd built together out of nothing had been ripped apart. It wasn't worth anything anymore.

My writing muse, I'd sighed in interviews. Christ, what an embarrassment now, when I looked back. Nathan, Grey, Riley, all my literary heroes had been based on Joe Hutton in one way or another. If it wasn't his looks or his love of squash and running, they'd shared his dimpled smile or his career. Joe had been part of the character jigsaw that I'd created for each of them, elements of him living and shining through them and dancing onto the pages.

I found myself drifting down the hallway and into our sitting room like a lost ghost, gazing at its panoramic views over Hampstead Heath. The trees would soon begin to look like black twiglets in the starry sky. My six published novels so far were propped side by side on the bookcase by the back wall, their colourful, embossed spines grinning out at me.

Bronte trotted over and I dropped down to pat her. Racking sobs were stuck in my throat. I raised my head and glanced at the sixty-inch plasma TV on the facing wall and at the splashes of expensive landscape paintings in their heavy frames. Then there was the Murano hand-blown glass lamp on the coffee table in the corner.

This was such a far cry from my hometown of Ealing. Working in the library, admiring all the books that stood to attention on the shelves, dreaming that one day my books might sit there too. Then I'd slave over my ideas in the evenings, trying to write novels that I ended up cringing over, travelling home on the bus, listening to snippets of conversation to try and get ideas, scrawling plot lines in cheap notebooks.

God, how I wished Mum was here, I thought with another painful pang of grief. We were like Thelma and Louise. She would've known what to say, what to do.

I didn't want to be here. The thought of staying in this apartment a moment longer made my heart wither. My attention fell on our designer sofa again and the sumptuous rugs.

I had to get away. Even the smell of the autumnal potpourri I'd placed in the hallway was making me gag.

I shoved my hands in my coat pockets and strode out of the sitting room. Joe was everywhere and I didn't want to be near the echoes of him.

I drew up at the doorway of our bedroom at the end of the hall. I would pack, go somewhere, and take Bronte with me. Where were we going to go? I'd no idea. I certainly wasn't going to go near the Peak District cottage I had booked for me and Joe to spend Christmas in – Mia had kindly cancelled it, as I couldn't face it.

But as I stood there in our hallway, there was one thing I did know: I couldn't stay here anymore.

Chapter Four

P ain iced up my veins as I reached our bedroom and made straight for our wardrobe.

My purple case was sat on the top of it.

Trying not to think too much about what I was doing; I produced Joe's St Christopher from my jeans pocket and dropped it onto the top of my mirrored dressing table. Joe's parents could have that. Then I dragged my case from its resting place and dumped it on top of our king-sized bed. The case sent our dark chocolate and gold scatter cushions flying to the floor.

I kept my attention trained on the chest of drawers as my trembling hands reached for underwear, socks, jumpers and jeans.

I yanked open the door of our shoe cupboard next. A lump in my throat caught me unawares. Pairs of Joe's running shoes were nestled beside the black, shiny brogues he wore on our wedding day.

I scooped up my trainers, walking boots and a couple of pairs of my dressier winter boots. I reached for my travelling shoe bag and thrust them all inside and slammed the wardrobe door shut again.

Bronte came plodding up to me. She plopped her dear little bottom down by my feet. 'Don't worry, pumpkin,' I assured her in an emotional croak. She was eyeing me in my coat with suspicion. 'You're coming with me.'

I whirled back up the hallway and into the sitting room, gathering up a few of Bronte's favourite toys, before fetching her feeding bowl and water from the kitchen. As if on autopilot, I retrieved her bag of kibble and some treats. Her lead, harness and coat were next. I unhooked them from the peg in the hall cupboard. I was doing everything with what felt like ruthless efficiency, but I knew that if I dared to stop for a moment and try to unscramble what I was doing, my insides would be crushed. It was as though I was turning my back on my old life, but what else could I do? What other option had Joe left me?

I gripped Bronte's lead, harness and coat in my bunched-up fists and took in Joe's section of the wardrobe, with his assortment of shirts, suits, jeans and T-shirts.

I darted into the kitchen and dived into one of the cupboards where I kept black bin liners. My throat wobbled but I rubbed my eyes and returned to the bedroom. I yanked his clothes from their hangers and thrust them into the bin bags. I would donate them to charity. His parents could also have his favourite cuff links. A dead weight gripped my stomach. I still hadn't told them about their only son's affair.

I finished balling and stuffing Joe's clothes into the rubbish bags, dumped them in the hall together with Bronte's things, and turned back into the bedroom. As I reached the doorway, my attention strayed to my writing room next door. All of a sudden, my walnut, circular desk looked as destitute as I felt.

Foreign editions of my novels rested on the shelf above my desk and my stack of writing notebooks and glitzy pens sparkled beside my laptop. I had loved to watch the dappled sunshine, the silvery rain or the whirling snow from the window as I wrote.

I flicked a look at my silver laptop, which seemed to be waiting for me to flip up the lid and begin hammering away on the keyboard, conjuring up characters and places like I always did. Despite my reluctance when I spoke to Mia, she had pleaded with me to sign a new contract, and I said I would think about it, not wanting to let my team down. I'd already made good progress on book seven and was half a dozen chapters into the story.

But now... Cold fear stabbed me. I couldn't do it. I couldn't face it. Sitting there, extolling the beauty of falling in love, when my own husband had taken from me everything I believed in? And I'd been racked with guilt over his death. I thought I'd robbed us of our happiness, but his adultery had robbed me of my desire to write.

The happily-ever-afters, the breath-catching romance

and golden futures; I'd been peddling this to my readers, who'd inhaled it with relish. But then came real life.

How the hell could I even contemplate throwing myself into my worlds of meet-cutes, enemies to lovers, and bubbling, passionate forced proximities anymore?

What was it Mia had said to me? That she wasn't going to make me do anything I didn't want to do? That my heart was broken and I had to mend? My back stiffened. This was me from now on. I had no heart left. I had nothing left.

I ignored my laptop, snatched up an empty box near my office door and picked up Bronte's bits and pieces where I'd left them in the hallway.

I cradled the box in my arms with Bronte's things jiggling about in the bottom of it, and made my way to our apartment door. I tugged it open and propelled myself towards the communal staircase. I'd come back for my case and the bags of Joe's clothes.

I raced down the stairs, the sound of my trainers thundering on the steps and in my ears. I didn't even want to hang around for the lift. I didn't want to set eyes on my reflection again in its glass panels. I kept seeing me and Joe tangled up in bed together instead.

I pointed my car keys at my bright blue Mazda and watched it light up and open in the descending dark. I dumped the box of Bronte's bits and pieces inside the boot.

I gave a shiver under my denim jacket.

My brain was clouded with pain. Where was I going to go? Where could I go?

Chilly realisation took hold. I'd no idea. I didn't know where I was headed.

A hotel? A bed and breakfast somewhere?

I wanted out of London, that much I knew.

Then it came to me, as pictures of my grandmother drifted into my head. Of course. Somewhere comforting and peaceful… Why hadn't I thought of it before?

I could take Bronte to my late grandparents' cottage in Rowan Bay.

It was situated hundreds of miles away and was a long drive, but it would be worth it. In fact, it would be perfect. Quiet solitude by a harbour in the Scottish Highlands. The cottage was just sitting there unoccupied anyway.

I'd spent so many of my school holidays there, combing the beach for shells, dolphin spotting, having windy, salty picnics and spending my pocket money on the assorted sea inspired paperweights and stationery in the local gift shop.

And seeing a friendly face like Barclay's was just what I needed. He'd suggested I go visit him anyway.

The more I thought about it, the more it made sense. I kept the spare key to the cottage in the top drawer of my bedside table.

I was tired of loss, and events being taken out of my control. I was sick of loving people and having them ripped away from me. At least this would be something that I was in control over. Leaving London would be my decision.

Joe had decided to cheat on me with another woman for the past three years. Now I was making this decision to leave what was left of our married life behind me. I had no idea what the future held for me, but at least I could do this right now.

No more trusting people or giving them my hopes and dreams, only for them to crush them. From now on, my life was just about Bronte and me. I had to protect myself. I wouldn't allow myself to be vulnerable to loss, hurt and pain ever again.

I dashed back up to the apartment and scooped up Bronte. Still cuddling her to me, I hurried back down the hallway to the bedroom to retrieve the cottage front door key. I found it and stuffed it into my right coat pocket.

Then I rang Barclay. 'I've decided to come for a visit. That okay with you?'

'Don't be daft, lass. Can't wait to see you. I'll make sure there are a few provisions in for you.'

'Thank you.'

'When you heading up?'

I straightened my back. 'I'm setting off tonight.'

'Well, you drive safe, Red. There's no rush.'

I finished speaking to him, a rush of adrenalin powering through me. I'd head there now. More tears trickled down my face and I flicked them away.

I set down Bronte and deposited the black bin bags outside the flat door. Then I took off my rose-gold wedding ring and my diamond engagement ring and dropped them in a drawer in the hall cabinet before leaving the apartment and locking the door.

It was dark now and a chilly autumnal night, but it was

as if I couldn't feel anything anymore. I didn't feel tired, only empty.

Bronte and I would hit the road now and take our time. There wasn't any rush. I'd stop somewhere overnight; take a couple of stops. Bronte would need feeding and to do her ablutions anyway. If I took it steady, we could be there at a respectable time later on tomorrow morning.

An image of Joe appeared phantom-like near my car, with that bright smile of his and his exploding dimple.

I wrestled my phone out of my bag and located the number of the local cancer charity shop. They were closed but I left a message and details of my address, so they could come and collect Joe's belongings.

Chapter Five

I lowered Bronte onto her pink-checked blanket on the back seat and secured her in her harness and seatbelt. Her little, furry face peered back at me.

I gripped the steering wheel. My knuckles tensed. I didn't feel like me anymore. I didn't think I would ever again.

I picked up my phone once more from the passenger seat and located Mia's number. I didn't give her a chance to say anything when she picked up. 'Just to let you know I'm about to head off to Scotland.'

'What? Now?'

'Yes. To my late grandparents' cottage.' I swallowed hard, the stars misting over through the windscreen. 'I need to get away for a bit, Mia. Bronte and me.'

'I get it,' she said softly. 'I do. But please. Let me drive you there. Can you hold fire till tomorrow morning? I'll come straight over first thing.'

I realised I was shaking my head, even though Mia couldn't see me. 'No. Thanks. I need to be on my own.' I gulped. 'You understand, don't you?'

'Yes. Of course I do.' She hesitated. 'Just take it steady, okay? There's no rush. Just please let me know you get there okay and keep in touch, otherwise you'll be in my bad books.'

'I will. Just please don't tell anyone where I am. I'll call Joe's parents and tell them I'm going away for a while, but I'm not even telling them where I'm headed.'

My heart felt like a piece of ripped paper, twisting and turning in the wind.

'I won't tell anyone anything, Rosie. Not if you don't want me to. And don't worry about your apartment. I'll hang on to the spare key and keep an eye on the place.'

'Thanks. I don't know what I would've done without you.'

Mia's voice splintered down the line. 'Don't be daft.' I could hear her fighting back tears. 'Please give Bronte a hug from me.'

'I will.' I paused. 'Can you tell Lola about all this for me? She'd want to know.'

'Of course I will. Don't worry about that.'

I finished the call and jabbed the button that controlled the driver-side window. I took a few greedy gulps of the night air and rubbed my face. Then I clicked the window closed again.

Behind me, Bronte let out a little whimper. She could sense my ping-pong of emotions.

I reached one arm into the back seat and ruffled her warm head. 'It's okay, sweetheart.'

I pushed my automatic into drive.

And then, dismissing the tears trickling down my face with the back of my hand, I concentrated all my attention on the road ahead and vanished into the night.

I managed to put a couple of hundred miles between London and us, before more huge waves of weariness and heartbreak gnawed at my bones.

Even Bronte, snuggled down on the back seat, looked in desperate need of a proper sleep. She let out a couple of Scooby-Doo type yawns.

I located a Premier Inn just outside Leeds which welcomed dogs, and eased into the car park.

For a few moments, I just sat at the wheel, staring out of the windscreen at the streetlamps and the concrete space I was parked in. I couldn't even remember arriving here.

Bronte let out a couple of irritated barks, which snapped me out of my stillness. I attached her lead and let her have a good wander around. Then I checked us in and gathered our things from the boot.

Our accommodation was small but clean, with dark wooden furniture, red, plump cushions on the king-size bed, and the lights from Leeds dazzling through the long, hessian curtains.

I glanced down at my watch. It was approaching one o'clock in the morning.

I peeled off my jeans and stripey sweater and tossed them onto the floor.

I fed Bronte her kibble and once she'd hoovered up the contents from her bowl, she jumped up beside me and pushed her squirming body against me on the bed. I wrapped both arms around her and buried my face in her coat.

A weariness gripped me. I threw on an old T-shirt and slipped under the bed covers. I was slumped against the pillows in a snotty, crying mess and despite thinking I'd never be able to sleep again and certain I had no more tears left, I finally fell into fits of restless sleep.

I lay in bed the next morning, staring listlessly up at my aertex guest room ceiling.

Pictures of Joe burned in my chest. It was as if I'd undertaken last night's journey here in a mixed-up, hallucinated fog.

Bronte was still curled up beside me on top of the bed, her ears sagging as she looked at me out of her mournful eyes.

I didn't want to get up. I just wanted to cocoon myself under these covers and push everything away, wallow in my desperation and anger.

But I got a whiff of my fruity armpits and decided that wasn't an option.

I was struggling to think about anything, let alone getting myself sorted out. The day was stretching in front of me like one long empty tunnel. It was dark and there was no chink of light to brighten it up. I showered and washed my hair on automatic pilot and threw on my clean, baggy, electric blue knitted jumper and jeans.

I scraped my red curls back from my pinched face into a messy ponytail trying not to linger in front of the steamed-up bathroom mirror.

God, I looked horrific – pale and blotchy.

I didn't feel hungry for breakfast, but I'd paid for it last night in my rush to get to my accommodation, so after feeding Bronte and whisking her out for a quick walk, I returned her to the room and slipped down to the dining area.

I took a napkin and stashed a blueberry muffin, a banana and a cereal bar inside it. I didn't want anything else. I didn't even fancy any of those, but I thought I'd better try and force something down. I'd been pecking and nibbling at food since Joe had died, and Lola and Mia had repeatedly warned me that I'd hospitalise myself, if I carried on this way. I'd already lost weight as it was. I'd always possessed a curvy, ample bottom, which Joe loved, but that was beginning to disappear under my jeans. I thought there were lots of things Joe had loved about me. Turned out I was wrong. He'd certainly loved the standard of living my books had been able to provide for us.

I screwed up my eyes. Even my face, leaning towards heart-shaped, was sharper.

When I returned to the room, I took Bronte out for another pit stop before we checked out and set off on the road again.

I sat hunched behind the steering wheel, my fingers digging into the leather.

The sky was bulging with tumultuous clouds. Upon arriving at a set of traffic lights, I shot one hand into the back seat and gave Bronte's ears a good ruffle. She responded by lashing my hand with her warm, flicking, pink tongue, which made me want to dissolve into an emotional, self-absorbed puddle.

The car was too quiet. It was like I was trapped in a silent bubble of torture. The silence was making me think too much. I couldn't focus on anything else except Joe and Greta.

I blinked and forced my attention on the road again. I knew where I was headed for now but what was I going to do with myself? What were my intentions once I reached Rowan Bay? I'd always written, but now…

I switched on the radio, keeping the volume at a steady, low hum, trying to drown out the noise in my head.

Oh brilliant. Road works at Newcastle.

We started to crawl along with other cars, vans and lorries wedged side by side like building bricks. When we eased to a standstill, I fetched my mobile from my bag beside me on the passenger side and reluctantly switched it on. I had kept it turned off since speaking to Mia and departing from Hampstead last night. I didn't want to have to explain to anyone what I was doing, where I was going and why.

I eyed myself in the rear-view mirror. The traffic started to move off again, a giant snake of metal, and so I took the opportunity to park up at the next service station to let Bronte relieve herself and to give my in-laws a quick call.

'Darling, how are you?' asked Nancy with concern.

I took in the grey and marble sky through my car windscreen and the motorway services which were rather attractive: all potted plants and shrubs, surrounding a modern-looking glass building with a café, newsagents and a mini supermarket. There was a big, lit-up pumpkin outside the entrance, and stickers of ghosts, mummies and witches plastered on the double doors. It wouldn't be Halloween for several weeks yet. Funny how everybody else's lives were just pushing on as normal. So many people were desperate to move time on, whereas I would've done anything to wind it back. 'I'm just outside Newcastle,' I said, refocusing. 'I stayed in Leeds last night. Now we've parked up for a bit to talk to you.'

'We?'

'Bronte and me.'

From behind Nancy, I could hear Joe's Dad firing questions at Nancy. 'Is Rosie alright?'

I jammed my lips together. I didn't want to cry again. I didn't want to make them worry or feel any more wretched than they already did, but I was struggling. I had to tell them about Joe. I couldn't keep this festering up inside me, pretending to be the grieving widow.

'Yes. Um fine. Well, not fine, but you know.'

'Where are you going?' burst out Nancy.

'To Scotland. For a bit of a break.'

'On your own?' Nancy's voice was wracked with concern. 'Look, why don't you come back to London? Stay with us. You and Bronte. Take all the time you need to get yourself together. You can relax here, decide what you want to do.'

I was touched by their kindness and concern, but the last thing I wanted to do was stay at theirs and be surrounded by more reminders of Joe.

'I needed to get away,' I started, blinking. I had to tell them about Joe. I took a breath. *Just tell them, Rosie.* Get it over with. 'I received a letter.' I paused. 'From Joe's mistress.'

There was so much silence down the line, I thought the reception had cut off.

'Sorry?' Nancy's voice was confused.

'It turns out Joe was having an affair with this woman for three years and kept promising he'd leave me for her.'

There was a strangulated noise from his mother. 'No… No… That can't be right. You don't know what you're saying.'

I lifted one hand from the steering wheel and rubbed at my forehead. 'It's true, Nancy. If you don't believe me, contact Mia. She has the letter.'

There were more startled protestations from Nancy.

She relayed the information to Joe's dad, who also proceeded to insist that this was all utter nonsense.

I'd heard enough. I couldn't handle this right now. 'Like I said, contact Mia. I'm sorry, but I have to go now. Speak soon.'

I slumped my head back against the driver's-seat headrest. Around us, other cars were easing to a halt into the unoccupied spaces. Retired couples, harassed business people and lorry drivers were milling around, availing themselves of the toilet facilities or returning to their vehicles with take-away cups of coffee and sandwiches.

Behind me on the back seat, Bronte was making light work of the chew stick I'd given her. There was the intermittent sound of crunching and snapping. The mention of Mia had brought me to another uncomfortable truth. It wouldn't be fair to make her think that I was planning to write again, that my previous outburst about not wanting to be an author anymore had been some impulsive whim and that given time I'd come round. I had to tell her that part of my life was over. She was my agent. But she was also my friend. She needed to know. Of course, she'd be shocked and saddened, but she'd have to understand. She would come to accept it in time, I reassured myself. The writing light inside of me had been blown out. The revelation of Joe's infidelity had seen to that. How the hell could I ever write anything again, let alone a romance, when the love of my life had made me think I mattered but it turned out I hadn't? Joe had been all my heroes rolled into one.

Writing didn't exist for me anymore.

My passion and heart for it had died the day Greta's letter and those photographs arrived.

I had to be truthful and honest, even if that meant disappointing other people. Writing romances didn't sit right with me anymore, and I wouldn't be able to face myself in the mirror if I didn't believe in what I was writing.

Up until this point, I'd been so invested in my characters, their lives and their experiences that they'd felt like old friends. I'd always had faith in love – up until now. My books were all about the happily-ever-afters and the belief that love conquered all. No matter what obstacles or difficulties I threw at my beloved characters, they always found a way to be together.

If only real life could be that way.

Despondency thumped in my chest. I took a steadying breath. *Come on, Rosie. Just tell her.* It would be like ripping off a plaster. Painful for a few seconds, but then the irritation would subside. Okay, probably far longer than a few seconds. Knowing Mia, her agony would last weeks. I eased into it first by telling her I'd just spoken to Joe's parents and told them about his affair.

'Jesus. Still, you did the right thing telling them, Rosie. I'm sure they'd much rather hear something like that from you, than someone else. What did they say?'

'Not much. They sounded stunned. In denial. I told them to contact you if they wanted to see the letter.'

'Of course. No problem.' She let out a rush of air. 'They're probably appalled and embarrassed. Their golden boy turning out to be not so wonderful after all.'

I glanced at my eyes in the rearview mirror. 'Look, Mia, there's something else I need to tell you. I won't be writing again. Not anymore.'

Mia sounded like she was struggling to breathe. 'Look. I can't begin to understand what you're going through right now, but please don't make any hasty decisions.'

'It hasn't been hasty. I've been thinking about nothing else.'

Mia's silence down the line was so prolonged I wondered whether she'd passed out.

When she did try to recover herself, her voice struggled. 'Dear God. You're serious, aren't you?'

I jammed my lips together and shifted in my car seat. 'Yes. Very.'

Mia blustered so much into my ear; she sounded like she was choking. 'But... But ... I thought you just needed time, and hell, no one would blame you if you did.' She paused. 'Rosie, don't rush into anything. You aren't thinking this through properly.'

'Oh, believe me, I've mulled it over so much I thought my head was about to explode.'

There was a desperate rasp. 'But we're on the verge of signing a new contract with Lola, and you said you'd started writing a new book. Listen, take all the time you need after signing the contract and we can work on...'

My frustration fired up. 'The light has gone out, Mia. I don't want to do it anymore.'

She let out a frantic squeak but I pushed on. 'I know it's

not what you wanted to hear, but I have to do what's right. No more falsehoods.'

'What falsehood?' Her tone became more conciliatory. 'Listen to me. What Joe did had nothing to do with you. He was the one who chose to have an affair.'

I swallowed and clamped my eyes shut.

'But your readers can't get enough of your stories. It's an escape for them.'

'Precisely. It's not real. What I write are fairytales. I've made my money from something that doesn't exist and I don't want to do it anymore.'

'But… But…' Mia's desperation seeped down the line. 'But it's all you've ever wanted to do.' She puffed out frustrated air. 'Rosie, take some more time to think this over, okay? I know Lola's keen to get you to sign on the dotted line, but I'll speak to her. Lay everything out. Then after you have taken some more time, we can talk again and iron out the contract.'

I shook my head, even though Mia couldn't see me. 'I don't need any more time to think it over. I know what I'm doing.'

'So, what are you intending to do if you're giving up being an author?'

'I don't know yet,' I conceded. 'I'll have to see what the future holds.'

The future.

It was stretching out in front of me, like this endless black hole that was swallowing me up and there was no light at the end of it.

My idea had been to get my next book written and then suggest to Joe we try for a baby.

I could hear Mia shuffling some papers around on her desk. 'What am I going to tell Lola? She and Jarred Roberts are going to be speechless over this. You're one of their highest-earning authors!'

'Just tell her the truth.'

Mia let out a defeated sigh. 'Yeah, that'll do it.'

I eyed the cloud-clotted sky. 'And it's not like you don't have a stable of other successful authors, Mia. That goes for Lola, too. Anyone would think I was the only writer around.'

Mia started to protest, but I steeled myself. 'I'll set off again now, okay? Can you update Lola for me please. I really don't want to have to talk to a lot of people at the moment.' I hesitated. 'Any calls from the Press?'

'A couple of journalists have rung, asking what your future plans are and how you're doing.' Mia's voice softened. 'But don't you worry about any of that. We're more than capable of handling all that on your behalf.'

Her kindness made me want to weep again. 'Thanks. I'll be in touch again soon. Take care. Bye.'

I ended the call.

I tried not to dwell on what Lola would say when Mia dropped the bombshell that I wouldn't be writing again. Oh, they'd probably think I was just grieving. Mia would say to Lola to let me sound off, advise her to make murmuring, reassuring noises at me while I did and then tell me that they'd give me however long I needed to get my writing back on track.

But they could say all that in neon lights, on printed T-shirts and hire out Wembley Stadium with a marching band. It was no good.

I forced my eyes open.

Cars were drifting backwards and forwards out of the parking spaces. Small children were squealing at their parents that they needed the bathroom.

I decided I'd had enough of trying to explain myself for now and switched my mobile off again. I dropped it back inside my bag on the passenger seat and stretched my arm over to pat Bronte. She'd demolished her chew stick and was sitting upright on her blanket, like one of those Chinese waving cat ornaments. 'Okay, poppet,' I sighed, switching the key in the ignition. 'Time to hit the road again.'

Durham, Newcastle, Edinburgh; they all zipped past in a cacophony of houses, retail parks, dew-tipped fields, the Angel of the North, tantalising glimpses of Edinburgh Castle and its stunning, craggy, grey stone façade, before Bronte and I finally reached Rowan Bay.

It was as if the last twenty-four-hour drive had happened to someone else.

Bone crunching weariness criss-crossed with a strange sense of relief.

Bronte was slumbering, in the back seat of the car, as we

approached the brown tourist sign proclaiming that we'd arrived in Rowan Bay.

There were pine trees lacing each side of the road before they petered out to reveal a swell of water to the left, rippling silver in the early afternoon autumn light. Beyond that, magnificent sharp rocks erupted at every turn, making their way down to the water's edge.

I drove on, for another couple of miles, until the centre of Rowan Bay opened out to reveal its myriad bijoux shops.

There were the usual seaside-type gift shops, selling everything from miniatures of the local lighthouse and postcards, to shell ornaments and even Rowan Bay clotted fudge. There was also the usual sprinkle of small, local supermarkets and newsagents.

Pictures of my grandparents and me meandering up this street, savouring ice cream cones, filtered through my mind like an old movie.

I clutched at the steering wheel. Even though I'd showered this morning, I felt grubby again. Well, I supposed I had been all but bathing in my own tears for the vast majority of the journey.

I hadn't eaten properly either. Before we'd set off, I'd nibbled at the banana and taken a few, reluctant bites of the cereal bar. If Mia had seen me doing that, she'd have been horrified.

My stomach let out an irritated, hollow growl so loud, Bronte's ears shot up. She let out an unsettled whine.

'Aww, it's okay, sweetheart. You've been such a good girl. We're almost there.'

My grandparents' cottage was located ten minutes' walk away from the main street on a higher enclave, which overlooked the bay.

The famous local lighthouse was situated almost directly opposite it, and perched slightly higher up, on the ragged cliffs. I gazed at it and felt the memories flooding back. I used to love it when, as a kid, Barclay would take Grandpa and me around the lighthouse explaining all the jobs that he did inside, everything from cleaning the windows and lenses, winding the clocks and sounding the deep, loud, trumpeting fog signal, to providing technical and historical information to any curious tourists. He'd been so proud of being a lighthouse keeper and never tired of reminding anyone who cared to listen that the role ran through the Hogan family's veins. Their DNA was virtually stamped into every crevice of Rowan Bay lighthouse.

Even though Grandpa and I had been on these excursions to the lighthouse with Barclay on numerous occasions, we never got bored. Each time he gave us a tour around the lantern room or stopped to explain how sturdy the glass storm panes were, we'd be as fascinated as if it were the first time.

'Thank Christ there's no bloody gift shop in here,' he'd often say to me, gesturing around. 'Can you imagine me selling sticks of lighthouse rock or pencils as well?'

I would sort out Bronte and then we'd go up to the lighthouse and see Barclay. I'm sure he'd be as pleased to see me as I would be to see him. I conjured up pictures of his twinkly, powder blue, lined eyes, white sweep of hair and a dashing moustache. I needed one of his fatherly hugs and to be regaled with sea-faring tall tales. Barclay Hogan was every much a part of Rowan Bay as the bay itself was, and it was such a comfort that Barclay had volunteered to look after the cottage after Grandma Tilda passed away.

My car crawled up the incline before it slid away and flattened out.

An emotional lump lodged itself in my throat and refused to budge.

Sat there on the right was the cosy, white-painted cottage, which had been home to my late grandparents for forty years, with its pillar box red front door and picket fence.

The windows were shining, but there was a stillness about the place that made my heart sag.

The last time I'd been up here had been six months ago for Grandma's funeral.

My grandparents had visited us in London on occasion, but I think they felt that down there they were like odd pieces of a jigsaw puzzle that didn't quite fit. They couldn't wait to get back to their beloved Rowan Bay, with its lighthouse, dramatic sunsets and crashing waves.

It was a strange experience, just being here with Bronte. Slivers of apprehension and disbelief took over. What the hell was I doing? Had I thought this through properly? I'd jumped in my car and driven hundreds of miles, trying to escape the pain of losing Joe and what he'd done.

A mixture of loss and anger brewed inside of me again and I tried to ignore it.

I eased my car towards the cottage and looked across the way to the lighthouse, balanced on the cliff face. It stood there like one, solid, white sentry. Its dome was painted sea blue as was its panelled door. Beside it sat its various, white-painted outbuildings, which included Barclays' living quarters, the fuel house, a boathouse and the fog signalling building, which housed the boilers needed for the loud, fog signal to operate. It was like a little world on its own up there: compact, self-contained and ready to protect the rest of us.

Despite the leaden sensation in my chest and my head screaming at me, *What the hell do you think you're doing*, my mouth managed another brief smile at the thought of coming face to face with Barclay again.

I'd last seen him in person in March, when Joe and I had come up to Rowan Bay for my grandma's funeral. Barclay had been wonderful then, hugging me, giving me a supportive shoulder to cry on and listening to my endless tales about what an enigmatic and wonderful woman Tilda had been. I remember standing outside the cottage, the hem of my black dress flapping in the sea breeze.

I craved a friendly face and a warm welcome from the memories of my past. I knew I could rely on sweet old Barclay for that.

I parked up at the side of the cottage and let a relieved Bronte out of the back seat for a run-around. Anyone would've thought she'd been incarcerated for the past five years, the way she was bounding about.

Below in the bay, the waves were sending white froth

spraying into the air. It was comforting to know that if those white horses became untamed and started crashing against the rocks, the lighthouse beacon would come on and pepper the top of the harbour and the horizon in a comforting, bright golden light. Barclay would be doing his duty as always and help those at possible peril on the sea.

I fetched the front door key to the cottage from my jeans' back pocket while Bronte zoomed ahead of me, up the crazy paved path.

There were modest hanging baskets at either side of the door, and tubs of heather frothed at the top of the path.

I slid the key in the lock.

Bronte hesitated as I eased open the door and gestured for her to go in. 'It's okay, honey.'

She sniffed the air, unsure of where she was. I knew how that felt. It smelled of fresh laundry and looked clean and welcoming. Barclay had done a sterling job of taking care of the place by the looks of things.

My heart stilled as I followed Bronte inside and took in my surroundings. It was like time had juddered to a halt. Long-lost holidays spent up here came rushing back to greet me while I stood, taking in the familiar hallway carpet with its black and red swirls.

Grandma Tilda had been a keen artist, especially with watercolours, and a few of her impressive artistic efforts remained on the walls. A painting of a vase of snowdrops hung beside a depiction of a robin on a bird table alongside a tea pot, cup and a bowl of apples.

It was as though her talented hands, with their unique

brushstrokes, had been captured for all eternity on those canvases. They seemed to breathe and move every time I looked their way, which gave me a shred of comfort.

I looked down the shadowy hallway to where my grandma's artist studio was. She'd turned the smaller bedroom into her own little painting haven. The door was closed. It looked forlorn somehow.

Sadness clung to me.

I couldn't face going in there. Not yet. At some point, it would be a good idea to start sorting through her paintings and the assorted bits she had stashed in there, but I couldn't do that right now. I didn't feel emotionally up to it. Being surrounded by her beloved paint brushes and easels was just too much to deal with. At the back of my mind lurked the realisation that this cottage would have to be cleared and put up for sale. This and then turning my attention to our flat and Joe's belongings.

The prospect of it all and what I had to do washed over me and snatched me up in its vice-like grip.

I tried to calm my breathing. It was as if the walls of the cottage were squeezing the life out of me.

I should've set aside some time after Grandma's funeral to travel up here and get the ball rolling. But time had slipped away from me. Edits, plotting out my next book, publicity and interview demands had consumed my weeks. Joe kept insisting he would be more than happy to come up with me and we could start making progress on getting the place sorted out, but the very idea had filled me with dread.

Joe had always given the impression of being so

supportive and empathetic. Even in his legal career, he'd carried this air of approachability and understanding, which made his clients relax and put their faith in him. How was I supposed to remember him like that now?

I remembered Joe's funeral service and what Charles Headley, his boss, had said about him in his regal-sounding but croaky voice. His hazel eyes had misted over behind his round spectacles as he spoke. He'd made a funny comment about Joe's reputation for running late; *'Many was the time Joe would come racing through the door, clutching his takeaway coffee cup,'* which elicited melancholy smiles and laughter from family, friends and colleagues. Then Charles had straightened his black tie. *'Joe Hutton was one of those people in our profession who didn't become a solicitor for the money or the prestige. He became a solicitor because he wanted to right wrongs. The legal community will mourn the tragic passing of a young man who didn't get the chance to fulfil his potential, and yet, he leaves a legacy of kindness and decency.'*

My shoulders sagged under my jumper, as I gazed around myself, feeling overwhelmed with the responsibility I was heaving upon myself. Had they all been taken in by him too?

I thought about my grandparents' furniture, books and my late mum's belongings; they would still be here too, boxed up and piled in the loft. There would also be the eclectic mix of bric-a-brac my grandparents had accumulated throughout their lives. Grandma Tilda, God bless her, had not been the most organised or tidiest of people. My grandpa was forever telling her to have regular sort-outs and get rid of anything she didn't want or use anymore, but Grandma Tilda would tut, grab the item out of my grandpa's arms and protest that said item was an heirloom/she used it/she might use it/it had sentimental value and that she'd hang on to it 'for the time being'.

I sighed. *One thing at a time, Rosie. One thing at a time.*

The house was silent, except for the ticking of a carriage clock on the heavy, grey stone fireplace in the sitting room, which was off to the right. There was also just the teasing rush of the waves from down below in the bay.

Bronte ambled around beside me.

I allowed my fingers to trail over the top of my grandparents' old cream leather couch and two matching armchairs.

It felt alien, being in this house without them here to greet me. I expected them to both come puffing in through the front door, complaining about the way the tourists insisted on parking along the main street.

Grandpa Howard had been an avid reader and a lover of horse racing. Copies of his dog-eared and much-loved Dick Francis novels nestled side by side in the bookcase at the rear of the sitting room, beside my grandmother's PD James's and her glossy, art tomes.

The white, fitted galley kitchen was opposite the sitting room to the left. A daffodil yellow scrolling blind hung at the window, and a mug tree and mugs in the same bright shade stood on the ledge.

Their old, wooden retro radio was resting on the kitchen windowsill.

I ventured a bit further down the hallway towards their bedroom.

My downturned mouth hinted at a smile as I gazed down at the crisp, lilac-patterned quilt cover and pillows. Everything was almost as it was when my grandma had passed away.

Next to their bedroom was the guest room where Joe and I slept when we came here and where I used to stay during the school holidays.

There was another one of Grandma Tilda's paintings on the opposite wall, of a bouquet of pink roses. It looked so lifelike; it felt like I could reach out and touch their frilly petals. A chair sat in the corner of the room; on it was a sparkly cushion with the words, *Be Happy*, emblazoned across it in sequins. Apart from that, the room carried a muted, understated edge.

I resolved to buy some pretty autumnal flowers for in here and pop them in a vase on the windowsill.

Despite the chill, I opened some of the sitting room and bedroom windows to clear my head.

I then hauled my denim jacket back on and took Bronte back outside with me into the sea-whipped air. I shuttled backwards and forwards between my car and the cottage, retrieving my belongings and all of Bronte's paraphernalia.

The weather was dry, but cold. The late September chill was evident, made worse by the exposed bay. It was still beautiful though, even on a gnarly, grey day like this.

I eyed the lighthouse across the way, stippled on the

broken cliff face. It would be wonderful to see Barclay again.

I clicked the front door closed behind me.

Realisation of what I'd done and what I was doing gave me a brutal shake. I wrapped my arms around myself. Had I just driven nudging five hundred miles to swap one empty property for another? One set of scenery for another? One set of ghosts for another?

I bit my lip, trying to stem another wave of emotion.

Bronte plonked herself on her bottom by my feet and thumped her bushy tail on the hall carpet. I dropped down beside her and nuzzled my face into her curly body.

I squeezed my eyes shut. For the first time in my life, I felt completely alone, like a shadow no one noticed. My stomach let out a gurgle of hunger.

Bronte gave me a knowing look. 'I know. I know. I need to eat something.'

I kicked off my trainers and padded through to the kitchen and opened the fridge. Oh, bless Barclay. He'd been shopping and had popped some essentials in; bread, milk, fruit, vegetables, fresh orange juice, cereal and a couple of ready-made meals to get me started.

I'd need some more kibble for Bronte, so I decided to pop down to the local supermarket and get that now, before having something to eat. Food was the last thing on my mind, but my stomach was telling me otherwise.

My insides sagged at the prospect. What if I got recognised? The last thing I wanted to do was engage in small talk with anyone. I didn't want to be pinned to the spot by doleful eyes, being asked how I was doing and listening to them talk about Joe. Folks around here must've heard about what had happened to Joe by now. When I'd rung him, Barclay had said that he'd mention Joe to a few of the locals and ask that I was given some space.

Mia, Lola and my in-laws had done a commendable job of trying to steer me away from the headlines, so I wouldn't be witness to photographs of Joe and me together or to the headshot of him on the publisher's website, looking all dapper and dimpled at the camera.

But all the same I would often get the urge to go on my phone – like an itching wound that was begging to be scratched – and end up coming across more comments, more headlines, more condolences; and they clouded my brain.

I thought again about stocking up on Bronte's kibble. Barclay didn't have a dog or any pet, so he probably hadn't thought to get Bronte some food. If I kept my head down and avoided eye contact, I might be able to do a quick smash-and-grab and get away with it. My proud grandparents would often remind the locals who their writer granddaughter was and how I visited them often as a small, red-headed, nosey child.

Some insisted they remembered me from all those years ago.

I sunk my teeth into my bottom lip. I just hoped none of them who remembered me happened to be knocking around when I went shopping. I wanted to be anonymous.

I wanted to be invisible. I just wanted to seek solace in the cottage, snuggle up beside Bronte and remain in the past.

Snatching up my bag from the top of the kitchen table, I returned to the hall and picked up Bronte's lead. A walk though would be good for the both of us. 'Come on then, honey. Let's go get you some more grub.'

'Rosie? Is that you?'

My hope of making a quick exit withered.

From the rear of the corner shop came Rhea Stafford, its owner and Rowan Bay's answer to the BBC.

She came barrelling down the aisle like one of the town's tourist boats, but with deep-claret-coloured, short hair. 'I'd recognise those stunning red curls anywhere! How are you? Oh, what a stupid question to ask! Oh God, I was so shocked and sorry to hear about that lovely husband of yours.' She tilted her head to one side, like a pet budgie. 'Barclay dropped by earlier. Said you were on your way. It's been a while since we've seen you around here.'

I gripped the handle of my basket. Was she ever going to take a breath? My brief smile was brittle. 'Thank you. But it's not that long ago since I was last up here. I came up in March, for my grandma's funeral.'

Bronte was poking her head into the shop door. I'd tied her up just outside and popped her quilted, waterproof, fuchsia coat on her for extra warmth. Maybe I should've gone to the large supermarket in the next town, Castle

Hamilton. I would've been less likely to be spotted there. But I'd done so much driving to get here and the walk to the next town would have taken me a good fifteen to twenty minutes. I knew I didn't have the energy or inclination.

'So sad,' she sighed, looking pensive. 'Your Joe was so young. Just goes to show we don't know the minute, do we? And they broke the mould when they made your grandma.'

My empty basket banged against my leg with frustration. 'Yes, they most certainly did. Right, sorry, I don't mean to be rude but—'

'Ah. So much to do when you lose someone, isn't there? The phone calls, the emails, the documents. It's never ending.'

It was like she was waiting for me to fill the space, but I couldn't dredge up anything to say. She carried on. 'I remember when I lost my Freddie; you feel like you're lost in this fog.'

She tried to push some buoyancy back into her voice to compensate. 'On another writing deadline, too, eh?' Her curious pale eyes studied me out of her ruddy, sixty-something face. 'I take it that you'll be getting back to writing all those books of yours. Best to keep busy. I love your stories. All those wonderful, gorgeous heroes of yours. I can't get enough of them.'

The inside of my mouth turned to sandpaper. I was having difficulty looking her in the eye. *Don't start crying, Rosie. Hold it together, at least until you get out of the shop.*

Rhea Stafford's features carried an expectant expression.

My attention fell on the pet section. I reached over and snatched up a brown bag of salmon flavoured kibble for Bronte.

I wasn't going to hang around here longer than I had to. Rhea Stafford was here for the foreseeable. Any minute now, I expected her to go and get a bright light and shine it in my face. 'Sorry, Mrs Stafford, but I really do have to go now.'

'Aye, you'll have that cottage to sort out too now, I suspect?' she continued, relentless. She folded her arms against her plastic grocery apron, making it crinkle. 'Is that why you've come up here? To clear out the cottage? You don't want squatters hearing about it lying empty. That sort will be in there and having orgies in no time.' She let out a dramatic breath. 'Tilda and Howard were such a sweet couple. She was a bit arty and unconventional perhaps, but her heart was in the right place.'

Unconventional? Arty? Of course she was. That was what made my late grandmother so special; so, her. She had the biggest heart of anyone I'd ever known.

Rhea Stafford's critical inference about my grandma nipped at me. She was known for her enviable talent of being able to weigh many a comment with a passive-aggressive undertone.

Spotting a display of tins of biscuits by the till, I reached for one and thumped it down on top of the counter beside my basket with the kibble inside. I would take the biscuits to Barclay.

My gaze was steely. Before, I might have just brushed off Rhea Stafford's niggling asides, but not now. Not today. 'If you're not going to go to the trouble of putting my groceries through your till, you can have this. That should cover it.'

I dived one hand into my bag, pulled out my purse and snatched a twenty-pound note from it. I threw it down on top of the counter. I didn't feel like me. I didn't sound like me either, but I realised I didn't care. I didn't think I'd ever feel like Rosie Winters or even Rosie Ward for the rest of my life.

Rhea Stafford gawped at me as I thrust the kibble and Barclay's biscuits into a carrier bag I brought with me.

'Well, there's really no need for that, I'm sure. I was just being neighbourly. In fact, I was just about to ask if Barclay had told you his news yet…'

But I was already whirling out of the shop and untying Bronte.

I was all for supporting local businesses, but I decided there and then that it'd be better for the sake of my privacy, blood pressure and Rhea Stafford's personal safety, if I shopped at the supermarket up the road next time.

Chapter Six

It was a relief to cocoon myself again in the cottage.

This place was quickly becoming my protective shell.

I replayed the heated conversation with Rhea Stafford again. I knew I'd been rude but I found I didn't care. Then again, what had I expected?

Rowan Bay was a close-knit community. My grandparents had been part of that ever since they'd moved from Edinburgh all those years ago.

I put Bronte's new bag of kibble in the cupboard under the oven. I didn't usually speak to people like that. Most of the time, it took a lot for me to get wound up and lose my temper. But her incessant questions and then that salty remark about my grandma… How often was this going to happen round here? Probably quite a lot. I would just need to get used to it.

Pictures of Joe fixed themselves in my head again. I'd

been plunged into this, exposed and made to feel vulnerable, because of him. I'd become a sour, snappy, heart-wizened woman. The polar opposite of who I'd been before. His death and then discovering his affair had twisted and contorted me into a version of myself I didn't recognise. And I realised I didn't care.

In the bathroom, I eyed my make-up bag propped up next to my electronic toothbrush. What would be the point of slapping on cosmetics? I was here in a cottage in the Scottish Highlands, not about to parade down the red carpet.

I hadn't felt any compunction to wear cosmetics since Joe's accident. But then something my mum used to say whirled around my head. 'Make-up is your armour. You might feel rubbish, but a dash of lippie works wonders.'

I concluded it was going to take more than some lipstick to stop my insides feeling like they were collapsing on top of each other, but I rummaged around to locate my rose-pink lipstick and my eyeshadow palette.

My eyes reminded me of two piss holes in the snow. Mascara would just be a step too far. I knew as soon as I saw Barclay, I'd crumple into his fatherly arms, so I dashed on some biscuit-coloured eyeshadow and decided to leave it at that for now. I didn't want to end up looking like a melted waxwork.

I pulled on my walking boots and white Puffa jacket and reached for the tin of biscuits I'd bought for Barclay. I slipped them into a shiny gift bag I found in my grandparents' utility cupboard and encouraged Bronte to follow me.

I locked the cottage door behind us and huddled into my jacket. The water below in the bay stirred in the wind, reflecting the pearly sky.

Barclay had come to our wedding in London five years ago and he and Joe had hit it off straight away. They'd teased each other about English and Scottish football and their camaraderie was formed. He'd been taken in by him too. We all had.

Bronte negotiated the steps up to the lighthouse. It was rocky and mossy, overlooking the spectacular swell of Rowan Bay and the fishing boats bobbing up and down. Houses stippled along the skyline on the opposite side of the bay.

I reached the lighthouse, raised my hand and knocked. I smiled down at Bronte. 'Barclay might give you a little piece of digestive biscuit, if you're lucky.'

As if on cue, I could hear thudding feet on the lighthouse stairs before his friendly shaggy, greying appearance materialised at the lighthouse door.

He took one look at Bronte and me and threw his arms open. Bronte jumped up at him, her tail thudding from side to side. 'Red! Oh, Red. Come here, lass.'

I fell into his arms, dropping his bag of biscuits down at my feet.

And out it came; a strangulated series of cries, as the waves in the bay slapped against each other.

Barclay smelled of sea and boot polish.

It was comforting.

Once we'd gathered ourselves, Barclay locked up the lighthouse and we ventured towards his white bothy close by, with its small windows and tie-back, red tartan curtains, where he stayed when he wasn't attending to his lighthouse duties.

He insisted on fetching me a cup of tea – or something stronger if I was so inclined – but I said tea was fine.

Moments later, he re-emerged from his kitchen and gave Bronte a tea biscuit. 'Is it a daft question to ask how you are?'

I shook my messy curls. 'I really don't know how I am.'

'Time, lass. We all need time.'

I buried my face in the steam of the tea. 'I don't think I'll ever be me again.'

Barclay tugged down his thick, beige jumper. 'You mustn't look too far ahead. Minute by minute, at the moment.' His lined eyes creased even more as he looked at me. 'In time, your memories of Joe will comfort you. You'll see.'

His innocent words stung. I cleared my throat and gazed around, taking in his heavy, dark wooden furniture, seascape paintings and old maps framed on the walls. 'That's where you're wrong.'

'What do you mean?'

I steeled myself the best I could. 'Joe was having an affair with a woman he met three years ago. She wrote to me. Sent photos of them together.'

Barclay's eyes widened. 'Are you joking?'

'I wish I was.' I sighed. 'I didn't want to tell you over the phone.'

Barclay fiddled with his floppy cap perched on his head. 'I don't know what to say to you, lass. What the hell was he thinking?!'

'Probably that he could have his cake and eat it.'

Barclay reset his expression. 'Well, you know what you ought to do from now on? Think of yourself, Red. Focus entirely on you. Take each day as it comes, and in time, you'll move forward and be happy again. You'll see.' He shook his head. 'Bloody idiot. You were always too good for him.'

I offered him a small, sad smile. 'And how's Mags?' I asked. 'Let's talk about you instead. I'm getting boring.'

The mention of the woman's name, elicited pings of colour on Barclay's sea-battered cheeks.

Mags Buchan was the landlady of Rowan Bay's most well-known pub, The Sea Shanty. She and Barclay definitely had a thing for one another. It was a will-they-won't-they situation and the locals of Rowan Bay had speculated for a while as to whether the two of them would finally admit how they felt about each other and do something about it. Barclay was in that pub so often; he should get shares in the place.

'She's good. In fact, very good.' Barclay shifted in his armchair. 'I didn't want to tell *you*, lass. Not over the phone. You've had enough to think about.' He performed a rueful little smile. 'Looks like we've both been waiting to see each other, before swapping the latest news.'

He raised his chin, glimmers of happiness appearing in his eyes. 'Mags and I have stopped dancing around each other. We don't know how long we've got left, so we've come to our senses and are making a go of it.'

I set down my mug, jumped up from the sofa and hurled my arms around him. 'That's wonderful! Oh, I'm so thrilled for both of you.'

Barclay's face bloomed even more. 'Thank you. I took the bull by the horns, asked her out a few weeks back, she said yes and that was it. We're officially an item, I think is the expression these days.'

I grinned at him as I sat back down. 'So come on then. What are your plans for the future?'

Barclay dropped his gaze for a few moments. 'I'm retiring, Red. From the lighthouse. Mags and I have decided to move to Loch Lomond. Enjoy what years we have left together.'

I blinked at him. 'Are you serious?'

'Aye. Never been more serious in my life.'

A mixture of delight and shock raced through me. 'So, no more Barclay the lighthouse keeper?' I threw my hands up in the air. 'I'm delighted for you. For you and Mags. But what will happen to The Sea Shanty? And this place?'

'Mags's nephew, Damon, is taking over the pub.' He took a considered sip of his tea, rubbed Bronte behind the ears and looked up at me. 'As for the lighthouse, there'll be a new lighthouse keeper in place very soon.'

'Wow.' I pushed out a smile.

I was thrilled for Barclay and his new future with Mags. Of course I was.

But it seemed incomprehensible that there would be someone new stationed here in the lighthouse, guiding sea mariners to safety and sending that buttered glow of light onto the water.

'I'll miss this so much,' murmured Barclay. 'But nothing stays the same, does it, and I've had a good innings looking after this place. Time for new blood.'

'Well, it's the end of an era, but hopefully, the start of a new one,' I said, hoping I sounded more optimistic than I felt. I raised my mug and leant across to clink it against Barclay's.

He twinkled over at me with mischief. 'How about a nip of something a little stronger? I think we both deserve it.'

Chapter Seven

Halloween had come and gone in a blur of tumbling copper leaves, flapping witches' costumes, scary clowns and Barclay and Mags' goodbye celebrations at The Sea Shanty.

All the locals had bid them farewell, in a riot of bagpipes, fresh seafood buffet and raucous sea-shanty karaoke.

Being surrounded by other people was the last thing I wanted to do, but I'd steeled myself, slipped in the back of the pub with its fishing nets and shells plastering the walls and given them both my best wishes for the future. I presented them with an ornamental lighthouse, which they loved. 'We'll keep in touch,' a watery-eyed Mags had said to me, her dangling, jewelled, raindrop-shaped earrings dancing under her purple-coloured hair.

Now the first of November was promising the imminent arrival of Bonfire Night.

I tried to keep busy, faffing around in the cottage, walking Bronte until we were both exhausted and trying not to think about Barclay no longer in situ at the lighthouse.

Barclay's replacement was expected to arrive anytime, but I found myself mentally comparing them – even though I had no idea who his successor was – and felt guilty I was being rather childish.

Mia had called to inform me that Nancy and Jeremy had been in touch yesterday and asked for a scanned copy of Greta's letter to be emailed to them. 'I sent it to them straight away,' she said. 'They probably decided they should see it for themselves.'

It was a crisp, brisk afternoon and Bronte was champing to get out to the woodland close by and investigate the carpet of leaves.

I bundled myself into my coat, hat and scarf and secured Bronte in her harness and lead.

I'd just closed the door behind me, locked it and was pushing my phone into my coat pocket, when another dog – a German Shepherd – came bounding over the garden picket fence and launched itself at me, its friendly tongue flapping around.

Its big paws were clotted with mud.

I found myself staggering backwards but managed to keep myself upright.

'Kane! Stop that! I'm so sorry! Come here!'

I brushed the mud off my coat.

The dog's owner was standing just a few feet away. He

was tall and dark-haired. He shoved his curly hair back from his face as he appraised me out of arresting eyes that were the colour of the Mediterranean. 'Are you okay? He's over excited. We've just moved in up there and it's all a bit new.'

Beside him, Kane gave a lash of his tail.

It took me a few moments for my brain to unscramble this. *Moved in up there.* 'Sorry, where?'

'The lighthouse. I'm the new lighthouse keeper.'

I could feel my eyes boring into him. My chest gave an odd clench of sadness about Barclay's departure. 'You've got very big boots to fill, I can tell you that.'

He eyed me. His attention flitted to Bronte beside me and back again. 'Sorry, who are you?' His Scottish accent was a deep rumble. I was aware that this man was studying me from head to toe. I straightened my back. 'I'm Rosie. Rosie Winters.'

He shifted from foot to foot in his heavy black boots. He hesitated. 'Are you a relative of Barclay's?'

'No. A friend. An old family friend.'

His dog, who was wearing a blue collar with his name, *Kane*, emblazoned across a gold disc dangling from it, trotted forwards a few paces and gave Bronte a curious sniff. Bronte eyed him and then did the same back. They were circling each other tentatively.

'I'm Mitch Carlisle.' He angled his head to one side. He continued to watch me from under his dark, arched brows.

My thoughts skittered around.

I was aggrieved that this man was standing where

Barclay should be. It seemed almost incomprehensible that there would no longer be a Hogan as the lighthouse keeper in Rowan Bay. Hundreds of years of continuity and tradition had been ended by love. It was bitter-sweet.

I found myself glowering over at Mitch, unable to disguise my disapproval of him. His broad frame cast a wintery shadow.

My jaw clenched. The testy, acerbic Rosie was back again in full force. 'Well, you certainly didn't hang around, did you?' Barclay was born and bred in Rowan Bay, grew up for a spell in industrial Greenock. I thought of his love of the sea, of his career in the merchant navy before he became Rowan Bay's lighthouse keeper in 1983. He was built into Rowan Bay's fabric, just like his lighthouse ancestors before him.

I knew I was being unreasonable, but I couldn't help it.

Mitch clocked my tight expression. 'I'm sorry if you think I've stepped into Barclay's shoes rather fast.' His direct gaze made me stand up straighter.

'Barclay was originally going to stay for the winter, but I wanted to start right away, so we agreed on first November.' He pointed back over his shoulder at the lighthouse. 'It can't just be left vacant.'

My mouth flatlined. I knew he had a point.

Bronte, seeming to sense my tumultuous emotions, pressed her head against my leg.

I fixed Mitch with a steely look. It wasn't his fault Barclay had retired. But this man, with his slicked-back, dark curls and serious stare, shouldn't be here. Barclay should. Of course, I was delighted about Mags and Barclay getting together, but looking at his replacement made everything more final. It was the end of an era where Barclay was concerned. My insides gave a lurch of desolation.

I should just have led Bronte away and returned to the cottage for a good, self-indulgent cry. I wanted to retreat to the armchair by the window, cradle a mug of tea, and wallow in the injustice of everything while the Rowan Bay waves swallowed the shoreline.

Mitch folded his muscular arms.

I curled my lip. I could feel tears banking up behind my eyes, ready to flow at any moment. But I was damned if I was going to crumble into an emotional wreck in front of this man. Hot lava of determination raced through me.

'I don't know if you've noticed, Ms Winters, but we have a dangerous stretch of water. I have to be here to warn mariners of the shallows. Can't you see how perilous this rocky coastline is?'

My mouth pursed with irritation. Sarcastic sod. Talking to me as though I was some idiotic tourist from the city. 'Yes, I'm well aware of what it's like around here, Mr Carlisle. My late grandparents lived in this cottage for forty years, and I spent all my summer holidays here in Rowan Bay.' I flashed him a white-hot look of anger. 'I've swum in this water more times than you've had a hot toddy.'

He looked supremely unimpressed, which only wound me up even more. 'I take it you're not from here?'

'No, I'm not. I'm from Strathyre in the central belt.'

I gave him a challenging look. 'I thought as much.'

'What's that supposed to mean?'

But I didn't reply. 'Now, if you'll excuse me.' And with that, I clicked my tongue at Bronte and began to make my way down towards the bay.

I didn't process the dramatic views as I stomped my way back down the cliff path. I failed to notice the water splashing against the rocks and the rippling edges of the coastline. I wasn't savouring the unmistakable scent of sea salt and the zing of the wind whirling in across the waves.

As I mooched along the shore with Bronte, my mind was cartwheeling. It was like my life was one of those tablets you pop in a glass of water and watch as it fizzles away to nothing.

I'd been so looking forward to reconnecting with Barclay, and now I had to confront the prospect of being alone here, with just the wild scenery. Shame pricked me. He was moving on with Mags, which was wonderful, but just like Joe, that was another person who was leaving my life.

After Bronte chased the waves and skittered across the sand, we made our way back up to the cottage.

I yanked the door key from my coat pocket and jammed it into the lock. Bronte stood beside me on the top step, her eyes wide like a Disney dog, taking in my every move.

I stepped inside and peeled off my coat. Bronte gave a little bark, waggled her tail and then ran to fetch one of her toys from her basket, which I'd popped into the sitting room.

I tugged off my boots and tossed them away from me.

I strode into the sitting room and made straight for the panoramic window, which provided enviable views of the cliffs racing along and the glistening sea lolling and waving in the light.

A couple of gulls dipped and weaved over the top of the water.

What was I doing here? Why had I come? What lay ahead for me? It was as though I was stuck down there in the water, thrashing around and not getting anywhere. The waves were pulling me down.

And what about the new lighthouse keeper? Captain Birdseye and his dog?

Nothing would be the same here. Nothing would be the same again. All I'd done, I came to the conclusion as the spray arched over the rocks, was change my setting for another one. I knew nothing ever stayed the same, but why couldn't Joe have come to his senses? Why had he thrown away what we had? Six years together. Married for five. Having an affair for three of them.

It was no good. The awkward conversation with Mitch Carlisle just now, together with Barclay leaving the lighthouse and more jostling thoughts of Joe and his deception, was too much.

Surrendering to the torrent of emotion pressing down on me, I slumped onto the sofa and dissolved into tears.

Chapter Eight

I spent the next few days sleeping in fits and starts, taking Bronte on long walks down by the bay and watching the gulls perform acrobatic displays.

Nancy and Jeremy had rung me in a state of confusion and horror after reading Greta's letter. 'We're so sorry,' stumbled Nancy down the line. 'We feel so let down by Joe.'

'If there's anything we can do,' chipped in Jeremy, 'you only have to ask.' He coughed. 'We want to see you, Rosie. Stay in touch.'

'There's no need for either of you to feel guilty,' I'd emphasised, watching from the sitting room as the waves tossed over one another down below. 'This was all Joe's doing.' I forced a smile. 'And yes, we'll do that.'

I'd exchanged a few more phone calls with Mia and texted Lola; Mia had spoken to her about my decision to give up my writing, but she was more than open to giving me a leave of absence. I'd rolled my eyes up to the cottage ceiling. Weren't they listening? Were they just trying to humour me? Didn't they realise that I was serious about this? How on earth could they expect me to station myself at my writing desk and rattle off a couple of thousand words a day about romance, when my own relationship had been a sham?

No doubt she and Mia would do everything they could to try and make me think again, but my mind was made up. I wasn't a three-year-old in a strop about her favourite broken toy.

It wasn't like I needed to write from a financial point of view either. My generous advances and royalties over the past few years had made sure of that. I'd been very, very lucky and I never took that for granted. Plus, Joe had been very canny with stocks and shares investments, which meant he'd left an additional cushion of money for me, should I ever need it. My mouth curled up at one corner. The truth was, I didn't want it, though. I was determined to manage by myself.

I mentally tried to brush aside the yearning in my chest for my old life before all this mess had happened and decided instead to visit my late grandparents' final resting place at Rowan Bay Church and take some flowers to their grave.

Rowan Bay Church was a stout little Gothic-style place of worship set a couple of miles further up the country road from my grandparents' cottage.

Its old graveyard, studded with headstones ranging from simple markings to elaborate and artistic carvings, was an echo of the community and its links to its past. The final resting places of sailors who'd perished at sea a hundred years ago jutted out of the grass beside the graves of a couple of local doctors and former reverends of the church.

The church's stained-glass windows glistened out of its ruddy, steel-grey Coade stone. The images depicted sea farers battling the elements. The church doors were open and the stained-glass windows shone down like precious jewels. Intermittent strobes of sunlight caught them, sending shafts of ruby reds, golden yellows and bottle greens onto the polished church floor.

On the way, I'd dropped by the local florists, Petal Power, and bought a big bouquet of amber and russet roses to leave at their grave.

I hugged it tighter to me as I made my way towards the cemetery. The air from the church was a heady scent of candle wax, flowers and musty bibles.

I glanced down at the pine cones and berries of the bouquet I'd bought, interspersed with the blooms. The florist was talking about taking Christmas orders, even though it was still early November. I'd arrange the flowers on their graves and have a few moments to myself with them.

Oh God. I was struggling to think about tomorrow, let alone Christmas. The prospect of that iced my heart over.

The colour and the cosiness of it; spending the holiday snuggled up with Joe, making Christmas dinner and having warm almond croissants for breakfast; taking brisk woodland, Boxing Day walks with Bronte and watching National Lampoon's Christmas Vacation. That was all gone now. Just a series of memories tied together.

The tissue paper my flowers were wrapped in let out a flutter.

I buried my face in my bundle of dark green woollen scarf. I didn't want a repetition of Rhea Stafford's incessant interrogations. The way I was feeling, I was likely to bite someone else's head off if they happened to spot me and ask me anything remotely personal. I didn't need the questions, the head tilts and the sympathetic looks. At least there didn't appear to have been anything new in the newspapers or magazines so far about Joe's death and me. That was something. And Mia, bless her, would deal with it anyway.

I was constantly and acutely aware of my life being a lie. I didn't need to be reminded of it in newspaper and magazine headlines.

The wind had dropped and I could hear the waves slapping in the bay against the rocks.

A couple of gravediggers were chatting quietly a few feet away from me. They both nodded their heads, before resuming their conversation.

The last time I had been here was for my grandma's funeral; it seemed a lifetime ago.

Odd bursts of pale sunshine strobed through the clouds. I offered the two gravediggers a fleeting, watery smile of gratitude and weaved my way over to where my grandparents were.

My booted feet crunched on the chipped gravel along the paths snaking between the headstones.

My grandparents were resting together at the other end of the churchyard, close to a couple of majestic Scots pines.

I studied their black and gold headstone and knelt down to arrange the flowers in the flower flute.

I flapped out the hem of my long coat. 'What am I going to do?' I asked them in a broken voice. 'Joe died while cheating on me; Barclay has moved away; I'm staying in your cottage with Bronte and as for writing anything ever again … well … that's done. I can't. I won't.' I moved a couple of the flowers. 'I feel like I don't know who I am anymore or what I'm supposed to be doing.'

I laced and unlaced my gloved hands. 'I honestly thought my life was sorted. I believed Joe loved me and that I had a marriage like yours and Mum and Dad's.' My fingers tightened around each other, as I continued to crouch there. 'But it turns out that Joe was just playing me for a fool. I thought I was writing about us. About him.' I shook my head. 'I don't have faith in love anymore. I don't have faith in romance and everything that's supposed to go with it.' I studied their granite headstone and the gold, swirling letters of their inscription. 'I won't allow myself to become vulnerable like that again. I've learnt my lesson. No more trusting anyone.' I gave the top of their headstone a gentle stroke and stood up.

I was rearranging my scarf around the bottom half of my face again to conceal it just in case anyone might recognise me, when a flicker of movement to my right, drew my attention.

Oh bugger! It was him. The new lighthouse keeper. Mitch Carlisle.

He had Kane with him and they appeared to be taking a walk. Panicking, I shoved my scarf further up my face and crouched down again at my grandparent's headstone, mentally willing him to go away. He was the last person I wanted to speak to.

I was likely to give him another terse mouthful.

When I slowly rose a few moments later and peeked over, I was relieved to see they'd gone.

Chapter Nine

The weekend vanished in a haze of long walks with Bronte and another phone call from my lovely, concerned in-laws pleading with me to go and stay with them.

I assured them I was fine, under the circumstances. What did fine actually mean? In my case, it meant limping from day to day, seeking some sort of twisted comfort in the beauty of the angry waves.

Over the weekend, there had been fleeting glimpses of the new lighthouse keeper and his dog. I liked Kane, but as for him, if I never saw him again, it would be no hardship. If Mitch thought he could just sweep into Rowan Bay and erase the legacy of Barclay and the other Hogan lighthouse keepers before him, he was in for a shock. The Hogan family's history was stamped into the fabric of not only the lighthouse but the town itself and no new broom could change that.

November was well and truly here. There was a crackling, sparkling frost lacing everything from the heather in my late grandparents' garden to their picket fence.

I padded around the cottage in my pink and white checked pyjamas, dressing gown and fluffy thermal socks. The heating system in the cottage worked well, but being so close to the bay meant that the sharp wind could still worm its way up and in.

After letting Bronte out into the garden for a run around and to do her first ablutions of the day, I shoved down a slice of toast with a lash of butter and made a pot of tea. I was forcing myself to eat, just to keep going for her, really.

I showered and dressed in automatic mode.

Out of the sitting room window, the tips of the waves glinted under the chilly, marmalade sunshine.

I switched on my phone and caught sight of one of my favourite photos of Joe in my photo gallery. He'd been running and his shock of blond hair was dishevelled. He was grinning at me, his animated eyes sparkling with love.

I snapped my attention away from the screen and dropped my phone down onto the sitting room table, as though it was scorching my fingers.

I thought about what I was doing here and why I'd come. It was to escape, run away from the nightmares that had besieged me in London. But they were still there; the dark reality of it all. What Joe had done and the implications of it were lingering, even though I'd driven hundreds of miles, in the hope they'd vanish in the rear-view mirror. I'd been naïve. Visions of my six book covers, with their embossed lettering and colourful, escapist artwork paraded in front of my eyes next. That side of me was gone. Not just the trusting, romantic side, but the passionate, enthusiastic, romance author, too. Joe might have been happy to pretend he was someone he wasn't – live a double life – but that wasn't who I was. I knew that much. Maybe I could write a serial killer or a slasher thriller and have Mitch as the villain? No. Tempting though that was, it wasn't me either.

My scattered thoughts were interrupted by Bronte startling me. She'd sprang up from the rug and burst into a fit of frantic barks and growls.

'Whoa, young lady! What's up with you?' Maybe she was picking up on my tension.

Bronte ignored me and continued to fix her furious stare across the sitting room and out of the window behind me.

Her tail was static and her paws pounded into the mat again and again as she let rip with another stream of noise.

'You really don't like those seagulls, do you?'

I rolled my eyes and turned around, expecting to see a brazen gull strutting up and down on the window ledge, deliberately winding her up.

But it wasn't an arrogant gull.

There was a man staring at me through the sitting room window.

His black and grey hair was lifting off his craggy face in the wind. He had sharp features and the upturned collar of his checked coat was flapping against his cheeks.

It took a few seconds for my brain to catch up and process what was happening.

That was when I screamed.

Chapter Ten

Seconds froze as the older man realised I'd spotted him.

With a look of horror gripping his face, he took a few stumbling steps backwards in his hurry to get away.

Bronte careered towards the front door, her body tense and her barking frantic.

I hurried after her, my heart pumping. What on earth did he think he was doing, peering in like that? Who was he and what did he want?

Despite my insides twisting with shock and fear, I yanked the door open to peer up and down to see where he'd gone.

There was no sign of him.

Bronte appeared by my leg and shot out in a blur of ears, tail and curls. 'Bronte! Stop! Here! Come back!'

But she was gone, leaping over the little picket fence and to the right, down towards the path that led to the bay and its modest strip of sand. She seemed to be on a mission to find whoever frightened me.

'Shit!' I gulped, whirling around and flapping about on the step, feeling helpless. What if she got lost or got into trouble in the water? I couldn't lose her. I'd lost enough.

I dived back inside the cottage for my coat, boots and scarf. I shoved them on and snatched up my front door key and mobile. I raced out the door, slammed it behind me and locked it. 'Bronte!' I screamed into the biting wind. I let out a few fierce whistles in the hope of attracting her attention, but there was no sign of her.

I raced down the garden path, not bothering to close the gate behind me. I called her name again, whipping my head in all directions as I searched for her.

'Excuse me? You, okay?'

Flustered, I jerked my head round.

It was Mitch. Kane was by his side, sniffing the air.

My voice was all wobbly. 'No, I'm not. I just had a prowler staring in through the sitting room window, and now Bronte's chasing after him.'

Mitch pulled a sceptical face. 'A prowler? Around here? Are you sure? Maybe it was a salesperson or a cold caller?'

I glowered up at him, in a mixture of panic and frustration. I could feel myself prickling under his turquoise stare. 'Oh, is this a new thing? Cold calling by gawping in people's windows rather than knocking on the front door? I must've missed that.'

Mitch gave me a measured look from under his dark brows. 'Or perhaps it was someone who was lost?'

I started to pick up even more speed towards the path. My voice was cracking. 'Sorry, but I don't have time for this. I've got to find her.'

Mitch's voice kept on behind me. 'What I mean is, he could've been a tourist, looking for directions, maybe?'

I peered down at the bay and then nodded my head so hard. I was in danger of snapping my neck. I couldn't see Bronte anywhere. 'Yep. You're right. Of course. Someone would be looking for directions by staring into my sitting room. He wouldn't have knocked and asked the way, would he? That would be too normal.'

I could see my sarcastic comebacks were making Mitch's teeth grind, but I didn't care. I cared about very little at the moment. All I wanted was Bronte to come barrelling towards me, with her tongue flapping out of her mouth.

'What I'm saying to you, Ms Winters, is are you certain it was a prowler?'

'No, I just made it up. I've lost everyone and everything I've ever loved and I'm bored so I decided I needed to…'

One of his dark brows shot up to his hairline. He gave me a long look. 'I'm sorry.'

My cheeks blanched. I was struggling to look at him.

'About your husband.'

I drew up at the top of the path. Hurt rippled inside me. 'Well, the broadcasting service around here has been busy.'

Mitch looked at me.

'I take it Rhea Stafford in the corner shop told you.'

He nodded.

My voice trembled. 'Well, it would help if some nosey buggers like Rhea Stafford minded their own business!'

I swung away from him, so he couldn't see the embarrassed look on my face, and yelled Bronte's name one more time. It was none of his business either. Why choose this moment to repeat gossip he'd heard? Fine. Maybe he was trying to be kind, but right now, the nicer people were to me, the more I seemed to want to lash out. It was as if a voice was telling me that I couldn't handle it, so it was safer to reject their offers of empathy and kindness instead.

I called for Bronte again, but the sound of my desperate voice caught in the wind. The stretch of sand was deserted. Where was she? I should've been more careful when I opened the door.

Bronte and her safety were consuming my mind. Pictures of her getting into difficulty in deep water or breaking a leg in a rabbit hole shimmered in front of me. 'I've got to find her. I don't care how long it takes. I can't lose her. I just can't.' I swallowed. Tears bunched in the corners of my eyes.

'Hey, come on. Don't think like that.' Mitch gave me a measured look. 'You won't lose her. We'll find her.'

I watched as Mitch stalked past me at a brisk pace towards the path. He was a confident blur in his heavy boots and black winter Puffa jacket. Kane followed. 'And you're sure Bronte took off in this direction?' he called over his broad shoulders.

I blinked at him, my voice dry with worry. 'Yes. Well, I'm almost certain. But what are you doing?'

Now it was his turn to be sarcastic. 'I thought I'd go for a pint and a game of dominoes in The Sea Shanty. What does it look like I'm doing? Kane and I will help you look for Bronte.'

I reddened. I supposed I asked for that one. I'd been Ms Sarcastic to him for the last ten minutes. 'Okay. Thank you.' I frowned up at him, my panic for Bronte's well-being shooting higher and higher. 'But don't you have lots of lighthouse-y things to be getting on with?'

'For your information, I've already cleaned the windows and lenses, taken and logged the weather readings and swept the lighthouse stairs.' He strode off ahead, with Kane loping at his heels.

My thoughts were whirring as I hurried to catch up with Mitch and Kane and fell into step just behind them. The path down to the bay snaked between two grassy hills.

'Did you get much of a look at this guy?' Mitch asked. 'Your prowler?'

I fired a suspicious glance up at him. 'I thought you didn't believe I had a prowler.'

There was the faintest trace of black, peppery stubble on his jaw. 'I didn't say that. Well, not in so many words.' He shook his head, exasperated. 'Anyway, like I was saying, what did he look like?'

I didn't feel like being communicative with anyone, let alone Mitch, but we had to work together to locate Bronte. Greater tides of worry swamped my chest at the thought of Bronte getting hit by a car. Oh no. What if the intruder had taken her? Would he hurt her? I might never see her again.

Panic flooded through me. I called out her name and whistled. *Oh, just appear Bronte. Please!* I squinted against the steely morning light glancing off the top of the water, willing a brown, curly blob to appear in the distance. I was struggling to quell the rising doom. I dragged my attention back to Mitch's question. 'He looked like he was in his late seventies with greying hair.'

'Well, that narrows it down around here.'

I hurried along behind him, my worry for Bronte consuming me. I whistled again for her. 'You did ask.'

I eyed the sliver of vanilla sand down below. Where was she? I called her name repeatedly. 'Bronte! Where are you?'

We reached the start of the bay and I lifted one hand to my eyes and scanned the horizon, praying that a bundle of Labradoodle would come bouncing towards me.

Kane took off ahead of us, his head down and sniffing the ground.

'She won't have gone far,' reassured Mitch. 'Please try not to worry.'

'But she doesn't know the area.' I buried my wobbling chin into my scarf. 'She hasn't been up here that often. If anything's happened to her, it's my fault.'

Mitch gestured to Kane, his tan and black limbs moving faster ahead of us. 'He's great at finding things. I'm sure he'll locate her.'

'We're not in an episode of Lassie!'

He gave me a look, but didn't say anything.

'I've just lost my dog, and it's all my fault. You don't

understand. I opened the door and she shot out.' My voice was raspy with emotion.

'I'm sure it wasn't your fault. If they spot something they want to chase, it's often very difficult to get them to obey.'

There was still no sign of Bronte. The beach was quiet. A couple of gulls shrieked, making me jump. 'Thank you for that dog analysis, Captain Birdseye!'

Mitch took a moment to digest what I'd just called him. His handsome face was impassive. Then he started to laugh. His eyes crinkled. I noticed he had white teeth and prominent canines. 'Captain Birdseye?!'

It wasn't like me to be so rude, but I didn't feel in control of anything anymore.

'You've put me in the mood for a fishfinger sandwich now.'

'Oh, I'm delighted you're finding this situation so amusing.' I threw him a look. 'There's really no need to help. I'll find her myself, thank you.'

The sand was melting with the splashes of the water, and the rocks glistened. The wind was unforgiving. What if Bronte had ventured into the water and got into difficulties? I remembered my grandparents speaking about the depth of the water being deceptive. They always used to warn me not to venture too far out and would never let me come down to the bay to swim on my own.

Fearful tears were on the brink of slipping down my cheeks. All I wanted was my Bronte back, safe and sound.

I should never have burst out of the front door like that.

To lose Bronte, my little constant companion, was a horrific thought at any time, but right now it was especially inconceivable.

Bronte had always lain beside my chair whilst I was toiling over a book, acting as my sounding board when I was debating character names or convinced that my latest plot wasn't working. She'd lie there, her fluffy paws like furry trousers, lifting her head to look up at me with those curious eyes of hers while I ranted and raved about my latest draft being crap and that the plot had more holes than a tea bag.

Oh well. At least she wouldn't need to do that anymore.

I yelled Bronte's name into the sea air, as did Mitch. I snapped round to look at him.

'I'm not leaving you here in this state, trying to find your dog on your own.'

I opened my mouth to protest, but Mitch was unrepentant. 'Stop being so bloody-minded and accept help when it's offered.'

My cheeks flamed with colour.

'Look, I know you were close to Mr Hogan and that I have big boots to fill, but I'm only trying to do my job.'

I flashed him a chilly glance from under my curls.

God, he was annoying. But he was helping me.

Mitch shouted for Bronte again, but there was nothing. No answering barks. No sign of her flapping ears as she charged towards me. No waggling tail thrashing from side to side in greeting.

I craned my ears, hoping against hope that I'd detect her

cheerful yaps or she'd come scampering out from somewhere, but all I could hear was the water and the odd screech from the gulls. 'This is down to me,' I gulped, picking up speed along the sand. 'It's my fault she's lost.'

'No, it isn't.'

I rubbed at my face. 'Yes. It is. Please stop trying to make me feel better. She was trying to protect me.'

'Ms Winters. Stop beating yourself up over it. We'll find her. Hey! Look at Kane.'

I turned around, shoving my hair out of my frantic eyes. Kane had gone from snuffling his big, black, sooty nose along the shoreline, to suddenly picking up his pace. His tail wagged.

With a glance back at Mitch, he took off across the top of the sand like a speeding gold and black bullet. His muscly back shifted as he moved, almost galloping on his sinewy legs like a racehorse.

He was flying, jumping over the odd rock in the sand and stippled clumps of grasses as though they weren't there.

He stopped, raised his proud head and savoured the sea air. Then he bounded away again.

There was a bigger, broader set of rocks sandwiched together at the further end of the bay.

Kane paused and looked straight at them. Mitch shoved his black hair back from his face. 'He's found something.'

We started running towards the rocks, in hot pursuit of Kane.

My heart dared to lift, as Kane concentrated on the cluster of grey rocks at the far end of the beach.

The sea air lashed through our hair and against our faces as we raced across the wet sand. Kane scrambled over the top of the rocks, vanishing with one brush of his tail over the other side.

A series of excited barks and yelps shot into the air. It felt like Kane had also been missing forever. I let out gulps and frantic pants as the rocks drew closer and closer. *Please, God,* I prayed silently in desperation. *Please let Kane find her. If he does, I promise I will try and not be so sarcastic to people ever again.*

Time seemed to slow down to a treacle pace, before both Kane and Bronte's heads popped up like meerkats from the other side of the bank of rocks.

'Oh God!' I broke into another delighted run across the sand. 'Kane! Thank you! You found her! Clever boy!'

Bronte scrambled up and over the rocks and came tearing towards me, her ears streaming behind her. I crouched down and she knocked me backwards onto the wet sand but I didn't care. I lay there, a series of odd laughs and sobs erupting out of me as she jumped on my chest and lashed my face and hands with wet, warm licks. Sea water was seeping into the waistband of my jeans.

I struggled to my feet, my hair tumbling over my eyes, and scooped her up in my grateful, relieved arms. I buried my emotional face into her. 'You naughty girl. Please don't ever run off like that again.' I scrambled around inside my coat pocket, set her down on the sand beside me, located her lead and clipped it onto her collar.

Kane materialised beside me, his long, pink tongue lolling out of his mouth. He looked like he was smiling. I bent down and fussed over him. 'Thank you, you big, handsome guy. I owe you one.'

'Och, it was nothing,' teased Mitch.

I glanced up. Mitch was watching me. His Mediterranean-coloured eyes danced. 'I'm glad you finally appreciate me.'

I slid him an embarrassed but grateful look. 'Thanks for your help.'

'It wasn't me who found her.'

Kane trotted over to be by his master's side. The German Shepherd still looked rather pleased with himself.

'Hold on.' Mitch darted over to the rocks where Kane had found Bronte, peered over them and came trotting back. 'Nope. No elderly miscreant prowlers lurking behind there.'

I clutched onto Bronte's purple lead. 'You still don't believe me, do you? About the prowler, I mean?'

'I do believe you saw someone, but as for an over-seventies prowler, I have my doubts.' He hesitated. 'Do you have any idea what he was doing, looking in your window?'

I tutted. 'I wasn't about to ask him in for a cup of tea and a slice of cake.'

The strip of sand we were standing on continued to be teased by the rush of the waves. Dinky fishing boats slicked with paint in candy pinks, electric blues and zinging greens creaked and bobbed. Their masts fired upwards, piercing the milky winter sky.

Mitch studied me from under his brows. He looked like he was trying to weigh me up. 'Are you always this sarcastic?'

I bristled, feeling self-conscious under his intense gaze. 'Not unless I get asked stupid questions.'

A corner of his mouth twitched, which infuriated me even more.

I glanced up at the sky. I'd just made a promise that I wouldn't be this sarcastic if Bronte was alright. Bugger. I wasn't doing very well.

We made our way back towards the cottage and the lighthouse. Kane skirted in and out of the frothing waves and Bronte paddled beside me on her lead, giving me imploring looks to let her run free. I decided not to for the time being.

'Would you like me to give your cottage the once over when we get back? Just to reassure you that there's no one about to jump out of your wardrobe?'

'I thought you doubted what I'd seen.'

I spotted him flex a brow. 'Och, not this again! Is that a yes or a no?'

'No, thank you. I'll be fine.' If this character did reappear and try anything, he'd get bashed over the head with one of my grandma's easels.

'Okay. But you know where I am if you're worried about anything, Ms Winters.'

'I appreciate that. Thank you.' Mitch's kindness touched me. I hesitated. 'And there's no need for the Ms Winters. It's Rosie.'

Mitch gave me a long look and whistled over his shoulder at Kane. He was still preoccupied, leaping about and barking in the spray. 'Okay, Rosie. Please call me Mitch.' He bent over and gave Kane a solid pat on his flank. 'I'm sure that guy just took a wrong turning. I bet you won't clap eyes on him again.'

I tightened my scarf around my neck. I really hoped I didn't. There had been enough excitement for one day.

Chapter Eleven

C hristmas.

A word that used to fill Joe and me with sparks of anticipation. It was descending on me now like a black fog.

It was growing ever closer, taunting me, reminding me of the wonderful Christmases Joe and me had had. Or at least, I had thought they were wonderful. How many times did Joe make up an excuse and slip away to see Greta over those festive seasons? Where was he, when he was claiming he had another post-work Christmas drinks do to attend?

Christmas was five weeks away now, and I was already sick of the sight of festive selection boxes, chocolate figures of Santa, snowmen and reindeer, not to mention the sparkly greeting cards.

At the entrance to the local garden centre, miniature Christmas trees and festive wreaths glowed everywhere.

I adjusted my moss green crocheted hat and clamped it down tighter over my curls. Even the weather seemed to be hinting at the festivities to come. Doughy clouds sailed overhead, with the water in the bay laced with white horses as it struck the pelt of sand.

I blinked furiously as pictures of Joe and me decorating our six-footer silver Christmas tree last year exploded in my mind. Him kissing me under the mistletoe; both of us savouring hot chocolate in Hyde Park and sharing a bag of roasted chestnuts; our breath colliding and mingling in the frosty air as we did our Christmas shopping, arms draped around each other. Did he repeat everything with Greta? A Christmas replay of all things romantic? When he was kissing me, did he taste her too and vice versa?

I tried not to dwell on how I would always insist on wrapping rose-gold fairy lights along our apartment balcony and station another decorated tree out there too.

Inside our apartment, the air would be filled with the scent of cranberry and cinnamon potpourri, and pictures were draped in more lights and garlands of holly and ivy. I didn't think you could go over the top at the most magical time of the year and Joe was every bit as crazy about Christmas as I was.

I tried not to register the empty feeling tripping through me, as I saw myself and Bronte stumbling out of the apartment and me slamming the car door shut, me imagining Joe's face in the rearview mirror.

I gripped Bronte's lead tighter in my right hand.

I'd stashed a couple of reuseable carrier bags in my shoulder bag. I wanted to get some air and decided to walk to the supermarket, rather than jump in the car.

No corner shop for me today. I didn't want a repeat performance with Rhea Stafford. Hopefully, no more nosey parkers would leap out and interrogate me. I know people meant well and only wanted to pass on their condolences about Joe, but all the kind sentiments in the world wouldn't wipe out how I was feeling and what he'd done.

———

At the supermarket I secured Bronte's lead around the nearby railings, grabbed a basket and dropped my chin into my scarf, just in case.

As I stepped inside, a display of Christmas selection boxes caught my attention. I glowered at the reindeer glitter design. Jesus, I was turning into Scrooge.

Gathering my resolve, I proceeded to scoot up and down the aisle locating bananas, bagels, more milk, pasta and assorted vegetables.

My lip curled up when I saw mince pies and Christmas puddings for sale.

There were a few other customers around, but it wasn't busy. Relief swam through me.

I surmised that nine o'clock on a Tuesday morning in November, wasn't the most popular time to conduct your weekly grocery shop. Perhaps a lot of people had ventured into the bigger towns to start their Christmas shopping. I groaned inwardly at the thought of it.

I hurried up another aisle under the strip lighting, reaching for a bar of 90% dark chocolate. On the shelf below, was Joe's favourite – Oreo. A pang of something hit me in the chest.

I pulled my eyes back up to the fluorescent ceiling. Was this what my life was going to be like from now on? Feeling like I was taking part in an episode of Supermarket Sweep every time I needed to restock my fridge? Stay cooped up in my grandparent's cottage for the foreseeable? Hiding from people? Trying to avoid awkward situations and probing questions? Worried that I'd dissolve into a torrent of tears, if anyone so much as asked if I was okay?

I glanced back at the bar of Oreo chocolate he loved.

I had to accept that there were going to be reminders of him and of what I thought we had, lurking around every corner. I would just have to learn to deal with them. A song we both liked or a film we snuggled up to watch together. Someone with hair similar to his, running in the park.

And that was precisely why I'd fled from London and dashed up here to Rowan Bay. It was so I could try to give myself time to heal in private and learn somehow to deal with the pain and the deception. It wasn't going to be a quick fix. At the moment, it felt like I was going to be fumbling through this airless, dark torture forever.

With my basket brimming with food items, I rounded the bottom of the next aisle to the pet section and picked up a new, squeaky apple toy for Bronte. Joe hadn't been keen on getting a dog to begin with. He insisted he wouldn't have time to devote to them and that it wouldn't be fair.

But that all changed the day I brought her into the apartment three years ago. She was a squirming, licking bundle of ten-week-old fluff and I'd fallen in love with her the moment I set eyes on her at the breeder's house in Camden. She'd wiggled over to me, licked my hand and then sat down behind my boot, as if to say, 'When are you taking me home then?!'

As soon as Joe clapped eyes on her, she wrapped herself around his heart and decided she loved us both unconditionally.

I plopped the latex toy into my basket, dropped my head and started to make my way towards the tills. That was until I barrelled into a tall, broad figure. 'Oh, sorry!'

'Hey. How's it going?'

It was Mitch.

'In a hurry?' he asked.

I pulled my eyes from my shopping basket. 'Er. Yes. Just wanted to do a smash and grab. Bronte's outside.'

He was smiling down at me, a sort of friendly, expectant smile that was making his eyes shine.

I fidgeted on the spot. 'Anyway, I'd better go. Sorry for almost knocking you over just now.'

Mitch grinned at me, while brandishing the litre of milk he was clutching. 'I think I'll recover.' He gestured outside. 'I only came in for this and I've got my car parked nearby. I can give you a lift back, once I get some more petrol.'

I was aware of his sculpted shoulders under his long coat and the breeziness of his smile. He was being friendly, twinkly. But I didn't want friendly. I didn't want anything from anyone. 'Thanks, but it's fine. Bronte and I could do with the walk.'

'Are you sure? You've got a couple of bags worth of shopping there, I would guess.'

I flapped away his concern. 'Like I said, thank you, but we'll be fine.'

And with that, I wheeled away towards the tills.

The cashier attempted small talk about the icy wind and whether I'd started my Christmas shopping yet, but all I could manage were grunts or stony silence.

My head was mashed and I just wanted to get back to the cottage.

I stashed my groceries in the reuseable carrier bags I'd brought with me. I hoped nobody noticed me. I kept flicking surreptitious glances around, but the couple of other shoppers also in the supermarket were too preoccupied with their own business. Mitch had gone by now.

I thrust my credit card at the cashier, whose name badge informed me that she was called Eva. She glowered as she directed me to swipe it against the machine. Then she muttered something sarcastic under her breath about the joys of working with the public. Bronte leapt up at me when I reached the exit.

I ruffled her warm, solid flank and let out an exhausted sigh.

I couldn't be around anyone.

As if detecting my morose thoughts, Bronte let out a whimper as she gazed up from the pavement. I crouched down and rubbed her head. 'Well, okay. Apart from you. You're the exception.'

I stood back up again, adjusted the strap of my bag on my shoulder, and was just about to untie Bronte's lead from the railing, when I noticed an older man emerging out of the newsagents a little way up the opposite side of the street. He was approaching a car, an old petrol-blue Ford Escort.

There was something familiar about him.

The man, with a newspaper under his arm, unlocked his car and tossed the paper onto the vacant passenger seat. He yanked open the driver's side and proceeded to clamber in.

Bronte was making impatient whimpers to get going, but I stood there and continued to examine the man. I couldn't get a close-up view of him, but…

It was as he fired up his car that my brain caught up.

Wait. I did know him. It was him. The dark, greying hair and long, sharp expression.

It was the same man who'd been staring at me through the cottage sitting room window!

Chapter Twelve

I ran to the end of the pavement. The stranger's car vanished up the road, and it was only after he'd disappeared that it occurred to me that I should have taken a note of his car registration and gone to the Police, but what would I have said? 'This man was looking into my cottage window.' He could have a perfectly innocent explanation. I was struggling to think of something plausible, though.

I returned to Bronte, who was stationed beside our two shopping bags outside the supermarket entrance.

I made my way back clutching the shopping with Bronte trotting beside me like a little pony, secured on her lead. I peered up the road, in the same direction as the mysterious older man had headed in his car only moments ago. Was he local? Did he live here in Rowan Bay? Or was he a tourist? Or maybe he had a holiday home here?

Maybe Mitch had been right. Perhaps he'd simply been

out for a stroll, taken a wrong turning and was going to ask for directions. But then, if he had, why not knock on the door, instead of peering in the sitting room and frightening me half to death and then running away.

I turned everything over in my head as I bumped my shopping along gripping Bronte's lead at the same time; I wasn't prepared to take any chances and let her off her lead again just yet.

I thought again about the older man I just saw.

What if Mitch had been right after all? What if I'd overreacted about the man at the window? What if my imagination had run away with me and the poor soul had just been lost or looking for someone? I was a writer, after all.

You were, reminded a dark voice in my subconscious. And my head wasn't in a good place right now. In fact, I wondered if it would ever be again.

I glanced up at the marbled, miserable sky. The weather in Scotland round these parts could change in an instant.

It seemed like only yesterday that I'd arrived here, my face swollen with crying; the hundreds of miles between me and London a distant memory.

I completed the walk back to the cottage in a mental fog.

Would I ever be able to get my life back on an even keel? How could I move on from this? What had happened had delivered a severe kicking to my heart and splintered it into tiny pieces. How the hell could I manage to push everything into the past and pick my life back up?

Would I ever be able to do that?

The thought struck me like a huge, forked bolt of lightning. I never, ever would've imagined me living my life without Joe by my side. The very thought had seemed incomprehensible. People say it takes time and you never learn to get over your grief. You just learn how to deal with it from your own personal perspective.

But after all this – the revelations about him and Greta; me scrambling to face each day; struggling to put one foot in front of the other; abandoning London and our home and fleeing to Scotland with just a few belongings in the boot of the car – maybe I had to face up to the reality that this was my life now.

I didn't know if I had the energy or the heart to try and start again. Everything seemed such a monumental effort and I didn't have the passion.

How I hated it that he'd died and left all this car crash of emotions behind him.

I gave my head a mental jolt and crossed the road with Bronte and my groceries.

My grandparent's cottage sat there, framed by the exploding clumps of heather in the garden and the bay water swishing about down below. Barclay had been tending to Grandma's plants and mowing the lawn. It looked picture postcard pretty, even at this time of year.

Opposite and perched up on the cliff face was the lighthouse and its assorted, accompanying little outhouses. It fired upwards into the grey day in a solid white and blue statue.

Pictures of Barclay doffing his cap, shaking his white

head of thick hair, and belting out that gusty laugh of his, skipped through my mind. He'd been an excellent listener. He would have left me to sit there to wallow in my self-pity for a few minutes, before handing me a shot of his glistening, amber whiskey and instructing me to pour my heart out.

My downturned mouth trembled at the thought of the sweet, elderly man. I was delighted for him and Mags. They deserved to be together and live the rest of their lives as a happy, contented couple.

I wished he was still here, though. He and Mags had given me a call the other day and ordered me to visit them in Loch Lomond once they'd got their little cottage sorted, and I promised I would.

If Barclay could see me now, he'd have a few choice words to say to me about dusting myself down and taking each day as it came. But I didn't even feel capable of doing that. Everything felt like a marathon that I had to limp through, and at night I'd fall into bed, dismissing visions of Joe spooned beside me.

Then I'd wake up with the sickening realisation of what had happened and the cold, brutal truth that I had to face another day in the knowledge that Joe had loved someone else.

It seemed like everything was happening at once – and not in a good way.

I eyed the lighthouse as I locked the garden gate behind me and negotiated my way up the path with my carrier bags. I let Bronte off the lead, and she pelted around the lawn for a few moments, then screeched up to the front door.

I opened it and allowed Bronte to skitter inside first, before I angled my way in with my shopping and locked the door behind me.

I began to deposit my spoils on top of the grey marble breakfast bar.

Bronte sensed that something was afoot and came darting into the kitchen. 'You're not stupid, are you? You know I've bought you something.'

She let out a thrilled little yap.

I delved my hand into the second carrier bag and located the squeaky apple. I tugged off the price tag and she sat bolt upright, her tongue lolling with excitement. She hitched up one paw for good measure. 'Here you are.'

She took it in her mouth and trotted off towards the sitting room with a series of frantic squeals coming from the latex toy.

I finished stashing the groceries in the fridge and reached for Grandma's spotty little teapot resting on the window sill.

I was just about to fill the kettle, when there were a couple of loud knocks on the front door.

My hand stilled, the kettle poised under the tap.

Bronte had heard someone, abandoned her apple and was already at the door, barking her head off.

I dumped the kettle on the counter and made my way up the short hallway. There was an old umbrella of my grandfather's propped up in the corner. I eyed it. That man at the window had made me jumpy, there was no denying it.

I grasped the wooden handle. I must've looked like Mary Poppins, but I was ready to give anyone a bloody good thump with it, if need be.

Bronte continued to bark and growl as though her life depended on it and I flexed the fingers of my other hand around the door handle.

I tugged the door open, half expecting to see the grey-haired mystery man standing there.

But it wasn't him.

Instead, I was face to face with a tall, thinner, younger man, who reminded me of a matchstick.

He was wearing a rumpled, grey suit under a long, woollen coat that was flapping open. I reckoned he was in his late forties.

He was clasping his mobile phone and gazed expectantly up at me from the doorstep. 'Sorry to disturb you, madam, but I'm looking for a Mr Mitch Carlisle.'

'He doesn't live here. Well, not in this cottage, He's the local lighthouse keeper—'

The man cut across what I was saying. 'Aye. I know. But there's no answer up there.'

I stared past him and up at the lighthouse. 'Have you tried his accommodation at the rear of the lighthouse? He might be in there or in one of the store rooms?'

The man shook his head in an irritated manner. 'Been round there. No sign of him.'

'Ah. Oh. Well, he's probably just popped out.'

Relieved that this stranger wasn't a reporter looking for me or the prowler coming back, I felt my shoulders relax a little. 'You can leave a message with me if you like and I can pass it on to him?'

The man pulled an anguished face. He bent down and gave Bronte a friendly stroke. 'I really do need to speak to him.'

'Well, I don't know how you're going to do that if he's not around at the moment. Like I say, if you give me a message, I'll be sure to pass it on.' Blimey. This guy had no patience. What was so pressing that he had to speak to Mitch straight away?

The stranger's long face broke into a gleaming, if somewhat intimidating, smile. It didn't reach his eyes as he looked back up at me. 'My name's Harvey Flanagan. I'm a journalist with the Glasgow Mail. I really would appreciate a word or two with Mr Carlisle.'

At that moment, there was a bark to the left of the woodland and Mitch and Kane emerged. Mitch had overheard him. 'Who wants to know?' asked Mitch, giving the reporter a suspicious look. Mitch nodded at me. 'Hi, Rosie. Everything okay?'

'Er… Hi,' I faltered. 'This gentleman was looking for you.'

The journalist spun round to see who I was talking to. 'Mitch Carlisle?' he asked, his voice rising with hope.

Mitch's sea-coloured eyes narrowed. 'Yep.'

The reporter strode up to Mitch and introduced himself.

'Good to meet you, sir. Harvey Flanagan. I'm with the Glasgow Mail.' He extended one hand.

Mitch stopped dead. His eyes turned to flint. He ignored the reporter's outstretched hand. Mitch looked like a dark, avenging angel in his heavy, long coat. 'How did you find out I was here?'

Harvey Flanagan dismissed the question. 'We don't reveal our sources, sir.' He gave Mitch what he probably hoped was an endearing smile. 'Now I won't take up too much of your time.'

'You won't be taking up any of my time, I can assure you. I don't speak to reporters.'

Unperturbed, the journalist continued. 'If you could just spare a few minutes, Mr Carlisle, please? I'm writing a feature for the paper about civil action cases and the impact they have on business people like yourself. I'm sure many readers would be interested to hear what happened to you after—'

Mitch didn't give the journalist any more time. He pushed his chiselled, glowering face into the reporter's. 'Are you hard of hearing? I said I don't speak to journalists. Now, sod off before I ask Kane here to see you off.'

Kane let out a low, menacing growl.

Staring down at the German Shepherd's fixed attention on him, Harvey Flanagan took a few eager steps backwards. 'There's no need for threats, Mr Carlisle.'

'Oh, they aren't threats,' clarified Mitch.

The journalist straightened his askew, navy and silver striped tie.

'And don't bother coming back here again.'

Kane took another deliberate step towards Harvey Flanagan.

The reporter took this as his cue to retreat to his car – a battered, tomato-red Kia – parked up further past the remote woodland. He wasted no time in jumping into his vehicle and speeding off.

Mitch stood there, his shoulders and back ramrod straight, watching the shabby car disappearing up the road. Bronte and Kane meanwhile were having a high old time chasing each other around the front of the cottage.

I eyed Mitch with confusion. What on earth was all that about? And what was it that reporter had started saying about the effect of civil court cases on business people like Mitch? Whatever it was he hadn't wanted me to know.

Mitch flashed me a look from under his black beanie. He offered no explanation about why a reporter from a big newspaper like the Glasgow Mail wanted to talk to him. He cleared his throat. 'I hope that character didn't give you any grief?'

I eyed him. 'No, not at all. I'm fine, thanks.'

There was an awkward silence, with just the water in the bay sloshing down below.

'And your prowler?'

It was clear Mitch was keen to move the conversation on to another topic.

'He hasn't been back since, although I did see him in the high street, after I'd been shopping.'

Mitch's thick, dark brows flexed under his hat. 'What, just now?'

'Yes. I spotted him across the road from the supermarket. He'd bought a newspaper and was going back to his car.'

Mitch digested what I'd just told him. 'Well, any more issues, you know where I am. Where we both are.' He gestured to Kane, whose tongue flapped. 'I mean it, Rosie. You aren't on your own.'

An odd flutter of gratitude took me by surprise.

Mitch gave Kane an affectionate scratch behind one ear. Then he turned and strode off back up the path towards the lighthouse, with no explanation offered about what had just happened – or why.

Chapter Thirteen

There was a hailstorm the next morning.

White, golf ball-sized stones rained down on everything, battering against the cottage windows, as though eager to break in. They pelted the top of my car and landed in the garden.

I watched the relentless winter weather, while I finished rinsing out the teapot.

Bronte was sat by my feet in the kitchen, giving me an expectant look as if to say, 'Right. I'm ready for my walk, so kindly get a move on!'

I turned round and smiled down at her. 'Just give it a few minutes, will you, sweetheart? I don't fancy having my head caved in.'

Sure enough, around ten minutes later, the white bullets stopped as quickly as they'd started and the watery sun forced its way through the bank of angry clouds.

It glided across the top of the bay making it look like it

was being touched by golden fingers. That was Scottish weather for you!

I wrapped myself up in my heavy winter coat, scarf, hat and boots before popping on Bronte's fleecy purple coat and her harness and lead. Thoughts of Mitch's confrontation with that newspaper journalist yesterday crept into my mind again. Well, whatever had happened, it was clear Mitch didn't want to talk about it. All very odd.

I also remembered what he'd said to me. 'You're not on your own, Rosie.'

I realised my mouth was slipping into a small smile at the memory.

I'd made the mistake earlier, just after breakfast, of going onto social media, and there were a lot of comments from my reading fanbase, asking if some of the rumours were true, that their favourite author had decided to stop writing.

A frisson of guilt zipped through me, but I dismissed it.

It was the right thing to do.

I meandered over to the kitchen window, from where I could see the garden. Stubborn leaves were spinning over the lawn and the path.

I remembered where my grandparents kept their garden tools and decided to occupy myself by sweeping up the leaves now that the hailstones had stopped. Bronte could keep me company.

Once I'd fetched the rake from the back hall cupboard, I got myself togged up in my coat, hat, scarf and boots, and Bronte sat on the cottage step, watching me sweep the rake this way and that, until the soggy leaves slowly began to pile up.

I was stooping down to gather up another satisfying pile for the green recycling bin when Mitch's voice made me start. 'Hi, Rosie.'

I almost dropped my armful of leaves. I stuffed them into the open bin. 'Hi, Mitch. Hi, Kane.'

Kane stood beside him, tongue flapping.

Mitch pointed at the leaves on the grass. 'You look like you might need a hand there.'

'No, I'm fine, thanks.'

Mitch folded his sinewy arms. 'What is it about you refusing help?'

His words hit home. I dusted my garden-gloved hands together. 'I would accept help if I needed it.'

'Something tells me you wouldn't.'

I angled my head to one side, my curls spilling out from under my winter hat. 'I would,' I insisted, a little too quickly.

Mitch's mouth hinted at an amused smile. 'Well, don't forget you've got a tall, strong and handy lighthouse keeper at your disposal. Twenty-four seven.'

My cheeks whipped themselves into a pink frenzy, which annoyed me. 'Don't forget to introduce me to him when you see him.'

Mitch's face split into a dazzling grin. 'Ouch. You'll hurt my feelings.'

'Something tells me you'll get over it quickly.'

He and Kane continued to watch me under the churning clouds while I dragged and pulled the leaves. 'Catch you later then,' he said. 'But I mean it: just shout if you need me.'

There was that arch of a brow again, the tremble of a cheeky smile.

'Thanks, Mitch, but I'll be fine.'

He offered me a little salute. 'Come on, Kane. Let's go.'

I waited a few moments until they reached the woodland before taking a sneaky peek. Then I focused my attention back on rounding up more leaves.

After a satisfying session of leaf collecting, I picked up my mobile from the hall table and locked the front door behind me. Then Bronte and I set off towards the path that led down to the bay.

It was so wild and beautiful here. Too much had happened. Joe's death had happened. His infidelity. Barclay's retirement. My crisis of confidence. Real life had taken over and slapped me in the face. But at least Rowan Bay was a constant. The sea was often moody, the beach was always buttery, and the lighthouse was the local beacon of comfort.

Bronte meanwhile jumped around in the waves, frustrated that I wouldn't let her off the lead. Once she'd got more used to the area and I felt more confident about letting her off, it would be a different story.

More used to the area. I considered what that implied. Did that mean I was planning on staying here? Was I going to settle in Rowan Bay permanently? Right now, I was struggling to decide what to make myself for dinner, let alone what my future was going to look like. Maybe I was trying to move too fast. Perhaps I was trying to walk before I could run. I was under no pressure to decide what I was going to do next. Any pressure that was there, I was inflicting on myself and that had to stop.

I was in Rowan Bay now, with its foamy waves and looming lighthouse, not London.

After a few more minutes of Bronte splashing about in the water, we headed back up the path towards the cottage.

As we neared the top of the path, Bronte performed another series of frantic tugs on her lead and let out a whine. She implored me with those eyes of hers. I gave her a stern look. She was like Mia and Lola. They wouldn't take no for an answer either. I sighed. 'Right, young lady, I'll let you off the lead, but don't you dare take off! Straight to the cottage, okay?'

She let out a cheerful bark and did as she was told, picking up speed on her furry legs to get back to the cottage gate.

I eyed the lighthouse, the solitary, white and blue column prising the clouds apart, with its associated buildings pressed into the cliffs behind it.

I frowned.

Mitch Carlisle was a strange one. Closed off. He gave off this air of being a lone wolf, but there was something about the way he'd bundled that reporter away; a mixture of fury and something else racing across his features. Perhaps I wasn't the only one trying to deal with my problems by hiding away from the world?

I fumbled around in my coat pocket for the front door key as I began to approach and open the cottage gate.

Bronte had zoomed off to have a good sniff of the garden fence. 'Come on, sweetheart. Let's go inside,' I called to her, without looking up. Then I heard her let out a sudden series of sharp barks.

Oh no. Don't tell me she'd spotted a rabbit or a squirrel in the garden. I couldn't face the prospect of her tearing off again.

I snapped my head up as I retrieved my key, only to barrel into the prowler.

Chapter Fourteen

The man almost tumbled backwards, circled by a yapping Bronte.

'Please! Miss! Call her off! Put her back on her lead! She's going to go for me!' His voice was a panicked but educated Scottish burr.

I hoped I could disguise the fear in my voice. 'She won't bite, unless I tell her to.'

That was a blatant lie, but he didn't have to know that. Bronte was far more likely to lick him to death after a few minutes.

The man flinched. 'Please. Miss. I'm not dangerous. Honestly!'

'Yes, well, you would say that, wouldn't you?'

'Do I look like a serial killer? I'm a pensioner with failing eyesight. Just please call your dog off.'

I studied the man from top to bottom. 'Well, you tell me what a serial killer looks like.'

The man continued to recoil from Bronte, as though she were a foaming-at-the-mouth, ten-foot-tall creature from another planet. I rolled my eyes. 'Oh, for pity's sake!'

I stooped down and clipped Bronte's lead back on. 'Right. Now I've got my Rottweiler under control, the least you can do is tell me what you were doing the other day peering into my cottage window?'

The man looked like I'd slapped him across the face with a wet fish. 'So, you live here now?' His voice sounded flat, resigned.

Did I? I supposed I did. I found myself nodding, not sure of what the official answer was.

His brows gathered. He appeared thrown for a few moments, as he slowly dusted himself off.

I took in his layered, greying hair and heavy, dark coat. He wasn't a journalist either, was he? Had he found out where I was and thought he could get an exclusive interview with the grieving wife? Or was he another journalist on Mitch's trail? I was still curious about that and why Mitch had been so keen to see that journalist off. 'Are you a reporter?'

'What? No! What makes you ask that?'

I narrowed my eyes at him.

'I'm telling you the truth. I'm not a journalist.'

'Then who are you and why are you hanging around here?'

The man, I noticed, was studying my face with keen interest. A glimpse of a faraway smile flirted at the corners of his mouth. 'Your hair,' he faltered in his Scottish brogue.

'It's so like someone else's I used to know when she was young.'

'Sorry?'

He dragged himself back from wherever he was. 'I'm rambling. Forgive me.' He shot out one hand. I looked at it, bemused, before shaking it.

'My name is Reece Stewart. I was a close friend of the lady who used to live here. I understand she passed away eight months ago.' His eyes dimmed.

I angled my head at him, curious. 'What was her name? The lady you're looking for?'

'Tilda Winters.'

I stared at him. 'Tilda Winters?' I repeated. 'That's who you were friends with?'

'Aye. At least Winters was her maiden name.' Reece Stewart studied the cottage. 'This is her house, isn't it?' He swung back to look at me. 'I was coming to visit her. Wanted to take her out for a slap-up lunch and catch up over old times.' His voice grew softer. 'But that day you spotted me at the window, I'd just learnt from one of the locals that she'd passed away.' He shrugged. 'So, I bought some flowers from the local florist and took them to her grave.' He coloured. 'Then I came up here to see her house. Probably sounds daft, but I wanted to see where she'd been living before she passed.'

I processed what he was saying. 'No. It doesn't sound daft at all.'

He gently appraised me again. 'I hope you don't mind

me saying, but you look very much like her when she was younger.'

Down by my feet, Bronte had hunkered down and was listening to the conversation.

I examined the man again. I didn't recognise him, and his name didn't mean anything to me either. Was he an old friend of Grandma's? He must be. Glimmers of sadness shimmered through me. 'Yes, we're related. I mean, we were. Tilda was my grandmother.'

He gazed at me and back towards the moody water of the bay below us. He turned back to me, his mouth downturned. 'I'm so sorry for your loss.' His mouth hinted at a smile. 'You're her double when she was your age.'

I found my voice cracking. It was the stunned look in his washed-out, blue-flecked eyes. 'Thank you.'

Reece's attention shifted from my hair back to my face. He stood there, gathering his thoughts. 'When I saw you through the window, I thought for a moment that I might've travelled back in time. It was as though I was looking right at her again, after all these years.' An emboldened colour bloomed in his cheeks. 'I didn't mean to scare you. I thought the property would be empty. Sorry, I'm wittering on.'

'No,' I assured him. 'It's alright. I still expect both of them to come through the door any time.'

I basked in the sudden burst of lemon sunshine drizzling through the clouds. 'She was married to my grandfather, Howard Michaels, for sixty-five years.'

'Yes. She told me. Quite an achievement.'

My curiosity was alight. 'Sorry, Mr Stewart, but how did you know Tilda?'

He sighed, his shoulders sagging. 'We were close, years ago… Er… Sorry … I didn't ask your name.'

'Rosie. Rosie Winters.'

'Ah. Well, nice to meet you Ms Winters.' His eyes were soft, sentimental. 'You use her maiden name?'

'I've always liked it.' I offered a smile. 'My original surname was Ward but I've gone by Rosie Winters for years now. Please. Just call me Rosie.'

Reece hesitated and shuffled in his coat. 'Alright. Thank you, Rosie. Call me Reece.' He fidgeted on the spot. 'Me and your grandma, we were close once, very close.'

My eyes widened at his inference. What?! When was this? It must have been a long time ago, seeing as Grandma and Grandpa were married for sixty-five years.

There was an expectant hush. I was mentally willing Reece to tell me.

'I take it from your reaction that she never mentioned me?'

'Sorry, she didn't. At least not to me.'

Reece nodded, resigned to the fact. 'I thought as much. I'd have been surprised if she had, after what happened.' He set his shoulders. 'I wouldn't blame her for not wanting to think about me, after the way I treated her. She didn't deserve it.'

'Reece, please tell me what happened. How did you know her?'

Reece looked troubled. He forced a hand through his windswept, collar-length hair, sending it flying back from his forehead. 'When we were young, Tilda and I were engaged to be married.'

Chapter Fifteen

I thought I'd misheard for a moment.

My grandma had been engaged to another man before my grandpa?

Reece nodded at my shocked expression. 'Aye. It's true.'

My eyebrows fired up.

'I was madly in love with her and she with me.' He glanced up at the tumbling clouds over our heads. 'That's why I still think about her and have done over the years. It's why I regret what happened.'

I shook my head. 'Well, this has come as a bit of a shock.'

Reece gave me an embarrassed glance. 'I expect it has. I'm sorry, lass.'

'Look,' I faltered, thrown that my late grandmother had never told me anything about this before. 'Why don't you come in, Mr Stewart ... sorry ... Reece, and I'll make us some tea?'

The older man's eyes widened with gratitude. 'Thank you so much. I'd appreciate that.'

I encouraged Bronte on, and she followed Reece and me up the cottage garden path. Reece was taking everything in, examining my late grandparents' plants and the colour of the front door.

He studied the cottage over my shoulder.

I unlocked the front door. I couldn't quite believe what he'd just told me. Talk about a bolt out of the blue. My grandma and I had talked about everything, and I'd confided in her about my teenage crushes during the holidays and my hormones raging.

But never once had she mentioned to me that she'd been engaged to another man before she'd met my grandpa. The name Reece Stewart had never passed her lips.

I turned in the hallway to take another look at Reece, but he was unaware I was checking him out. He was too preoccupied, appreciating my late grandfather's green fingers in the garden. He hesitated at the doorstep.

Bronte leapt inside. 'Please come in,' I said to him.

He offered me a gentle smile of gratitude and bowed his head almost reverently as he stepped through the doorway.

His attention turned to my late grandmother's paintings in the hallway. 'She was always so very talented,' he remarked with a wistful air. 'I don't think your grandmother realised how great an artist she actually was.'

I beckoned Reece into the sitting room and he took up a seat in one of the armchairs.

My head was brimming with questions. My

grandmother had been engaged to someone else before my grandfather? It seemed so unlikely somehow. And why hadn't she mentioned this before? Had she ever said something to my mum about it? If she had, Mum had certainly never breathed a word to me.

I realised I was staring at him again, with fascinated curiosity. I supposed it was because he was a connection to my grandma, one that had just erupted out of nowhere. Another part of her past. 'How do you take your tea?' I asked him, trying to visualise him as a young man. I could picture him now, all long, lean legs and thick hair. Handsome, in an intense, long-nosed sort of way.

'Just a dash of milk please.'

I hurried off into the kitchen and busied myself with making the tea. Bronte, meanwhile, had melted. She'd morphed from Satan's hellhound back into a wriggling ball of fun.

She'd picked up her new, squeaky apple toy, clamped it in her mouth and proceeded to push it against Reece's leg in an attempt to get his attention and coax him into playing with her.

I kept mulling over thoughts of my grandparents.

It was almost incomprehensible to imagine Tilda with anyone other than my grandfather, let alone contemplating marriage to them. I knew she'd had other boyfriends when she was younger, before settling down with my grandfather, but she'd never mentioned Reece, let alone another engagement.

She and Grandpa Howard had been like two bookends.

Even when the odd argument erupted, it would soon blow over with laughter.

They were demonstrative and affectionate, cajoling each other. Just like Joe and I had been. Or so I thought.

I fetched the milk from the fridge and dashed some into Reece's mug.

I could hear Bronte thumping her toy with her paw.

'I think we're friends now,' he smiled up, with a hint of awkwardness, as I came back into the sitting room.

I handed him his mug of tea. 'She's a softie, really. I think she was just trying to protect me.'

Reece gratefully accepted his mug of tea. 'Well, you can't be too careful. Thank you.'

'Would you like a biscuit with that?'

'No, thank you. My doctor wouldn't approve.'

I sank down on the sofa opposite Reece, cradling my mug in my hands.

Reece took a long, considered mouthful of his tea and relaxed a little in the armchair. His fingers, I noticed, were gripping the mug and he delivered a few cautious glances at me from over the top of it. 'I'm so sorry again for scaring you the other day. I didn't mean to.' He sighed and stared around himself again. A soft look enveloped his periwinkle blue eyes. There was that melancholy air about him once more. 'I'd hoped to be able to talk to her again face-to-face. I know it's been a long time, but I wanted to explain to her and apologise. I owed her that much.' He drank in the sitting room surroundings, from another couple of paintings lining the walls, to the framed family photos in the sitting room cabinet. It was a home that had been carved out of nothing by a couple devoted to one another.

Reece craned his neck up to her artwork. 'She's everywhere, isn't she?'

I nodded. 'They both are.'

Reece eyed me. 'Do you mind me asking what happened to her?'

I gathered myself. 'It was a heart attack. Fourteenth March. Very sudden.'

'I'm sorry to hear that.' He clutched the handle of his mug, more regret flickering through his eyes. 'And your grandfather?'

'He passed away five years ago now. A stroke.'

'My condolences.'

God, I was sick of hearing that phrase, even though I knew people were only being thoughtful and kind.

Reece hunched over and began to ruffle Bronte behind her ears. She nuzzled her nose against his age-spotted hand. You would never have thought she'd been snapping at his heels ten minutes ago. 'And were they happy together? Your grandparents?'

'Very. Oh, they had their moments, believe me, but they were devoted to one another and woe betide anyone who tried to come between them.'

A sad ghost of a smile travelled across his face. 'That's lovely. I'm glad Tilda was happy. She deserved it.'

That sounded like Reece hadn't been? Or was I trying to read too much into his words?

I sipped my tea. Outside, the late November sun danced around and through the clouds and onto the water.

'How did you find out about my grandmother living here?' I asked him.

'I found your grandmother on Facebook last year and she gave me her address. We messaged each other from time to time.' He glanced out of the sitting room window. 'I was living in Italy – Florence – at the time, when I discovered her on social media.'

My eyes pinged open. Good grief. I thought I knew most of what there was to know about my grandmother – until now. Turned out I'd been wrong. Reece had tracked her down and yet she'd never mentioned anything about this to me.

She had been a keen painter, a lover of hill walking and adored Neil Diamond. But there had been this other side of her life that I never knew existed. A combination of shock, admiration and disbelief was firing through me. 'I hope you don't mind me asking, but can you tell me what happened? Between you and my grandmother?'

Reece shot a considered, lost look to his right, out of the panoramic sitting room window again. His gaze looked as unsettled as the clouds.

Then he reached into his trouser pocket and pulled out his wallet. From it he produced a black and white photograph and handed it across to me. It was of him and my grandmother up by Edinburgh Castle on a foggy day in what looked like the early sixties, going by my grandma's long leather boots and short winter coat and Reece's bushy moustache and collar-length hair. They were cuddling and laughing at something. It was a captivating scene, catching them in an intimate moment. A young couple sharing love. I kept looking down at the photograph and then back up at Reece. She did look like me in the picture, with her snub nose and riot of tumbling, red curls. I handed it back to him. 'It's a gorgeous photo of both of you.'

'That was taken a few weeks before I proposed to her.'

'So … where did you meet her? What happened?'

Reece slid the photo back inside his wallet. 'I met your grandmother in nineteen sixty-three. I was twenty and she was eighteen.' He took a considered gulp of his tea and carried on. 'I'd gone into the centre of Edinburgh with a few friends, but all they wanted to do was hit the pubs, so I slunk off by myself and decided to visit The Royal Art Gallery instead.' Reece rolled his eyes. 'My parents were horrified that I wanted to become a painter and study fine art. I was studying law at The University of Edinburgh to get my degree, but it was really just to placate them. My heart wasn't in it. It never was.'

'I don't blame you for choosing art instead.'

His lips twitched. 'My life up until I met your grandmother had been somewhat directionless. I kind of drifted around, not really knowing what my purpose was. My parents were snobs.' He let out a wry laugh. 'Och, don't get me wrong. I loved them but they came from very comfortable families and had very set ideas about things.'

'What kind of art do you paint?' I asked, intrigued.

'Did paint,' corrected Reece with a small, sad smile.

'I was more of an abstract artist. Cubism. Pushing the boundaries a bit or so I thought. But I lost my passion for it after what happened between me and your grandmother.'

I eyed him. 'So, you didn't pursue it? Your art career, I mean?'

'No. Not after losing Tilda. I ended up in the bespoke furniture business after that and made quite a success of it.'

'I see. Sorry to interrupt. Please do go on.'

Reece hunched over and patted Bronte on the top of her head. 'No need to apologise, young lady.' There was a light in his blue eyes as he continued to talk. 'On the day I met your grandma for the first time, I'd noticed there were a few exhibitions on, but there was one in particular at The Royal Art Gallery that appealed to me. It was the works of John Duncan Fergusson, so I decided to check that out.' He gave his head a shake. 'I still can't believe that it's been sixty-two years since I first saw her. It only seems like yesterday.' He paused. 'I can still see it now. It was February and bloody cold. It was a relief to get back into the warm and wander around, marvelling at all the stunning paintings of Paris in gilt frames.'

Reece paused and then continued, 'I'd only been in there about ten minutes when a blur of red caught my eye.'

Reece cradled his mug in his hands and nodded over at me. 'Like I said before, she had those wild, red curls just like you and she was wearing a bright pink beret.' Reece let out an embarrassed laugh. 'I should've been admiring the artwork, not your grandmother, but goodness me, she was beautiful.'

My heart shifted at Reece's words. I found myself shuffling forward in my chair. Even Bronte appeared to be listening. She'd stopped squeaking her toy apple and was gazing up at Reece, bewitched.

'I was as nervous as hell, but I managed to pluck up enough courage to go over and talk to her.' He reddened. 'Well, that's not exactly true. I deliberately dropped some loose change to get her attention.'

I let out a laugh. 'And then what?'

'Tilda scrambled around the art gallery floor to help me pick up the pennies. Then I insisted on taking her for a coffee to say thank you. She said yes.'

I raised my brows, encouraging Reece to continue with his story.

'We fell in love so quickly. It was as if I could see myself reflected in her. Does that make sense?'

I gulped back a tide of emotion. I'd thought the same thing about Joe at one time. I pushed out my chin to reset myself. I nodded. 'Yes. It makes perfect sense.'

Reece spoke again. 'Your grandmother was everything I wasn't. She had so much promise and ability and wanted to become a successful artist. I did too, but...' His voice faltered. 'I wanted to be as brave as Tilda. But I was nowhere near. Compared to her, I was a coward, and because of that, I lost her.'

There was a heavy silence. Reece took his time before continuing. His attention swam to the scenery outside the cottage's sitting room window and the cold ripple of the sky. 'I took a part-time job at a legal firm not long after Tilda and I got engaged on that Christmas Eve. It was a friend of my parents who got me in. Mum and Dad thought that getting legal work experience would stand me in good stead after graduation.' He flashed me a look. 'Once again, I did it just to keep the old folks off my back.'

'And how did they react to your engagement?'

'They were furious. They couldn't accept Tilda. They didn't even try to get to know her. They just saw this young, struggling artist and decided she wasn't good enough for me.'

Reece grimaced. 'I kept insisting to Tilda that everything would settle down and that they just had to get to know her. Then they'd realise how wonderful she was, how much in love we were, and then everything would be fine.'

'But?'

Reece eyed a seagull swooping around outside. 'But I underestimated what they were capable of.' He shook his head in disbelief. 'They said if I went ahead and married your grandmother, they'd disown me.' He exhaled. 'It meant I wouldn't get a penny from their publishing business. I'm embarrassed to say I capitulated.' His eyes took on a haunted expression. 'I regretted it for the rest of my life. I still do.'

My sympathy gathered for Reece and for my grandmother. 'And how did Tilda take it when you broke off the engagement?'

'She was heartbroken, but she did what she always did. She tried to act like she could deal with anything, if she set her shoulders and smiled.' Reece's mouth flatlined. 'I never saw her or heard from her again, until I came across her Facebook profile last year.'

I gripped my mug of tea. 'Did you end up marrying someone else?'

Reece nodded. 'The daughter of a business acquaintance of my father's. Five years after Tilda and I broke up. Nice girl. Her name was Lilian. I was fond of her, but I wasn't in love with her.' He considered what to say next. 'I think she knew it too, that my heart belonged to someone else and always would, but we both tried to make the best of it.'

'Are you still married?'

'No. I'm a widower. Lilian passed away ten years ago from dementia.'

'I'm sorry to hear that. Any children?'

He shook his head. 'No. Never happened for us.' Reece drained his tea and set the mug down on a coaster on the occasional table. He looked agonised. 'Rosie, you can say no if you want to. I wouldn't blame you if you did.'

'What is it?'

He fidgeted while giving Bronte another fuss. 'Would I be able to buy one of your grandmother's paintings? I'd love to have one to remind me of her.'

He dropped his eyes to the carpet for a few moments. 'I don't care what it's of. You can choose which picture I could have. I'd just like to have something of hers, something she painted herself.' He flashed me a look of embarrassment. 'I'm sorry if that sounds selfish.'

I realised that despite the fact he'd called off his engagement to my grandmother and hurt her, I felt touched by his openness and honesty. The way he was sitting there now in front of me, racked with regret, made me feel sorry for him. 'No. It doesn't sound selfish. Not at all.'

There were several of Grandma's pictures on display here in this room. But I could sense my attention shifting from Reece and down the hallway to my grandmother's makeshift art studio. 'I'm afraid I haven't had the heart to go into her studio and begin sorting things out yet,' I confessed. 'I just haven't been able to steel myself and what with other things going on...' I didn't elaborate. Reece wouldn't want to hear my woes. This poor man was still haunted by memories of my grandmother. I'm sure the last thing he wanted to hear about was me recently losing my adulterous husband.

I turned over his request. 'But perhaps we could go in there together and you can take a look? Then you can choose one yourself. Oh, and I'm not accepting payment for it.'

Reece's watery blue eyes sparkled with a mixture of relief and apprehension. 'Are you sure? I'm more than happy to pay you for the painting.' He sat forward. 'I don't want to impose or force you into doing something you don't want to or don't feel ready to do yet.'

I shook my head. 'You're not. On either of those counts. And, like I said, it has to be done at some point, so why not now? It won't seem as bad, having someone here with me.'

Reece offered me a small, flickering smile of gratitude.

'No time like the present, and like I said, at least I'm not having to go in there on my own. I have moral support now.' I got to my feet and gave my hands a decisive clap, hoping that would charge me up for entering Grandma's studio. We both moved off together down the hallway, with an intrigued Bronte bringing up the rear.

The wooden, panelled door to my grandmother's studio was closed. I approached it with Reece behind me.

He gazed at the closed door as Bronte skittered around my heels. 'When was the last time you ventured in here?'

'I haven't been in since she passed away.' I turned and half smiled over my shoulder.

Reece shook his head. 'I should never have asked you for one of Tilda's paintings. It's remiss of me to expect you to do this. I'm sorry.' *He* started to move back up the hallway. 'Please forget I said anything.'

I reassured him. 'No. It's fine. I can't keep avoiding it. I have to bite the bullet and do it some time. As I said, at least I'm not doing this on my own.'

I reached for the gold-coloured door handle and cranked it upwards. It let out a subtle creak and I entered.

The rattan blind at the window on the left was pulled down. The room smelled of turpentine and paint.

Reece hovered in the doorway as I tugged up the blind, allowing the light to spiral in. The coastline rising upwards, with the bay swaying in front of it, became visible.

My grandmother's heavy, wooden desk sat on the right, creaking under the weight of assorted papers, and beside that was another, slightly smaller table, with piled-up paint palettes. Jars of brushes in assorted sizes were thrusting out in all directions and a couple of easels were propped over in a corner.

Various pieces of artwork leaned against the back wall in two separate rows. Above them ran a couple of long shelves, the first of which was dotted with an assortment of the ceramic butterflies my grandmother loved so much, and a few family photographs.

There were a couple of shots of my mum and dad, together with a few of me. One showed me as a gappy-toothed schoolgirl; in another I was beaming on my wedding day, grasping my bouquet of gerbera, eyes shining with love for Joe.

I forced my attention away. I didn't want to be reminded of how happy I'd been then. It seemed like a lifetime ago now, as if all those special, treasured memories and moments had only been lent to me for a short time until they had to be returned – a bit like borrowing a favourite library book.

I turned my eyes instead to a few photographs of my Grandpa Howard, tall, proud and distinguished, with his lopsided smile and kind, crinkly eyes.

My mind shot back to when I was younger, and I would visit here during the holidays. My grandmother would allow me into her art studio on the proviso that I'd be very careful. She would entrust me with some paper, paints and a brush and encourage me to produce my own little pieces of artistry.

I gazed around, taking in her desk, the empty velvet chair and the Tupperware boxes she stashed with various bits and bobs sitting on the lower shelf above the old, disused fireplace.

I still expected her to come bustling in, bursting with ideas for her next painting, her earnest, navy blue eyes glowing and her messy, silvery curls bouncing on top of her shoulders.

It felt as though I'd taken a momentous step coming in here, finally. The relief that I'd made it through the door without collapsing into an emotional heap was a step in the right direction. That was down to Reece.

He was still lingering in the doorway, as though debating whether he should be here at all.

What would my grandmother say if she knew Reece was here now? Something told me she wouldn't mind. No doubt, she'd be shocked. But she had never been the sort of woman to lash out and be spiteful just for the sake of it.

I knew I should follow her lead. I beckoned him in. 'Please look at Tilda's paintings and take one. Whichever you like. There seems to be quite the eclectic mix.'

Reece's cheeks coloured. 'Thank you.' He pulled up an old, rickety chair from the corner while I knelt down beside him.

We sat in silence for a time, revelling in the quiet, serene atmosphere with my grandmother's presence everywhere.

The various swirling flower arrangements, angry sea landscapes and the odd, dynamic portrait she'd painted of people I didn't recognise leapt out of the canvas. Reece was stationed in front of the first stack of paintings whilst I was looking through the second.

My attention drifted over each one, appreciating the swirls of colour, the dancing shadows and the textures.

I shot a sideways glance at Reece. He was studying a still life of a small vase of bluebells, together with a bowl of apples, an old wine bottle and a half-filled glass sat beside it. It gave the impression of some French, louche lunch.

Reece's lips quivered. He raised one finger. 'I see she still continued with her unique little moniker.'

I followed his gaze to where there was a discreet, tiny, yellow butterfly just visible on one of the table legs. 'Oh yes. She'd never sign her name on any of her paintings, but she always slipped that little butterfly in somewhere.'

One of Rowan Bay harbour at dusk made me stop. It was the way my grandmother had made the sky look spilt with raspberry and rose golds. The water on the canvas seemed to swish under my fingertips.

Grandma had always been rather shy about her capabilities. Despite being a confident, together person, when it came to her creative prowess she was reticent. She would ignore our protestations that she should try to sell her work or attempt to have them exhibited. Instead, she insisted she wasn't good enough and that gaining satisfaction and enjoyment from her art was what she cared about, not having them suspended from a wall or being bid for in some opulent auction room.

I admired a few more pictures. One was of a little girl with a pink flower in her hair and another was of a vase of sunflowers by a rainy bedroom window.

Reece was sighing with appreciation at a watercolour of the harbour lights at dawn.

I'd just started to take a look at a painting of a half-empty milk jug alongside a bowl of glossy pears when, beside me, Reece let out a gasp that made me jump.

'Oh my God... Oh, Tilda...'

His eyes were big and glistening. He continued to stare at the painting for a few moments as if he couldn't believe what he was looking at.

Finally, he took the portrait in both hands and turned it round to face me. His eyes were wide and shining. 'Look what your grandmother painted, Rosie. Or should I say, who?'

Chapter Sixteen

I stared at the portrait Reece was holding.

It was of him as a young man.

It was a spellbinding, intense painting.

His dark hair was swept to one side, hiding his brow. His light, wise eyes shone, and he was wearing a white, crisp shirt open at the neck. The backdrop was the palest blue, making his eyes even more captivating. He carried a devilish air. There was something intimate about the way my grandma had him looking out of the canvas.

Reece kept gazing at the painting in disbelief and then at me. I thought at one point he might crick his neck. 'It's amazing,' he managed. 'When did Tilda paint this?'

I admired the smudges of ghost grey she'd captured in Reece's eyes and the strong angle to his chin. I shook my head. 'Goodness knows. Grandma was very private and protective about her paintings. You never knew what she was working on until you saw it. That's if she felt it was good enough.'

Reece marvelled at his portrait. 'She was so talented.' His voice was laden with awe. 'I can't believe she took the time to paint me.' He let out a long breath. 'She never forgot me and I never forgot her.'

Reece sat back in the chair, his attention still lingering on the painting of his younger self. 'She never told me in the messages we exchanged, that she'd painted me. Maybe she felt embarrassed about it. I wish she had told me.'

He rubbed at his chin. 'All these gorgeous pieces of her artwork; how many exhibitions did she do?'

'None,' I replied with a simple shrug.

Reece's jaw dropped. 'What? Not at all? You mean never?'

'No. She always said she painted for her own enjoyment. I think it was more of a confidence issue. She never considered herself a good-enough artist. She was always so self-critical.'

I sat back on my hunches and stretched out my legs.

Reece leant forward on his creaky chair. I assisted him to prop the portrait back.

He looked pensive. 'I had hoped she might change her mind about that. I used to encourage her to try and sell her work but she was even apprehensive about trying to do that.'

Reece gazed in wonder at his former fiancée's volume of work. His kaleidoscope of expressions changed again from sadness to shock and then to a melancholy smile.

He pointed at his portrait leaning in front of him. 'I hope you don't think I'm being presumptuous, but I don't suppose I could buy this one?'

'Please take it Reece, but like I said, I'm not accepting any money for it. I'm sure my grandmother would have wanted you to have it.'

Reece's weathered face broke into a delighted smile. 'Thank you. That's so kind of you. The fact that Tilda painted this…' His words tailed off.

We both stood up and I handed Reece the painting. We angled it out of the open studio door.

Reece jerked his head towards the windows and the bay below. 'I can understand why Tilda felt so inspired living here. Rowan Bay has such stunning scenery.'

'Yes, she and my grandpa were very settled here. They loved Edinburgh, but I think they wanted somewhere more rural.' As we departed the room, I took the opportunity to steal another appreciative look around. My grandmother's desk was littered with papers, clotted pots of paint and fine brushes. The intermittent sun fighting its way through the window, glancing off her glass butterfly ornaments, brought them to life.

I almost felt like an intruder, having ventured into my grandma's hallowed space. Even my grandfather had only been allowed limited access to this room, except to bring her a cup of tea or tell her about some breaking news item. She would vanish in there, singing along to her radio through the closed door.

But a glow of satisfaction and relief burst inside me.

I hadn't been able to face going in there after losing her, and I had avoided it since my arrival, but thanks to Reece, I'd finally done it.

Reece and I reached the top of the hallway, carrying his portrait between us. Bronte was scampering beside me.

It was like a weight had shifted; I could begin to leave the grief of her passing behind for a little while at least and allow life to once again start its ebb and flow.

My thoughts drifted back to the top of her desk scattered with assorted papers. It looked like a mish-mash of rough sketches, receipts and to-do lists which were only half completed. My lips promised a smile. Grandma Tilda had tried to be more organised, but failed. Her often scatter-brained approach to life used to drive my grandfather and mother mad. Mum had always been the epitome of efficiency.

I liked to think I was a crazy hybrid of them both.

I helped Reece to place the picture beside his armchair in the sitting toom. Bronte was gazing up at him again, her apple toy now back in her mouth, making her look like one of Henry VIII's stuffed boars.

This afternoon, I would make a start on tidying up my grandma's desk.

Little wins, Rosie. Little wins.

Reece shrugged on his winter coat and lingered in the hallway with his painting beside him. 'I hope my presence here today hasn't upset you, Rosie. I'd hoped to see where Tilda lived, but you've given me so much more.'

'It's fine. I mean, it did all come as a bit of a shock. I'm just sorry you weren't able to see my grandmother before she…' I didn't finish the sentence.

Reece gave an understanding nod and picked up his portrait. 'Me too. How long are you intending on staying here for?'

A sliver of panic raced through me. Sooner or later, I would have to take decisive action and decide what I was going to do.

I forced a smile. 'I'm not sure yet. Just playing things by ear at the moment.'

I gestured to his portrait in his arms. 'I know the weather is alright at the minute, but let me see if I can find something to cover your painting with, to protect it from the elements.'

I darted back down to the art studio and after a bit of rooting around in my grandma's cupboard, I came across a couple of sheets of canvas rolled up and stuffed in the far corner. One of these would be big enough to cover the portrait of Reece.

I returned back up the hallway with it rolled up and tucked under one arm. 'Here. Let me help you.'

'That's very kind of you, Rosie. Thank you.'

I assisted Reece with the painting and held it, while he draped the canvas down and over the top of it. 'You don't have to if you don't want to, but would you like to give me your contact details?' I asked him, jerking my head down the hallway, indicating the art studio and its door now ajar. 'I'm intending on making a start on tidying it up this afternoon, now that I've managed to step inside the place.

If I find anything else that might relate to you, I could pass it on?'

Reece's face blossomed with gratitude. 'Would you? Oh, thank you so much. I'd appreciate that.' He hesitated. 'I don't deserve your kindness. Not after how I treated your grandmother.'

'That was over sixty years ago.'

'It still only feels like last week to me.' His eyes clouded. 'Believe me, I regret it. I never stopped loving her, you know.'

I took in the pain wavering in his eyes. 'I can see that.'

I dashed into the kitchen, located an old envelope and pen and asked Reece to scribble down his contact details for me.

'I'm staying in one of those Airbnb places a bit further up the coastal road. It's an apartment and very nice. I was planning on staying here a few more days and then heading back to Edinburgh.' He handed the envelope back to me, containing his temporary address and mobile phone number. His writing was all loops.

'Thank you.'

Reece looked like he wanted to say something else. He fidgeted on the spot in his winter boots.

Bronte circled us both.

'Tilda's granddaughter,' he sighed at me, as though reluctant to leave. 'I can scarcely believe it. Could I visit again before I leave?'

'I'd like that,' I reassured him. I helped him out of the cottage door with the painting, even though he insisted he could manage, and angled it down the garden path and out of the gate to Reece's car.

He clicked open the expansive boot and was lowering it in with reverence when a flicker of movement to my left caught my attention.

It was Mitch and Kane, who looked as if they'd just returned from a walk. They were up by the lighthouse.

I raised one hand and gave a brief wave. I found myself noticing the way the wind was rifling through his dark curls, before checking myself.

Mitch did the same before burying his face into the upturned collar of his coat.

Kane followed obediently.

Chapter Seventeen

After waving Reece off, I returned inside the cottage and rustled up a baked potato with grated cheese and salad for lunch.

Bronte hoovered up the grated cheese I'd given her as a treat with obvious delight.

Then it was a walk with Bronte down to the harbour savouring the icy blast of wind across the water, before returning to the cottage.

I towelled Bronte after her insistence on splashing about in the waves and then made myself a warming mug of tea.

Cradling it in both hands, I made my way back down the hallway to begin sorting out my grandma's studio. I decided to start with her desk first.

I studied the painting palettes, rolls of kitchen towels and brushes again. Her digital radio sat on top of some of the detritus, so I clicked it on. American rock wound out of it as I began to gather up the first few papers.

The rising wind gave the cottage windows a good shake and Bronte slumbered by the art studio doorway.

I wanted to keep some of her handwritten scribbled notes about the pieces of art she'd been working on: *more blue tones needed for seascape; order two more of those horsehair brushes; check when pastel chalks are back in stock*. They were random, but they were pieces of her. My throat constricted at the sight of her scatty, swirly handwriting.

I found an empty, pale pink envelope amongst her odd bits of stationery and slid the notes I wanted to keep inside.

I stretched and rose out of her desk chair. It was almost four o'clock in the afternoon now and darkness was beginning to swallow up the cliff faces and the harbour.

I strode up to the kitchen to get myself a glass of water. From the kitchen window, I could see the lighthouse, dazzling with its swivelling golden eye washing over the horizon and lighting up the choppy waves. It was a strangely calming sight in the descending dark, providing a warm, yellow hand of comfort. I bet Mitch was wondering who Reece was, after seeing him leave the cottage. I decided to keep that revelation to myself for now.

I poured myself a tumbler of water from the filter jug in the fridge, collected a few black bin liners from under the sink and slapped back down towards the art studio in my thermal socks.

Bronte stirred, so I let her out for a charge around the garden for a few minutes. Once she'd scooted back inside, I locked the door and gave her some kibble, before returning to what I was doing.

Sorting through the contents of Grandma's room was painful, but in an odd way, comforting.

It made me feel even closer to her somehow, being here in her hallowed place and beside her chaotic art processes. It was also temporarily blanking out Joe and giving me a little respite from the pain. Every so often, my heartache would rear up like one of the big harbour waves and crash over my head, swamping me. It could catch me off guard, as though I were drowning, stealing the breath from my lungs.

I pulled down the blind and switched on the main light. It was encased in a fancy, glass shade.

My grandmother's desk contained three drawers, which were all shut. I tugged at the ornate, brass handles. The first two glided open revealing more tat. I smiled to myself. Broken pens, elastic bands and Post-it notes in the top one, and straws, blotters and pencils in the second.

I got one of the bin liners and deposited the broken pens in it together with pencils that had seen better days and some of the bent straws.

Once I was satisfied I'd got rid of what needed to be discarded from the first two, I reached for the third drawer and attempted to open it.

It wouldn't budge.

I took a sip of my water and set the glass back on a coaster on top of the desk. The coaster said, 'Painters know their art from their elbow.'

I tried to open the third drawer again. Maybe it was just a bit stiff?

Nope.

It seemed to be locked.

I frowned.

Why were the other two drawers not locked but this one was? And where was the key?

I searched around the desk and in the other two drawers in case she'd concealed it there. I also checked behind her glass butterfly ornaments and in her purple desk tidy. The irony of that wasn't lost on me.

But there was no sign of a key.

I moved towards the window and checked along the window sill, just in case she'd placed it there. But I knew that if she had, I would've noticed it when I opened the blind earlier.

I proceeded to root around in a few of the Tupperware boxes stashed along the second shelf above the old fireplace, but there was no sign of a key in any of these either. Only tacks, blue tack, paperclips and Sellotape.

I was about to give up looking for this elusive key, when my attention alighted on something peeking out from behind one of her glass butterfly ornaments: the Swallow Tail, with its lemon and black markings.

I gently pushed it to one side.

It looked like a small, dark jewellery box.

There was an ornate motif of two peacocks on the top of the marble, oval box, their plumed tails entwined around each other in an elaborate display.

I couldn't recall ever seeing this before. Although to be fair, it could've been in here for years and no one would have known, so protective of her art space was my grandma.

I picked up the little box. It was beautiful.

I lifted the lid to reveal a red velvet interior and some of my grandmother's earrings inside. There were two pairs of simple pearl studs and a pair of dazzling, party-style earrings which looked like Roman gold coins.

I was about to close the lid again, when something made me caress the party earrings. They moved and I noticed an item move underneath them. It was a small brass key.

I carefully removed it out of the jewellery box and examined it. Could this be it?

I set the little box back on the shelf and moved over to the desk. I slid the key into the lock of the third drawer. It let out a satisfying click and eased open.

Stashed inside this drawer were a series of floral notebooks, all tied together with a strand of tartan green and blue ribbon.

I angled the notebooks out until a wodge of them were resting in my hands. I set them down on top of the desk and gently tugged the tartan ribbon. It slithered off.

Were they more notes about her art? Tough, self-critical observations about what she could do better? But if they were, why conceal them in here? What might be so special about these?

I sank back down into the desk chair, with its scuffed arm rests and weary, floral cushion, and slid the first notebook from the top of the pile. It had a daisy imprinted on the cover.

I opened it and my grandmother's frantic handwriting stared up at me from the lined pages.

I'd expected maybe some random sketches, suggestions for possible titles for her art pieces, or notes about the best HB pencils.

But this notebook contained nothing like that.

It appeared to be a diary.

I started to read and as I suspected, it was a journal, detailing her thoughts, dreams, worries and hopes for the future.

Guilt tugged at me when I realised what I was holding in my hands.

As I took in what she'd written, turning page after page and allowing her words to sink into my head, I let out a troubled gasp.

Oh, Grandma.

Chapter Eighteen

I read on, oblivious to the darkness smothering everything outside and the time slipping by.

The journals mentioned my parents, my grandpa, me and her artwork.

The first few notebooks, from what I could make out, covered the last twenty years. Beside some other entries were random sketches and little drawings: thistles, small fishing boats, daisies and her beloved butterflies.

But what jumped out at me from the pages again and again, was the edge of disappointment at not having tried to have her work displayed; or more to the point, taking a risk and putting her paintings out there.

I continued to read.

13 September 1999

I've finally finished my sunflower and gardening tools painting. I'm pleased with it. A tiny part of me even suggested it might be good enough to exhibit but I'm not deluding myself. I'm not prepared to take the risk and be rejected. I've had enough of that feeling.

Hmmm. Rejection. Was she referring to Reece there?

Settling back in the desk chair, with Bronte snoring by my feet and the glimpse of the lighthouse beam drizzling through the blinds, I returned my attention back to Grandma's journals. The years fell away as I turned the pages.

There were some days when she hadn't written anything. Others were more mundane. Some consisted of a couple of sentences, whilst in other entries she expressed her frustration at not being more ambitious or was far too hard on herself.

Bloody shadows are all wrong, she'd grumbled on 3 January 1982. *I don't know what I'm doing with this damned piece!*

I eased over a few more pages, my grandmother's handwriting and the faint scent of fusty vanilla emanating from the paper.

I put the notebook I was holding down on the desk and picked up another. This journal appeared older than the others. The pages were much more yellowed and it had a faded, suede, baby pink cover. Crikey! How many were there?! I'd no idea Grandma Tilda had been such a prolific journaler.

I opened it up. The first entry was 10 June 1963.

I love Reece so much, but I'm not sure it's enough. His family disapprove of me. No matter what I do or what I say, they treat me like I'm a nobody. I can see it in their eyes. They think I'm beneath him. I keep mentioning it to Reece, but he says they just haven't got to know me properly yet and just brushes it off. He insists that once they do, they'll fall in love with me like he has. I won't hold my breath!

Even though Reece had already alluded to this, anger lit up inside of me. My grandmother had been the most loving and compassionate woman. She was kind and considerate. How dare Reece's jumped-up family be so judgemental?

I turned over the next few pages, my heart going out to my grandmother. It must've been awful for her.

There were details of dates that she and Reece had been on. Descriptions of the music they loved at a dance hall in Edinburgh; her saying how much Reece loved *The Four Seasons* and The Ronettes. My grandmother had written how she'd watched the movie *Cleopatra* in the cinema with Reece, and that he had teased her that the next choice of film they went to see would be *The Great Escape*. Then there were more frustrated comments about her art and also annoyance at her job in a picture framers in Edinburgh.

I know some of my paintings aren't as good as the ones we sell in here, but others are.

I skipped over a few more entries until I arrived at Christmas Eve 1963.

Reece proposed to me tonight – and I said yes! We were admiring the huge Norwegian Christmas tree just off Princes Street, when he suddenly dropped down onto one knee. Stupid me, for one moment, I thought he was tying his shoelaces, but then he plucked this small, glossy box from out of his coat pocket. I opened it up and there was the most gorgeous yellow diamond ring.

I'm so, so happy! I honestly could cry right now. I did when he proposed. But his parents keep looming in my head. I know they aren't going to be at all pleased about this. Reece still insists I'll win them over, but why should I have to? I'm a good person and I love their son deeply.

I lowered the journal, a mixture of fury and sadness battling it out inside of me on behalf of my grandma. You could sense her fear and apprehension underneath her happiness and delight at her engagement to Reece.

I looked over several more entries and then stopped. Under the date 16 April 1964 was scribbled just a few, frantic sentences.

It's over. Reece has called off the engagement. I love him so, so much but it's not enough. I'm not enough. I knew I

wouldn't be. I'm not enough for him, as it turns out, and
certainly not enough for his parents.

I shook my head.

Outside, the stars blinked over the bay and the
lighthouse was beaming its protective eye across the boats it
was guiding in the rough swell.

The journal had no more entries for a long time after that
last one, just more random sketches of pieces of fruit and
birds.

In fact, there were no more diary entries for another six
months, until 30 October 1964.

> *The thought of Reece still hurts but perhaps, on reflection,*
> *he did the right thing by ending our engagement. His parents*
> *would never have allowed us to be happy anyway.*
>
> *I'm trying to move on. It's still difficult. I loved him more*
> *than life itself. But I'll get there. I have to.*
>
> *I'll get there. I have to.*

I traced one finger over these particular words. I just
wished I could believe them for myself.

More dates were missing – no more new entries for ten
days, until 10 November. Then my grandmother had
written.

> *Whilst I was working in the shop today, a young man*
> *came in, asking about having a picture framed for his*
> *grandfather for his birthday.*

The picture was a painting of the older man in his younger years whilst serving in the army. Whoever had painted it had captured a determined, steely spark in his eyes.

Anyway, the young gent kept staring at me, going red and smiling.

He was attractive in a kind, boyish sort of way. When Ms Townsend disappeared into the back office and I'd taken the measurements of his picture and processed his order, he thanked me for my help and said his name was Howard Michaels.

I let out a delighted, stunned little gasp that made Bronte jerk her head up to look at me.

My grandpa. That was the day she'd met him. The day she'd recounted again and again over the years, describing him blushing furiously across the counter and smiling at her. I rubbed at my eyes. They were beginning to feel gritty. I'd done far more sorting and reading than I'd intended.

Weariness was tugging at my bones. Even Bronte let out a very unladylike yawn, as she rested by my feet.

But I couldn't resist. I decided to push on with reading just a few more pages, before calling it a night.

Details of their subsequent dates – meeting for coffee; going dancing and ten-pin bowling; strolling through Princes Street Gardens; catching a concert by The Hollies – followed. My grandmother's happiness at their blossoming romance wafted from the pages.

Howard is trying to encourage me to display my work or sell it. He says I have great talent. But then he would, wouldn't he? I've had comments like that before. I'm happy for the first time in a long time and I'm not prepared to risk that. Perhaps I'm not meant to have my work seen by a lot of people. Maybe my painting is just meant to give me happiness and contentment – which it does. So, so much. Perhaps I'm not as talented as I think I am, or those around me believe me to be. Still, I do dream about having an exhibition of my work, people in the arts admiring my brush strokes and sketching abilities, appreciating what I'm trying to do.

Art makes me feel alive, and thinking that my paintings could make other people feel the emotion I do is almost too wonderful to imagine.

I know my darling Howard means well, but for me to take that further step and try to get my paintings exhibited somewhere … well, I just can't. I'll hold that dream in my heart though. Always.

Fascinated, I flicked through more entries: my grandparents' meeting, falling in love, marrying and then eventually leaving Edinburgh to move to Rowan Bay.

31 May 1985

Leaving Edinburgh behind was difficult, but both Howard and I have decided we wanted a change of scene and Rowan Bay is certainly that!

Tessa has gone travelling with a few friends in Europe, before she begins her English degree at the University of York, so it seemed like the perfect time to start a new chapter.

Rowan Bay is breathtaking, with the majestic waves, rippling cliff faces and even a lighthouse just across from our cottage and up on the opposite cliff! It will certainly be an inspirational setting for my art.

The lighthouse keeper is a flirty, funny gent about the same age as Howard and me, called Barclay Hogan. He's promising to lead Howard astray by taking him on a tour of some of the local hostelries. I don't think my dear Howard will take much persuading!

The locals, just like Barclay, seem welcoming and friendly. Or at least, most of them are…

I frowned. I wonder what Grandma meant by that? I resumed reading.

There's even an art gallery here, called the Lumiere Gallery, which I've heard so many wonderful things about. Apparently, almost every famous Scottish artist you can think of has had paintings exhibited there at one time or another. Oh, to have a piece of my own work hanging on its famed walls! What a dream that would be.

Anyway, it's been another busy chaotic day, unpacking more boxes after we arrived earlier in the week.

I hope to go and check out more of Rowan Bay and its inhabitants tomorrow.

I smiled fondly at Grandma's dancing handwriting and her mention of meeting Barclay for the first time. I turned over the next page.

3 June 1985

I suppose life never goes truly smoothly all the time.

Some people don't seem to need much of an excuse to take against you.

I dared to ask about the possibility of joining The Rowan Bay Artists' Society and almost had my nose taken off. I was told in no uncertain terms that it was full to capacity at the moment and couldn't accommodate anyone else. I find that very hard to believe, for a town this size. Talk about not very encouraging!

Oh well. I suppose it's to be expected to come across folks who you don't like as much as others.

I frowned. Who was this person who my grandma seemingly had issues with? She'd never mentioned anyone like that before. Grandma Tilda had rubbed along fine with most people throughout her life, so for her to refer to it wasn't like her.

Oh well. Probably some old local gossip who my grandma had taken exception to.

That night, I lay in bed thinking, with the water rolling under the chipped stars and the lighthouse glancing across the top of the waves.

My grandmother had been so talented and yet she'd stifled her own ambition. She'd harboured regret, as it turned out, and doubted her own capabilities so much she'd refused to even try to release her artwork into the world. I had no idea she'd been engaged to Reece and also hadn't known that, underneath it all, she'd wanted to try and get her artwork noticed, despite her insistence over the years to the contrary. I believed Reece's parents had a part to play in this. They'd crushed her confidence. They'd made her think she wasn't worthy.

As I continued to lie there, huddled under my beige and cream duvet for warmth, my mind turned to the stack of paintings in the art studio.

They deserved to be seen. They were sitting there, propped up against one another, only glimpsing the light of day if I hitched the studio blind up. Grandma Tilda's talents should be appreciated. But how?

After a few more moments of frustrated thoughts, I finally fell into a fitful sleep.

I woke up the following morning, with my grandma's melancholic words still whirling around my head. *Perhaps I'm not as talented as I think I am.*

I remembered her as a stoic woman, who could be a tigress when she needed to be, especially where her family were concerned.

And she was still all those things to me.

But after seeing her journals and digesting her innermost hurt and feelings, I realised there was a fallibility to her, underneath the perpetual smile and joviality.

Reece breaking off their engagement had affected her. It had made her question her own value and that had stayed with her for years.

Despite longing to make it as a serious artist, she had never felt able to reach those heights.

And Mum and I had no idea she'd been carrying this weight around with her. She'd never mentioned her dreams to us. Not once. She just kept them locked up inside herself, allowing them to slumber away and ignoring them whenever they happened to stir and threaten to wake up.

Grandma Tilda was gone. She wasn't coming back.

But her legacy of artwork was still here.

I pushed myself upright in bed, suddenly oblivious to the chilly November temperature. The central heating had gone off, and through the gap in my bedroom curtains I could see shreds of ominous grey clouds scudding across the sky.

My mind swirled, taking my thoughts down the hallway to Grandma's studio.

Could I help achieve my late grandmother's dream? Even though she was no longer here, could I fulfil something for her?

I shoved off the bedcovers and tugged on my towelling dressing gown from where it was draped over the chair in the corner.

I'd call Reece first and discuss my idea with him.

He might think it was a silly proposal, but there was only one way to find out.

Chapter Nineteen

I called Reece while I slid two slices of pumpkin-seeded bread into the toaster.

'Would you be able to pop round in an hour or so?' I asked him.

'Is everything alright, Rosie?' Reece sounded concerned.

'Yes, I think so. It's just there's something I'd like you to see.'

I wandered through to the sitting room and watched the chilly light slide across the cliff face outside. The water looked like a still, ice-blue curtain.

'Och, sure. I just need to pop to the supermarket to get a couple of things and then I'll drop by.'

I showered, dressed and took Bronte out for a walk in the woodland opposite. She bounded over the cross work of twigs and branches scattered over the woodland floor.

We'd just arrived back inside the cottage; I'd closed the

front door and was swiping off my hat, when there was a knock.

Bronte let out an excited bark.

I opened it to see Reece standing there on the step. He was sporting a snazzy tartan peaked cap like Peaky Blinders and was huddled in his winter coat and a matching scarf that was knotted at his throat.

His hands were behind his back. Like a magician, he produced a beautiful, festive looking bouquet of roses and carnations, interspersed with berries and holly and ivy. He proffered them to me. 'For you.'

I gawped at him, touched by his thoughtfulness. 'They're beautiful. Thank you.' A lump clotted in my throat as I accepted them. The fragrant, perfumed scent wafted up out of the red and white tissue paper they were wrapped in. A huge, silky green bow was holding them together. 'What have I done to deserve these?'

I beckoned Reece in from the cold.

Bronte jumped up at him as he entered and she was rewarded with pats on her head.

Reece pulled a dismissive face at my question. 'You were so kind and welcoming to me yesterday, even after I told you about what happened between your grandmother and me. I appreciate it.' He gave me a wink. 'And it's also to apologise for almost frightening you half to death.'

I gazed down at the delicate heads of the flowers. As if out of nowhere, everything hit me with brute force: Joe, Mum and Dad, Christmas looming, my grandparents no longer here, Barclay moving on, my writing career finished and my loss of direction. I tried to bury a tearful gulp, but it was no good. Out it came, followed by a tear sliding down my face.

Horror shone out of Reece. 'Oh no. Och lass, I'm so sorry. I didn't mean to upset you. I'm such an old eejit!'

I shook my head and swallowed. 'It's not you. I'm just letting things get on top of me, that's all. It's been rather a tough time of late.'

I dashed my face with the back of my right hand while still clutching the flowers. I hurried into the kitchen. I placed them in the sink and rooted around for one of Grandma's vases, which she'd stored in a cupboard under the plates.

I found a pretty, cranberry coloured vase with white dots painted around the rim, and filled it with cold water. I fetched a pair of scissors from the cutlery drawer, snipped off the ends of the stems and cut open the sachet of flower food. I watched it swirl and drift to the bottom of the vase – a bit like how I felt at the moment.

I gave my head a mental shake. Come on, Winters!

I set the flowers on the kitchen window sill and turned.

Reece was watching me with concern from the kitchen doorway. 'Are you sure you're alright? I know we don't know each other very well, but I'm a good listener. Well, actually, I think I'm beginning to go a bit deaf.'

I managed a laugh.

Reece cocked one greying brow at me.

I found myself fiddling with the flowers. 'My husband died in July. He was knocked over by a car and killed.'

Reece's jaw dropped. 'Och lass. I'm so sorry. I don't know what to say.'

I shrugged, not knowing what else to say myself. 'It's tough, isn't it?'

He nodded. 'It is. You just have to give yourself time. There's no textbook for this.'

I shook my head. 'No, there certainly isn't.' I gave him a long look. He was easy to talk to. A good listener, with those compassionate, world-weary eyes. I readied myself. 'I found out in September that he'd been cheating on me with another woman for three years.'

There was a heavy silence. Reece let out a long, low gasp. 'The bastard.' He coloured. 'Och lass, I'm sorry for speaking ill of the dead, but still.'

I flung my hands in the air for something to do. 'Please don't apologise. I've been doing the same thing.'

He shook his head in shock. 'And how are you doing? I mean, how are you coping with it all?'

'Sometimes I think I'm beginning to cope, and then other times I know I'm not. Sometimes I wish he was here, so I could scream at him. Other times a part of me is glad he isn't.' I managed a brief smile. 'Keeping busy helps. Right. Come on. Let me show you something.'

I led a still-stunned Reece down the hallway and back into Grandma's studio.

The light spiralled and twisted through the window and down onto her paintings resting there.

I reached over to her desk and retrieved one of the journals. 'I was tidying up Grandma's desk last night as you can see, when I came across these. There's a whole stack of them and they were all together in that bottom drawer. I couldn't open it at first. It was locked. But after a bit of searching around, I located the key.'

Reece shrugged off his coat and draped it over one arm. 'What are they?'

'Journals. Diaries. My grandma's.'

Reece's brows lifted. 'I didn't know she kept diaries.'

'Neither did I.' I picked up the pink, suede one in which I'd placed a few strips of coloured Post-it notes for reference, so I wouldn't lose the place. 'Take a look at the pages I've marked.'

Reece ran one hand over the cover, as though trying to connect, by touch, with my grandma. His fingertips caressed it for a few seconds. 'Are you sure?'

'Of course. Here, let me take your coat.'

I took it from him, while Reece eased himself into the desk chair and turned to the page I'd flagged up with a sliver of zesty yellow Post-it. He hesitated again.

'I didn't realise what they were at first, but when I started reading some of her entries... Well, I'm glad I did to be honest.'

Reece gave a silent nod of understanding and turned his attention to my grandma's loopy swirls of handwriting. He began to read.

I watched his faraway expression shift from sadness to surprise. 'Rosie,' he choked, jerking his head up to look at me.

'I know. Turn to the next page I've marked.'

Reece opened and closed his mouth a few times, but did as I asked him. His gnarly fingers moved the pages with the utmost care.

The next entry was the one I'd earmarked with a purple Post-it note.

Reece started to read again. An emotional crack escaped from the back of his throat. 'Och, no. Oh, my Tilda. My beautiful Tilda.' He set the journal down in his lap as though in slow motion. 'What the hell was I thinking of? What did I think I was doing?' His pale eyes shimmered. 'I loved her. I never loved anyone else the way I loved her. And yet I let her walk away. I ended our engagement and took the coward's way out.'

I reached out and patted him on his right shoulder. 'You were a lot younger then. You were under pressure from your parents. If you'd been a bit older and more independent, it probably would've been a different story.'

Reece's eyes shone with regret. 'I wish I'd come to see her sooner.' His heavy eyes dropped back to look at the journal he was holding.

Now it was my turn to have glistening tears. 'Take your time. When you're ready, turn to the page marked up with the blue Post-it note.'

Reece turned to the page I'd mentioned. It was the one where she'd poured out her heart, just after Reece had ended their engagement. She'd spoken of wanting to believe in herself and her art, but she didn't think she could do it. She didn't think she had enough self-belief.

Reece's eyes scanned the diary entry. As he took in what

she'd written, his shoulders sagged. 'So, she did want that after all.' His voice faltered. 'She did want to become a successful artist.' He closed his eyes and then spoke again as though murmuring to himself. 'I knew she was never satisfied, working in that bloody picture framer's shop.' His frustration changed to pensiveness for a few moments. 'What was the name of it again?'

'Picture Perfect.'

'Aye. Of course it was.' His small smile vanished. 'She'd always bat away my suggestions when I tried to encourage her.' He looked agonised. 'Was that because of me, Rosie? Because I never fought for her? Did I make Tilda feel that way about her talent? That she wasn't good enough?' His mouth became grim. 'My damned parents made her think she was beneath me, beneath us all, and I knew she was growing tired of me not standing up to them.' A dark expression clung to Reece's face and refused to let go. 'I didn't deserve her. Even after all these years, she still thought about me, though. She painted my bloody portrait, for heaven's sake!'

He let out a shallow, dark laugh. 'Some people go through their entire lives never experiencing a love like that, and I had it, but I ruined it. I was a coward.'

I blinked back more pictures of Joe and cleared my throat. I studied the older man, hunched over in my grandma's scuffed swivel desk chair, regret pressing down on him. 'Look, Reece, you can't keep dwelling on it.'

'I should've fought for her. I should've given her a

reason to come back to me. I was weak and cowed by my parents. If only I'd stood up to them.'

'Regrets are painful things,' I admitted. The irony of what I was saying lodged itself inside me. 'But they can be avoided, if only you grasp opportunities where and when you can.'

But Reece didn't reply. He was staring down, his gaze drilling into the pink journal still resting in his lap. 'Reece?'

He gazed back up at me, looking for a moment as though he'd forgotten I was standing there. 'Oh, sorry, lass. I was miles away then.'

I gave him an understanding smile. 'It's okay.' I paused. 'Look, there was something I wanted to talk to you about. After reading some of Grandma's entries, I came up with an idea.' I leant against the side of the desk. 'What if we could get some of Grandma's art exhibited?'

Reece looked up at me from the swivel chair.

'It's the least we could do,' I carried on, 'and her work does deserve to be seen, don't you think?' I dragged a hand through my hair. 'I don't know how easy it would be, but I think we should try.'

Reece's expression was one of bewilderment. He stared past me at the blank wall over my shoulder for a moment. 'Yes, of course it does. She possessed such talent. Anyone can see that.' He risked a look down at his lap again, at the notebook resting on it. 'But what gallery or galleries were you thinking of, though? Would they take us seriously? That sort of thing is very competitive.'

'I know it is, but I don't see why they wouldn't give her

work serious consideration. I know we're probably a bit biased, but her paintings are wonderful.' I could sense a kernel of optimism flourishing. 'There's that prestigious Lumiere Gallery on the outskirts of Rowan Bay for starters. I remember her mentioning how artists fought like rats in a sack to get their work exhibited there. She's even mentioned it in her journal.' What was it she'd said? *That it would be a dream to have a piece of work exhibited there?*

My enthusiasm started to fly. 'She said lots of prestigious Scottish artists have had their artwork showcased in that gallery: Jack Vettriano, William Turnbull, Joyce Cairns.' I could feel my excitement stacking higher in my chest. 'I know it's a bit of a gamble, but isn't it worth a try?'

I could see the cogs whirring in Reece's mind.

'What do you think? She lived here in Rowan Bay for forty years, so that might be an added advantage. Local artist and all that.'

Reece's attention slid from me, back down the journal in his lap. He gave it a tender pat. 'Aye. I think we should at least try. It would be a fitting tribute to her, if we could get this off the ground. Tilda deserves that much at least.'

Both his hands reached for the journal and placed themselves on top of it. 'I feel like I owe her, Rosie. Especially now. Especially after reading this. I want to do something to show her how sorry I am.' He sighed. It was a painful noise that burrowed in his chest. 'At least I'll feel like I've tried to make amends.'

I nodded and was about to reply, when my mobile

trilled in my back pocket. I pulled it out and peered at the screen.

It was Lola.

Reece's silver brows arched. 'Everything alright?'

'Yes, yes. Fine, thanks,' I trilled through a forced smile.

My phone then let out a series of frantic blips.

Texts from Lola rippled and glowed out of the screen.

Can we talk? No pressure, sweetheart, but readers are reaching out to us, begging you to write again. Maybe we could have an informal chat, you, me and Mia, if you feel up to it?

I couldn't help myself. 'Oh, piss off, Lola. Just leave me alone!'

Reece took his time. He gave me a look. 'Doesn't sound like everything's fine to me.' He picked up my grandma's pink journal from his lap and set it back down on her old desk.

I didn't want to talk about it, but Reece kept examining me with a soft, expectant expression that I couldn't ignore. I knew he was being kind, offering to listen to me wittering on.

I sighed in a defeated way and dragged over the other spare, rickety wooden chair in the corner. I flopped down into it, resigned to the fact that I was about to confide in my late grandma's ex-fiancé. I hadn't seen this coming.

'You don't have to tell me,' clarified Reece. 'But it might help.'

My chest deflated. 'Okay. Don't say I didn't warn you.'

And I proceeded to relay to him my decision not to write any more books.

Reece listened and nodded and murmured in the right places. 'You're an author?'

'Was.'

'What genre do you write?'

'Did. Romance.'

'Ach.'

'Exactly.'

When I finished talking, I slumped back in the chair, mentally drained by it all.

Reece contemplated everything I'd told him. He was silent for a long time. Then he finally spoke again. 'Do you know how proud your grandma was of you?'

I jerked my head to look at him. 'She told you about me?'

'Aye, she did indeed. Quite a lot actually. She mentioned you often in our Facebook messages.'

I let out a brief bark of laughter. 'So, you knew about me being a writer, but never said anything?'

He shrugged. 'We were still getting to know one another. I'd already frightened you half to death and I didn't want to come across as some deranged stalker.'

Our conversation was interrupted by a sudden, insistent knock on the door.

'Excuse me a second.'

Reece remained seated in the art studio, while I hurried

up the hall to open the door. Bronte was yapping behind me.

I jerked open the front door to be met by Mitch and Kane. He gave me a little salute. 'You, okay?'

I took in his angular mouth and glinting eyes. My stomach did a weird, wriggly movement, which caught me off-guard. What on earth was that? I swallowed and tried to reset my thoughts. 'Yes, thanks. How are you?'

'Och, not bad.' He hesitated. His attention lingered on my face. 'Are you sure you're alright?'

His eyes were glowing back at me in that stunning, bright sea colour. They spangled from under his ebony, long lashes.

I cleared my throat. 'Yes. Why do you ask?'

'It's just I was walking past the corner shop just now and the woman who works in there ... Rita?'

'Rhea.'

'Aye. That's right. Sorry. Rhea. Well, she saw me passing, dived out and said she was up here with her Pekinese for a walk a short while ago and she thought she saw a man she didn't recognise, hanging round.' He delivered a hint of a devilish smile. 'So, Captain Birdseye decided to don his cape and make sure everything was okay.'

I found myself blushing and smiling at the same time. 'Ouch. I asked for that one.'

Mitch continued to lock eyes with me. A quiver of something tumbled through my stomach. I banished any thought of it. Nope. Not even going there. I'd had enough of being let down and hurt to last me a lifetime, and not even a tall, dark, handsome lighthouse keeper could persuade me otherwise.

I pushed any lingering thoughts about how gorgeous Mitch was firmly to one side. 'Yes, it's all good, thanks. Honestly. I was expecting Reece, so everything's fine.'

An unfathomable look zipped across his stubbled face. 'Oh. Okay. Right.'

My heart gave an odd little squeeze of gratitude. 'Thank you for checking up on me. Really. That was very kind of you. I appreciate it.'

But to my surprise, Mitch was already walking away, Kane lumbering at his heel. His voice was brisk over his shoulder. 'No worries. I'll leave you to your company then, Rosie.'

Chapter Twenty

R eece materialised behind me in the hallway.
'Who's your knight in shining armour?'

My cheeks popped with more colour. 'The new lighthouse keeper. Tends to keep himself to himself.'

I knew I'd applied the same philosophy since arriving in Rowan Bay. I mentally dismissed more images of Mitch's green-ringed eyes and his thoughtfulness. 'Come on,' I urged Reece, watching Mitch's dark-haired, muscular frame vanish up the cliff steps. 'Let's give this art gallery a call. We should hit the ground running.'

Reece's eye's popped in surprise. 'What? Now?'

'Why not? No time like the present and all that.'

We returned to my grandma's studio and I fetched my mobile from the desk. I pulled up the Lumiere Gallery's website and located their phone number and dialled it. My stomach was flip-flapping around with a combination of nerves and excitement.

After several rings, a deep, modulated, Scottish female voice answered. 'Good morning, the Lumiere Gallery. How may I help you?'

I smiled down the line. 'Good morning, I was wondering if we might be able to make an appointment, please? We have some very impressive chalks and watercolours from a late, local artist. She was my grandmother. We hoped you might be interested in taking a look, with a possible view to exhibiting?'

'Oh, I'm very sorry for your loss,' replied the woman. 'We would of course have to see the artwork before making a decision. Are they landscapes, portraits, still life…?'

'A very eclectic mix,' I explained, hoping I was doing a good job of verbally selling them.

Reece stood opposite me, listening to the phone conversation with interest.

'My late grandma lived in Rowan Bay for years, so there's a lovely, local angle to many of the pieces. In fact, some of her pictures feature Rowan Bay harbour, the lighthouse, the cliffs…'

'Well, we could certainly take a look,' mused the woman. I heard her tap the keys of a computer keyboard. 'Could you give me some details first and then we can schedule a suitable appointment time for you to bring in a selection of your late grandma's artwork?'

I stuck one thumb up in the air at Reece, delighted by how the phone call was playing out so far.

Reece beamed and jerked his thumb up at me in response.

'Right. So can you give me your late grandma's name please?'

'Yes. It's Tilda Michaels.'

The excited twittering from the woman at the other end of the phone vanished. I thought the line had crashed. 'Hello? Are you still there?' I asked.

The woman let out a weird cough. Her voice had morphed from friendly and enthusiastic to brittle in seconds. 'I do apologise, but I'm afraid we won't be able to consider your late grandmother's work for exhibition. Our diary is very full right now.'

My shoulders stiffened in surprise. What on earth was going on here? Only a moment ago, she was all for it. 'Sorry? I don't understand.'

The woman was keen to wrap up the conversation. 'Thank you for considering the Lumiere Gallery and I wish you success with finding another gallery for the work. Have a good day.' The phone went dead.

I stared down at my mobile. She'd put the phone down on me!

Reece frowned down at my phone screen, back at me and then at my phone again. 'What's happened?'

I shook my head in disbelief. 'I don't know. She was so enthusiastic about seeing Grandma's paintings, but as soon as I mentioned Grandma's name, she realised their exhibition diary was choc-a-block and hung up!'

Reece's bristly brows fenced. 'Seriously? That sounds odd.'

'I know. Tell me about it.'

I set my mobile back down on the desk, my head racing.

Reece shrugged under his woollen sweater. 'Och, some of these arty types can be a bit unpredictable.'

I chewed my bottom lip. 'But it was only when I gave her grandma's name that she went all weird. Up until that point, she was charm itself.'

'Did you get her name? The woman who you just spoke to?'

I shook my head in frustration. 'No, she never gave it and I was so worked up about doing a good job of verbally selling the artwork, I never thought to ask.'

Reece brushed it off. 'Like I said, arty types.' He rubbed at his forehead. 'We'll just have to approach another gallery.'

I eyed my grandma's collection of paintings leaning against the wall. 'Maybe the Lumiere Gallery would change their mind, if they actually saw Grandma's work for themselves, appreciate how talented she was.' I set my shoulders in defiance. 'I'm not taking no for an answer, Reece. I received so many rejections when I was starting out as a writer.' My determination took off. 'I think we should just turn up at that gallery with a selection of Grandma's best works. Once they see it for themselves, I'm sure they'll change their minds and be chomping at the bit to exhibit her paintings.'

Reece didn't look convinced. He sighed. 'Okay. That's what we'll do, boss. But I wouldn't get your hopes up.'

After breakfast the next morning, I got ready and chose my smartest trousers, pink satin blouse and ankle boots that I was grateful I'd tossed into my case.

Reece was to meet me at the cottage at ten o'clock, so I could drive us to the gallery, along with some of Grandma's paintings.

When Reece arrived he was dressed in his long coat with a crisp, white shirt, paisley tie and dark dress trousers.

'You look very smart.'

Bronte sat, eyeing us both from the cottage sitting room.

I'd already loaded some of Grandma's paintings into the boot of my car. They ranged from her smudged, powder blue and lilac depiction of bluebells in the local woodland, to two different interpretations of the lighthouse at dawn and dusk, two contrasting portraits (one of an elderly woman reading and another of a little boy playing in mud) to a gorgeous depiction of cherry blossom swirling around on a spring day.

Once I'd reassured Bronte for the third time that I wouldn't be long, I locked the cottage door and we pulled away with our precious cargo.

I thought it might be best to arrive at the gallery just after they opened so that we could catch them unawares when they were quiet. Hopefully, they'd be able to devote more time to appreciating and ultimately approving Grandma's work.

The drive took us past stippled hedgerows and fields tipped with winter frost. Remnants of copper and russet leaves danced everywhere, and the scenery, with its glittery, silvery winter webs reminded me of an advent calendar. It was almost December and Christmas was drawing ever closer.

We caught glimpses of Rowan Bay sliding past us in a cool, steady line on the horizon as I negotiated my car along the country roads.

The Lumiere Gallery was a grand, white stucco affair, hugged by huge Scots pines.

It was situated just off the main road, on the outskirts of Rowan Bay, and was illuminated with subtle gold spotlights in the trees. In its panoramic window was a large, gilt-framed painting of a voluptuous, naked couple embracing.

Reece and I didn't say anything. We just exchanged bemused glances. My grandmother's artwork was streets ahead of that.

Once we clambered out of the car, we each took a couple of my grandma's pictures, which we'd covered with pieces of canvas for protection, and made our way carefully towards the arched, glass entrance. We could come back to the car and collect the remainder of the paintings shortly.

Inside, the air in the gallery was brimming with spiced apple and clove potpourri.

There was no one around, so Reece and I took the opportunity to set the paintings down for a minute and take in what was displayed on the silky, burgundy gallery walls.

It looked like more of the same artist's work that was in

the window; pink, wobbly thighs under tables, a sweating, bulbous-faced man loosening his tie and assorted others of mean-looking children gobbling sweets. These artworks would give you nightmares!

No sooner had we wrinkled our noses in unison, than a handsome, but austere-looking older woman, who I estimated to be in her early seventies, emerged from a closed white door at the rear of the gallery.

She was wearing a slash of glamorous red lipstick and a well-cut, black trouser suit with a striped shirt peeking out from underneath. Her hair was cut in a sharp, cheek-grazing, blue-grey bob. She made me feel shabby, despite the effort I'd gone to, to look professional. She offered a smile. 'Good morning. Can I help you?'

As soon as she spoke, I recognised her smooth, Scottish voice.

It was the same woman who I'd spoken to yesterday, the one who'd been keen initially to see Grandma's artwork, only to rudely close down the conversation moments later after she found out who my grandma was.

'Yes, I hope you can,' I replied. 'I don't know if you remember, but I spoke to you yesterday on the phone.' I pinned on a friendly smile. 'I'm Rosie Winters. I called you about my grandmother's paintings for possible exhibition.'

It took a moment for the woman to register what I was saying. Her friendly expression vanished. Her eyes flew to the covered painting we each had by our sides.

'There are more where these came from,' interjected Reece.

The woman's deep-set gaze hardened. 'I'm not interested in these paintings or anything to do with your grandmother.'

What the hell was going on here? What was this woman's problem?

I shot Reece a furious glance beside me. 'May I ask why?'

She indicated to the illuminated walls and the fleshy artwork taking centre stage. 'We only accept pieces of a certain standard.'

I could feel my ire being pricked. 'I can tell you that my grandmother's paintings are of a far higher quality than these.' I pointed one finger at my grandma's assorted, concealed pictures by our feet.

'Art is subjective,' clipped the woman. Her red slash of mouth twitched with a smirk. 'Rather like the publishing industry.'

My jaw tightened. The rude cow! She was taking a shot at my writing! She obviously knew about me having been an author.

We stared each other out.

I straightened my back and was about to give her a mouthful, but Reece jumped in. He shot out one rough hand and rested it on my coat sleeve. 'Thank you for your time. Come on, Rosie. We're done here.'

I whirled round so fast; I almost cricked my neck. 'What?'

But Reece was already steering me and the paintings back towards the gallery entrance.

I shot her a dark look over my shoulder. She folded her arms.

Once we'd set the pictures back in the boot of my car, I opened the driver's door, slumped heavily in the seat and then thumped the steering wheel in annoyance. 'Who the hell does she think she is? Did you hear the way she spoke about Grandma? Did you see the way she was looking down her nose at us?' I shook my updo in exasperation. 'Something isn't right about all this.'

Reece frowned out of his passenger side window. 'It does seem strange; I'll give you that.' He settled himself back in his seat. 'Let's not waste any more time or energy worrying about this place. I'm sure with a bit of research, we'll find another gallery that's more appreciative of Tilda's work.'

I fired up the car ignition. 'You're right.' I glowered out of the windscreen. 'But I know it would've meant so much to her to have her pieces exhibited there.'

'Rosie, it would mean a lot to your grandmother to know you're putting in so much effort to get her work exhibited anyway.'

I struggled to smile at him. I knew Reece meant well, but my frustration was at boiling point. That bloody woman! Who the hell was she anyway and what was her issue with my late grandma?

As I pulled away from the kerb, I caught a glimpse of the woman, her twisted red mouth examining us through the gallery window.

The journey back was shrouded in disappointment.

Reece and I exchanged the odd bit of chatter, but it was rather forced.

What the hell was that woman's problem? My late grandma deserved her talent to be recognised.

We arrived back at the cottage and I parked up beside Reece's car.

Bronte's delighted barks could be heard before I even unlocked the front door. There was a blur of movement up by the cliffs, which caught my attention.

It was Mitch, who was cleaning the exterior of the lighthouse. He was armed with a bucket of hot, soapy water, cleaning cloths, and his devoted Kane by his side.

Mitch Carlisle really was an enigma. He insisted on helping me search for Bronte and then checking in on me yesterday to make sure I was alright. He'd shown genuine concern for me but at the same time, he seemed keen to keep himself to himself.

I wondered what might have happened to him to make him be like that. A broken marriage? A deception of some kind? Friends ghosting him over something? Okay, I was giving this a bit too much thought. I had my own issues to deal with, without getting embroiled in other people's.

I found myself watching him clean the lighthouse, his long, muscular legs bending and stretching. He appeared lost in what he was doing. His movements were methodical and rhythmical.

I gave myself a mental shake, and Reece and I began to retrieve my grandma's artwork from the boot of the car to return them inside.

I was angling the last painting – one of the lighthouse scenes at sunset – back through the open cottage door when Mitch's intrigued voice startled me.

'Hi there. Wow. Did you paint that, Rosie? It's fantastic.'

I spun round, startled by his soft-footed approach. Mitch's appreciative expression drifted over the painting. There was an odd look on his stubbled face, which I couldn't decipher.

'No. If only. It was my late grandma. She was the artist.'

I was about to push the door open wider, but Mitch spotted what I was trying to do and gallantly jumped ahead of me. 'Here. Let me help.'

'Oh. Right. Thank you.'

Mitch eased the picture inside and set it down just inside the hallway. We were very close now, almost brushing against one another.

He was in no hurry to move.

I could see the sweep of his lashes and the way the corners of his mouth lifted when he was interested. We both stood there, our thighs almost touching. Mitch held my gaze. My breathing fluttered in my chest. Then I dragged myself back and moved away.

He swiped his hands down the front of his jeans. 'So, your grandma painted?'

I clasped and unclasped my hands for something to do. 'Oh yes. She was prolific. Mainly watercolours, but she dabbled with chalks, too. Her studio is full of her pieces and she painted these too.' I gestured to some of her artwork on the walls.

He nodded. 'So where were you taking her artwork?'

'Trying to get them exhibited,' I explained. 'We visited that posh Lumiere Gallery.'

Mitch angled a brow. 'We?'

'Reece and me.'

'Oh. Right, Your visitor from yesterday.' There was that odd, loaded look again. 'So, what happened?'

'No good. The stuck-up bint in there wasn't interested.'

Mitch blinked at me in surprise. 'Seriously? They turned her art down?'

'Yep. Without even taking a look at it.'

Mitch pulled a face. 'I mean, I'm no art expert, but from what I can see, your grandma's paintings are terrific. What's the issue?'

Mitch wasn't going to let this drop. He was looking at me like Bronte did whenever she wanted a treat. Shit. Oh, what the hell. What did it matter if I told him? It wouldn't make any difference anyway.

I shrugged. 'To be honest, I've no idea why they rejected them. I spoke to the woman at the gallery on the phone yesterday, and she seemed very keen. But as soon as I told her the artist's name, she changed her mind about taking a look at the paintings and put the phone down on me.' I shook my head in disbelief. 'I thought if she saw the paintings, she'd change her mind, but as soon as I told her I was Tilda's granddaughter, she was very rude and said she wanted nothing to do with the art or my grandmother.'

Reece had reappeared at the cottage entrance.

'Oh, sorry. Let me introduce you both. Mitch, this is Reece, an old friend of my late grandmother's. Reece, this is the new lighthouse keeper, Mitch. And this big, gorgeous boy is his dog, Kane.'

Both men swapped handshakes.

Mitch blinked and looked from me to Reece and back again. The strange expression he carried before cleared. 'Oh. Right. So, this is Reece?'

'Yes. Why?'

Mitch said, 'No, no reason.'

What was he going on about? What was the matter with him?

Having examined Reece sufficiently, Mitch concentrated again. 'Wow. That's odd that the gallery wouldn't even take a look.'

I ground my teeth. 'I know you'll think I'm biased. I probably am, but most of those paintings being exhibited in that gallery right now can't hold a candle to my grandma's.'

'Oh, I know that,' agreed Mitch. 'I've seen them for myself.'

'You go up there often then? To the Lumiere Gallery?' I asked him, intrigued.

'I do. Just for something to do. To get away from the confines of the lighthouse and the bothy for a bit.' His lips hinted at a small smile and I found myself fiddling with the hem of my coat as he looked at me.

'Nice and peaceful up there. Languid atmosphere and just the art for company. Suits me fine.'

I examined him again. He really did prefer his own company. 'Well, we'll just have to try and find another gallery who might be interested. It's just … the Lumiere Gallery was a place my grandma was rather in awe of, considering all the prestigious Scottish artists who've exhibited there.' A faraway look entered my eyes. 'Ever since I was small, she was always armed with a paintbrush. She was able to capture the essence and shadow of life.'

Mitch listened. Another indecipherable look passed across his face, which had adopted a sudden and serious edge. 'It takes such talent and dedication to be able to paint. I don't think it's something you can learn. You're born with it. It's a gift.'

I found myself surprised by his sudden openness. 'Yes. You're right. It is.'

I noticed he'd produced a stray cleaning cloth from his fleece pocket and was turning it over and over in his hands. His fingers began to knot it, wrapping the material around and around his fingers. If he continued doing that, he'd shred the thing. He noticed me watching his hands and pushed the cloth back inside his pocket. 'You've had a real time of it, haven't you?'

'Sorry?'

'Your grandma, your husband and then Barclay leaving.'

'Yes, I've had better times in my life.'

I was aware his expression had softened as he continued to study me. Bloody hell, those eyes of his. They were lethal.

I refocused. 'We just wanted to do something special for her, that's all. It turns out that she always wanted to have her work exhibited, but she was terrified of failing.'

I realised I was under scrutiny again from Reece's hypnotic, blue-green gaze. I shuffled from foot to foot in my ankle boots. I was doing it again! Reacting to this man. Well, that would have to stop. He carried on looking at me, a pensive expression clutching at his features. 'Let me help. Please.'

'You just did,' I assured him. 'That's all the paintings back inside now. Thank you for lending a hand with them.'

'No. I don't mean that.' He hesitated and pushed his hands into his jean's pockets. 'Could I come inside for a few moments please? I wouldn't mind taking a look at some of your grandma's other work, and I can help you back down to her studio with these ones.'

Before I could debate it, Mitch was inside, almost filling the hall with his tall, dark presence. I watched him pick up the lighthouse picture again. 'Her studio is at the bottom of the hall, you said?'

I shot a look at Reece, who offered me a small, cryptic smile. I didn't know what that meant. 'Er ... yes... Right at the bottom, facing you. Thank you.'

Mitch strode off on his long legs, clutching the painting with reverence. Reece had already moved off just ahead of him and was placing the bluebell painting inside the open studio door.

As I approached, the studio looked like a child's paintbox. The late morning light was sending strobes of winter sunshine across the wooden, paint-splashed floor. It glanced at her precious collection of glass butterflies up on the mantlepiece above the old, gothic-style fireplace.

'This is where it all used to happen.' I managed a smile.

But Mitch wasn't listening. He was too interested in Grandma's artwork. He set down the painting he was carrying and took in his surroundings. His attention zoomed in on my grandma's other paintings propped against the back wall. 'You said she always wanted to have her work on display?'

'Yes, she did, although when you asked her, she'd always deny it.' I took in her palettes of paint that I couldn't bring myself to pack away. 'She never knew how good she was.' I clasped my hands together. 'Anyway, at least we tried to get her featured in the Lumiere Gallery. I hope I can thumb my nose at that old bat when another gallery snaps up her work.'

'Let me help,' erupted Mitch, breaking through my thoughts.

I blinked at him. 'Sorry?'

His voice sounded almost desperate. 'Let me see if I can get her paintings accepted by the Lumiere Gallery. At least let me try.'

I stared at him and then at Reece, who'd been listening intently from the other side of the room. 'But... But that woman in the gallery gave us a flat no,' he said.

'Well, she might not if I ask her.'

I narrowed my eyes at him. 'What makes you think that you'll have more success than us?'

'My dark, troubled-poet good looks and scintillating personality?' His face was deadpan.

I rolled my eyes. My head was swimming with surprise. I tried not to acknowledge how good-looking he was. He definitely did carry a brooding, tortured Heathcliff vibe with all those thick, dark curls. 'It's very kind of you to offer. But why?'

Mitch looked at me and Reece. 'Why what?'

'Why offer to do this?'

Mitch gave a dismissive shrug. 'Can't someone just want to do a good turn for someone else?' His tone was verging on the defensive.

I knew I was still staring at him and looked away. Why was Mitch offering to do this? Why was he so insistent that he wanted to help?

'Look, just let me take a few of your grandma's paintings into the gallery and see what happens. You can come with me if you like. Conduct surveillance from the car.' Mitch arched his brows. 'You don't think I'm capable of nicking them and running off with the takings, do you?'

Reece let out a laugh. 'Of course not, young man. We don't, do we, Rosie?'

'No. Not at all.'

'Then why not let Mitch at least try?' suggested Reece. 'It's worth a go, surely. He might have more luck with the ice maiden than we did. What do you say?'

'Ice maiden?' asked Mitch.

I folded my arms. 'Yes. The witch who works in there;

all cheek-grazing silver bob and red lipstick. I don't know her name.'

'Ah. You mean the gallery owner, Ruth Mangan. Her bark's worse than her bite.'

'That's your opinion,' chipped in Reece with a rueful look. 'I think Rosie and I might need tetanus injections.'

I didn't know how I felt about any of this. Mitch was being very kind. It was just a bit left field, that's all. We didn't know each other very well and yet he was offering to do something like this.

I debated whether I should accept. I didn't want to have to rely on anyone, especially another man. In a weird way, living up here just with Bronte and with the bay swishing around at night, I was slowly becoming used to being on my own. I knew sooner or later I would have to face up to life's challenges and the bitterness of what Joe did. Although I much preferred to achieve this for Grandma just with Reece's help, I didn't want to appear unappreciative. I just wished I could understand why Mitch was so keen to get involved. How did he plan to help? What was he intending to do?

As if reading my mind, he carried on with his argument. 'I'm good at pitching. In my former life, it was something I did regularly.' He hesitated. 'I had my own business.'

Now it was my turn to look questioningly at him. If Mitch noticed, he chose not to expand on his previous employment situation.

'Just let me give it a go and if I don't manage to charm

Ruth, then you can say, I told you so.' He aimed his attention back at me. 'I'm confident I can persuade her to take the paintings. Like I said, I know what I'm doing.' He pulled himself up but didn't elaborate.

I was in danger of being on the receiving end of one of Mitch's hot looks again. I took a breath. His assertiveness and confidence were very attractive. Okay, I was acknowledging it. That was all. 'I don't think a lion tamer could handle that woman,' I ground out, my optimism deflating as I thought more and more about her attitude. 'But I don't suppose we've got anything to lose.'

Mitch cocked one brow.

I accepted defeat. 'Okay. Reece is right. Worth a try. Thank you.'

Mitch nodded his head. 'Good.'

I suspected that the gallery Rottweiler would refuse him too, even if he was a long, dark stream of good-looking moodiness. But he definitely didn't lack self-belief, that was for sure. I wondered what career he'd had before becoming a lighthouse keeper.

Mitch's voice cut across my thoughts. 'You free tomorrow?'

'Yes.'

'Okay. I'll drop by to collect you at just after nine-thirty. Have the paintings ready.'

Mitch bent down and gave an admiring Bronte a rub behind her ears. Was I imagining it or was she batting her eyelashes at him?

I watched Mitch stride back up the hallway. Just when I thought this reclusive lighthouse keeper couldn't get any more mysterious.

Chapter Twenty-One

Mitch stood on the doorstep the next morning looking dashing in a navy suit, pale lemon shirt and sky-blue tie under a long, military-style coat.

It took me a moment to recover myself.

'Will I do?' he asked.

'Yes, not bad,' I answered quickly, my cheeks stinging with colour.

Mitch brushed his hair back from his face. He eyed me. 'Come on. I'll help you load the paintings into the boot of my car.'

'I thought I was driving?' I asked with a frown.

'Well, I thought it might be better if I did. If Ruth Mangan spots you pulling up, she'll smell a rat. I want the element of surprise. And anyway, I've got more boot space than your Mazda.'

'It's no problem,' I persisted. 'I managed yesterday.'

Mitch cut me off. 'Rosie, will you just please accept my help?'

I inwardly flinched. Why didn't I want to accept anything from Mitch? What was the issue? He hadn't done anything offensive or bad to me. In fact, he'd been helpful and neighbourly. I chose not to examine the reason why; no more relying on men in my life, just to have them throw my trust in them right back in my face. I was done with that. 'Even if they were dark and gorgeous?' whispered a teasing voice in my ear.

'Well?'

I blinked myself back to reality. Jesus. He was so pig-headed!

I tutted. 'Alright. Yes. Have it your way.'

Mitch gestured to the side of the cottage. 'I've parked round the corner. Right, let's get this show on the road.'

I'd opted this time for Grandma's sunflower table arrangement, a chalk drawing she'd done of a few of the paint-chipped, peeling little boats in Rowan Bay harbour and a portrait of an old, haggard gentleman perched on a wall, smoking a pipe. Maybe Mitch might have better luck if he took different paintings to the ones Reece and I had taken.

Once we'd loaded the three pictures into the boot of Mitch's car, I assured Bronte I wouldn't be long and locked the cottage door.

We set off.

I eyed Mitch's serious, dark profile beside me. 'What are

you going to say to Miss Trunchbull when you get there?' I asked him.

'I'm still thinking about that.'

I widened my eyes at him. This was crazy. He hadn't planned anything? Why the hell did I think this might work? I stared out of the passenger side window and sighed.

Mitch concentrated on the set of traffic lights glowing ahead of us. 'Don't worry. I'll do your grandma's paintings justice.'

I slid him a sideways glance. No matter how often I turned this over in my mind, it still didn't make sense. Why had Mitch been so keen to help with trying to get my grandma's paintings exhibited? Something was telling me there was more to Mitch insisting on doing this than just being neighbourly.

I noticed his hands holding the black, leather steering wheel. He spoke, unaware that I was mentally trying to dissect the situation. 'Like I said, I've visited that gallery a few times since I took up the job as lighthouse keeper.'

He was deluding himself if he thought he could sweet talk that dragon Ruth Mangan into agreeing to exhibit Grandma's work.

Mitch eased his silver Lexus into a parking space at the rear of the gleaming white gallery and switched off the engine.

I turned to him. 'I guess I'd better stay here.'

Mitch gave me a look. 'I think that's wise. You're not supposed to be here. Just let me deal with this, okay?'

I could feel my eyebrows knitting together.

Mitch looked like he was on the verge of laughing at my pained expression. 'I know you letting someone else deal with a situation in your place must be a new experience, but just run with it.'

My back stiffened. 'Are you trying to say I'm a control freak?'

'No. What I'm trying to say is that you like to give the impression you can do everything on your own. There's nothing wrong with asking for help sometimes.'

I snapped my head away to look out of the passenger side window. 'I still don't understand why you're doing this, Mitch.'

Mitch clambered out of the driver's side as though he hadn't heard me.

Hmmm. There was something going on, but what it was I'd no idea, and he wasn't prepared to tell me.

I jumped out of the passenger side and huddled deeper into my quilted jacket. The air was icy cold and the sky a wintery marble.

I assisted Mitch to the corner with the three pieces of artwork. 'Good luck, commander,' I joked with a mock salute. 'Something tells me you're going to need it. Yell if you need reinforcements.'

Mitch offered me a withering look. 'Oh, ye of little faith. You haven't been on the receiving end of my charming pitch offensive.'

My cheeks sizzled. I whirled round and started to head back to Mitch's car to sit and wait. I'd only just scooted back around the corner when I heard a female voice. 'Oh hello. How lovely to see you again, Mr Carlisle,' she purred. 'My goodness! What do you have there?'

I rolled my eyes heavenwards. The two-faced madam! Funny what a six-foot four pair of turquoise eyes could achieve.

I jumped back inside Mitch's car and clanked the passenger side door shut, grateful to escape from the biting wind. I had to be patient. Not one of my qualities.

Today the sun was struggling again to find its way through the bank of clotted grey clouds.

For something to do, I clicked on Mitch's car radio.

The presenter was rambling on about some Christmas card design competition they would be launching for kids. It was December 1st next week, so I guessed the festive mania was to be expected.

I clicked it off and retrieved my mobile from my bag by my feet.

I let out a cross between a sigh and a groan. It echoed around Mitch's car. More messages from Lola and Mia. They were both still clinging to the hope that I'd change my mind, sooner or later, about returning to writing romance. Talk about having the bit between their teeth!

I dumped my phone in my bag and nestled back into my seat. I clicked the radio on again, but they were still burbling on about Christmas, so I switched it off.

I glanced down at my watch. Mitch seemed to be taking ages.

Joe often used to laugh that I was a big kid with no

patience. I pushed out my legs and stretched them. He was right. How long was Mitch going to take? Was that Ruth-whatsit trying to seduce him?

Maybe Mitch was just a passionate art lover and that's why he was so keen to get involved, I reasoned to myself. Perhaps it was as simple a reason as that, and I was imagining there could be more to it? Although didn't he confess he didn't know a lot about art?

I frowned to myself. All rather odd.

I'd promised Reece that I would ring him with an update about today. Mitch had said he was more than welcome to come, but Reece had declined, saying he didn't fancy sitting cooped up for ages in a car, as his bladder might start giving him the runaround.

My thoughts drifted back to Mitch. There was something so guarded and protective about him, like he'd wrapped this impenetrable force field around himself and he was adamant no one was allowed a peek inside. And yet, he was doing this for my grandma and for me. A little spark of something flared in my chest. I swallowed and ignored it.

But then again, I should talk. I'd been doing a lot of that, cocooning myself away in the cottage with Bronte. Trespassers keep out!

I was still mulling over everything – Joe, my life, what my plans for the future might be, the loss of my sham of a marriage, Reece – when Mitch's face appeared at my window.

I jumped. 'Christ! You scared me then!' I hollered through the glass. I wound it down.

The wind was rifling through Mitch's layered, black curls.

'What happened? How did you get on?'

Mitch moved round to the boot and began loading in Grandma's paintings. 'Crikey. Don't you have any patience?'

I shot out of the car and darted round to where he was. 'Are you doing this deliberately? You're not telling me anything.'

'You haven't given me a chance! Get back in, and I'll tell you.'

Mitch clanked down the car boot and we headed back round to our respective sides and jumped back in. It was lovely, getting back inside the warm, leather scented car, rather than being buffeted by the wind.

Mitch angled round in his driver seat to look at me. His lush, black lashes jutted.

'She said yes.'

My mouth sprung open. 'You're kidding.'

'Nope.'

I didn't know whether to laugh or cry. Exhilaration shot through me. 'You mean she said yes to exhibiting my grandma's work?'

'No, she said yes to my marriage proposal.' He raised his eyes up to the cream ceiling of his car. 'She said yes to exhibiting the paintings.'

I gawped out of the windscreen in shock. I turned back towards him, a slow, delighted smile breaking out across my face. 'I don't believe this. What on earth did you say?

What spell did you put on her? It was Ruth Mangan you spoke to, right?'

'If you stop asking questions for one second and let me explain.' It was at this point, that I noticed Mitch squirm in his seat. 'I showed her the three paintings…'

His voice had tailed off and he was having difficulty making eye contact with me.

'So, tell me what she said about the paintings. Oh, this is good. Did she like them? Oh, of course she did.'

Mitch was nodding, but he wasn't saying much. I was doing all the talking.

'I'm thrilled,' I burst out. 'And I'm grateful. You have no idea. Thank you!'

Mitch managed a smile, but there was something that he seemed to be holding back.

'So come on. Stop being so modest and tell me exactly what you said to this Ruth Mangan then. Did you use witchcraft or hypnotism? How did you succeed where we failed?'

Mitch fixed his alluring gaze through his windscreen. He appeared fascinated by the bright whiteness of the gallery wall.

'Mitch?'

He angled his head to look at me and there were spots of pink on his cheekbones. 'Now, I never told Ruth Mangan this or led her to believe it, okay?'

'Believe what?'

Mitch looked like someone had stood on his foot. 'Things have become a little complicated.'

'In what way?'

He squirmed in his driver's seat. 'She thinks I painted those pictures.'

'You?!' I sat up straighter. 'Are you joking? What did you say to her? You pretended you painted them?!'

'You're doing it again! Firing a volley of bloody questions at me!' He drummed his fingers on the steering wheel. 'I did not lie about painting those pictures. I'm not in the habit of going around passing myself off as Scotland's answer to Constable.'

I squinted at him. 'Then how the hell does she think you're the artist?'

Mitch let out a rush of exasperated air. 'I've no idea. You would need to ask her that. She just jumped to conclusions.' He looked rueful. 'She barely let me get a word in, rather like someone else sitting inches away from me.'

I glowered at him.

'She just assumed I'd painted them, and the conversation carried on like that.'

'And you didn't think to try and tell her that you weren't the artist, but Tilda Michaels was?'

Mitch rubbed the back of his neck. 'I tried. But she just went off on one, praising the paintings and saying how beautiful they were, that they were mesmerising. Then she said she wanted to hold an exhibition, and she hoped there were more where these came from.'

I made a noise that was a cross between a laugh and a snort. 'This is crazy. You can't pretend you're the artist and take credit for those pictures. It's wrong. We'll have to go back in there and tell her who the real painter is.'

But a nagging thought nipped at me, taking me by surprise. Hold on. If we did that, what were the chances Ruth Mangan would change her mind again, just like she did the other day? For whatever reason, this woman was determined that my grandma's pictures wouldn't be appearing in her gallery, no matter how great they were.

'Rosie,' said Mitch, his voice cutting through my internal deliberations. 'Let's grab this opportunity. I know it's a bit left field, but it might be worth taking the risk.'

'A bit?' I choked. 'That's an understatement.'

I avoided staring into Mitch's green-speckled aquamarine eyes. 'How is this supposed to work? You're a lighthouse keeper, not a painter.'

'We get the go-ahead to have the paintings exhibited, play along that I'm the artist and then on the opening night of the exhibition, I come clean.'

My stomach sank. Could my life get any more complicated? Could it become any more of a shit show than it already was?

And now I was about to get involved in an art deception. I rubbed at my face so hard; I thought I might remove a layer of skin. 'So, Picasso, what did the sabre-toothed tigress say about the exhibition?'

Mitch offered me a long look. 'There's no need for sarcasm.' He sighed. 'She checked the gallery's exhibition diary and said they'd just had an artist cancel their pre-Christmas exhibition due to family matters, and so there's a spot on December 13th to launch it. It would run for a month.'

A month? My grandma's paintings hanging in her favourite gallery under those spotlights, in all their glossy, bright glory? For four weeks? If she was here right now, she wouldn't believe a word of it. I drew up in the passenger seat. 'Hang on. Did you just say December 13th?'

'Aye, I did. Why?'

A mix of sadness and happiness took over. 'That was my grandma's birthday.'

Mitch offered me a knowing look. 'Then maybe this is serendipity?'

'Do you believe in that?' I asked him.

'I'm not sure,' he conceded. 'This is a bit of a coincidence though.'

Maybe all the stars were aligning. Perhaps it was all meant to work out this way: messy, chaotic, and all.

My eyebrows rose at Mitch. 'Bloody hell! You must've made a big impression on our Ms Mangan.'

'Well, like I said, I'm not bad when it comes to the pitching game.' No doubt she'd spotted his tall, dark, handsome looks the previous times he'd visited the gallery. He would be hard to ignore, I admitted to myself. I dismissed any further inspections of Mitch's maleness and wondered what kind of pitching he meant.

I waited to see if Mitch might expand again about his life before Rowan Bay, but he didn't.

I slumped my head back against the passenger seat.

Mitch did the same on the driver's side and appraised

me from under his lashes. 'I had a quick look at the paintings when the gallery phone rang, and Ruth darted off to answer it, but I couldn't see your grandma's signature on any of them.'

'You wouldn't have done. She never signed her work. Well, not in the traditional way.' I eyed him. 'She always painted a very small, yellow butterfly somewhere in her pictures. Often, they're so discreet, you struggle to see them.'

'Oh.' Mitch rubbed at his chin. 'Look, Rosie, I know this isn't how you probably imagined things to play out.'

'You think?'

'But it's still an opportunity for you to make your grandma's wishes come true. What if a chance like this doesn't come by again?'

Mitch was silent for so long; I wondered for a moment if he'd passed out. 'Life's too short. Dreams, opportunities, chances – whatever you want to call them. They might only come around the once, so you have to grab them with both hands.'

When I didn't say anything, Mitch trained his earnest gaze on me even harder. It reminded me of the lighthouse, casting its full beam across the dark night water. 'We're not going to deceive anyone longer than we have to.'

'Then we get arrested.'

Mitch let out a shout of laughter. 'Yeah. Right.'

I slid him another look. This was ridiculous. But then again, Ruth Mangan had sneered at Reece and me when she'd discovered my grandma had been the painter behind those gorgeous pictures. I wanted to find out why. Then there had been her bitchy comment about publishing being subjective.

'Rosie? Hello?'

I pulled my attention away from the car windscreen and the view of the stormy, ghost-grey sky outside.

Knowing my grandma like I had, all this would've made her laugh. A smile tugged at the corners of my mouth when I thought about her, and about the fact the exhibition would be on her birthday too. It would have been her eightieth birthday. What if Mitch was right? What if we decided not to go ahead with this and didn't get another opportunity with another gallery? I'd be sitting, kicking myself that I hadn't taken this chance. After all, that was what Grandma did. She didn't put herself out there and take a chance, and she'd spent the rest of her life regretting it. I could feel myself wavering. What if this was the only opportunity we had to have Grandma's art shown to the public?

I angled round to Mitch. 'You promise me that as soon as it's opening night, we come clean and tell Ruth Mangan the truth.'

'Oh, don't worry, we will. I'm bricking it in case she or anyone else starts asking me about perspective and tonal aspects.'

I ignored a warning voice whispering in my ear that I could very well be launching myself into an embarrassing situation. No, scrub that. In all likelihood, I was launching myself into an embarrassing situation. But the way I saw it, what other choice did we have?

'So, we're going to do this?' Mitch asked.

'Yes. Okay. I'll tell Reece, but no one else. Don't you either.'

'Don't worry, I won't. I've given Ruth my contact details, so she'll be in touch shortly with more information on how everything will pan out. We have free reign to have whatever sort of opening night we want.'

Mitch fired up the ignition.

My stomach somersaulted when I thought about what we were doing. Perhaps getting what you wished for wasn't always a good thing.

Chapter Twenty-Two

R eece let out a disbelieving gasp into my ear when I
rang him.

'Are you joking? But how the hell is that supposed to
work? Mitch isn't an artist as well, is he?'

'Don't worry,' I assured him down the line, trying to
sound far more convinced than I felt. 'Mitch has promised
me that he'll tell that Mangan woman the truth on opening
night. By then, it'll be too late for her to do anything
about it.'

Mitch sat close by in one of the armchairs, all long legs
and dark hair. He must have sensed I was looking at him
because he glanced up at me from his phone.

I averted my eyes.

'So, Mitch led that woman to believe he painted your
grandma's pictures?'

'No. Mitch said Ruth Mangan jumped to the wrong
conclusion.'

'She did,' interjected Mitch, overhearing both sides of the conversation. 'She just assumed the artist was me. I definitely didn't lead her to believe that.'

Reece let out an awkward noise. 'And you're happy about this, Rosie? You've got no qualms about it?'

'I wouldn't say I'm happy about it,' I confessed. 'But desperate times call for desperate measures, and for whatever weird reason, this Ruth Mangan rejected Grandma's art when she found out she had painted them.'

I wasn't prepared to let this go. I had to find out why.

'I know you think I'm jumping to conclusions, Reece, but Ruth Mangan has something against my grandma. I'm certain of it. I don't know what that is yet, but I'm determined to find out.'

Reece still didn't sound convinced.

More thoughts about Ruth Mangan pushed themselves to the front of my mind. 'Oh, and guess what date the exhibition is going to be on? Another artist cancelled for personal reasons, so the slot was empty.'

'Go on, tell me.'

I paused for dramatic effect. Would Reece remember the date of my grandma's birthday? 'The thirteenth of December.'

Reece let out a cross between a laugh and a gasp. 'You're joking?! Tilda's birthday.'

He did remember. I shouldn't have doubted him.

'Well, in that case, I think we have no option but to proceed. It seems like fate is on our side.'

Mitch jerked his head up. 'Be careful though, Rosie, with

regard to digging around Ruth Mangan. You don't want to mess this up.'

'I'm not going to mess anything up.' I was indignant. 'I'll be discreet.'

Mitch waggled a brow.

'I promise,' I protested.

'Mitch is right,' warned Reece into my ear. 'Just be careful.' He fell quiet for a few moments. 'I don't have anything to rush back to Edinburgh for. In fact, I've already checked and this place where I'm staying doesn't have any more guests booked in until 6 January.'

A rush of relief came over me. Christmas was looming ever closer and I wasn't relishing the prospect of spending it alone up here in Rowan Bay. I knew if I called Mia or Lola, they would be up here in no time with festive hampers, pampering gifts, bottles of Moët and an assortment of expensive advent beauty calendars.

But I realised I didn't want that. I wanted to be here with Bronte.

And even though Reece and my grandma had never worked out, I liked the older man. He was repentant, honest and still carried a torch for Tilda, even after all these years. 'So, you're planning on hanging around?' I asked him.

'If you have no objections.'

'Don't be silly. Of course not. It will be lovely to have you here.'

It was strange. At first, I'd experienced pangs of resentment towards Reece. I'd felt angry and disappointed in him, on my grandmother's behalf.

But then, after reading my grandma's diaries and witnessing Reece's pain and regret over what had happened all those years ago, he'd made me see that we all fumble through life at times, stacking up regrets, making mistakes, and carrying with us dreams and wishes we'd never realised. I knew that now only too well.

And it was clear just from seeing Reece's face whenever he spoke about Grandma, that he wanted to try and make amends. 'We'll keep you informed about how things are going with the exhibition planning,' I said, rounding off the call. 'When do you want to drop by again? You could come by for a coffee or we could have lunch if you like?'

'I was going to suggest tomorrow,' said Reece. 'Although, if the weather forecast is right, I think it might not be such a good idea to try and venture out.'

'Why?'

'Oh, a hellish snowstorm, snow bomb, or some such thing. Anyway, forecasters don't always get it right. Speak to you soon, Rosie.'

I hung up.

Mitch brandished his phone, having caught some of what Reece was saying about the weather. 'Reece is right. Awful snowstorm on the way, by all accounts.'

Mitch set down his phone on the arm of the chair.

'I'm sure it won't be as bad as they're making out,' I said, trying to sound hopeful.

Mitch didn't look convinced. 'Red warnings for this part of the country. Means the lighthouse and I will be busy.'

I flopped down in the opposite armchair.

Bronte took this as her cue to plonk herself down in front of me for some fussing. 'I appreciate you helping us, Mitch.' I paused. Was it a good time to ask him again his reasons for helping? Why had he been so keen to get involved? 'I know you're probably not going to tell me…'

'Then why ask the question?'

I ignored him. 'You still haven't told me why you were so insistent on helping us out.'

Mitch shuffled in the armchair. I watched him fiddle with his phone. 'Och, of course I have.'

'No, you haven't.'

He took a pointed look at his wristwatch. His wall was up again, deflecting any personal questions. 'I'd better head back and take Kane out. The big guy will be crossing his legs.' Mitch was an expert at dodging questions, refusing to open up. He rose from his chair and towered over me. 'You sure you're okay with everything?'

I wrapped my arms around myself. His gaze was intense. 'Yes. Well … kind of.'

When he frowned down at me, I nodded. 'I mean, yes, of course I am.'

'Good. When I hear from Ruth, I'll let you know.'

And in a whirlwind of dark hair and long, black, swirling coat, he was gone.

I woke up the next morning with a sense that there was whiteness through the curtains.

I clambered out of bed and peeked out of my bedroom window.

Sure enough, the forecasters had predicted the white stuff today. There were snowflakes being whisked in the air. It didn't look too bad, but I guessed snow was to be expected at this time of year.

Christmas was sticking its frivolous, glittery nose around the corner.

My head was whirring at the thought of that and what Mitch had got me into with this exhibition. It was my choice though and I'd said yes.

Mitch could be rather persuasive, I surmised. I felt myself blush and mentally changed the subject.

I drifted around, tugging open the cottage curtains in the sitting room and then hitching up the kitchen blind.

Bronte gave me her usual, enthusiastic welcome. Outside, the flakes were becoming fatter, as they spun down from the sky.

I'd finished giving Bronte her breakfast, eaten my cereal, and was just about to head for a shower when my mobile rang from my bedroom. I dashed down the hallway to answer it.

Mitch's name popped up on the screen.

I found myself wrapping my fluffy dressing gown tighter and fiddling unnecessarily with my bun.

'Hi. Sleep well?' he asked.

'Yes, I did, thanks, despite finding myself caught up in an art conspiracy.'

There was an impatient sigh. 'Och Rosie,' he growled. 'We're hardly stealing the Mona Lisa.'

He didn't give me a chance to come back with a reply. 'Are you busy this afternoon?'

My cheeks zinged. I wasn't busy. I was never busy now. I hadn't been busy since I got here. I was intending on doing a little more sorting of Grandma's studio after lunch, but I could do some of that this morning. 'Er … no… Not too much on today.'

'Well, in that case, you could come over about two if you like. I've had an email from our friendly neighbourhood gallery owner.'

'Was it written in blood?'

Mitch laughed. 'Not quite.'

'What did the email say?'

'She wants to start getting preparations underway for opening night. I think we should discuss it.'

'Okay. I can take Bronte out for a quick walk before coming over.'

'Great,' he replied. 'And feel free to bring her with you. She can keep Kane company.' He paused. 'Oh, and take care when you make your way over. The forecast said it's due to get worse later.'

I showered, threw on a cosy jumper, jeans and thick socks and after letting Bronte out for a charge around the snowy garden, checked out my emails on my phone.

Mia had sent me a message, to say that *Snow, I'll Always Love You* had shot up to number five in the Amazon charts. A glimmer of happiness lit up briefly in my chest, before fizzling out again like a firework. I'd been so preoccupied with everything, I hadn't even thought about checking out my book sales and rankings.

Before all this, I would've been glued to Amazon, checking my reviews and refreshing the rankings every half an hour.

I spent the remainder of the morning tidying up more of Grandma's studio for something to do and filling a couple more black bin liners with tatty stationery and threadbare paint brushes.

Then I began the difficult process of choosing which of her paintings should be exhibited. She had such a varied mix of artwork it was hard to decide which should make the cut. I did remember, though, the ones Ruth Mangan had already seen when Mitch had taken them into the gallery, and so I ensured they were put to one side. We didn't want to show our hand too early.

I ended up losing myself in more of Grandma's journals and time ran away from me.

I had intended to rustle up some cheese and tomato on toast for my lunch, but just grabbed an apple and a protein bar instead before taking Bronte down to the snow-encrusted bay for her afternoon walk. The water was swishing in a restless, icy blue motion, and the sky overhead was pearly white. Feathery flakes were still tumbling down and vanishing into the water. It was a magical, wintery scene, but there was a foreboding hush.

I clamped my crocheted green hat tighter down over my curls and buried my gloved hands into my coat pockets.

We started to head back up the path and in the direction of the lighthouse, Bronte skittering through the snow, her tail swinging from side to side like a brown feather duster.

She did a couple of zoomies and the chilly stillness stung my cheeks as we both carefully negotiated the winding path.

Looking down at Rowan Bay again, the cliffs sat there, hunched under shrouds of white. The snow was definitely coming down thicker and faster than it had been this morning.

I knocked on the lighthouse door, but Mitch was standing waiting for me at the entrance to his bothy. He shouted over from his accommodation. 'Hey! Over here!' A tail-wagging Kane was stationed beside him. 'Come in. Quick!'

He beckoned me inside and helped me remove my coat. I was aware of him standing right behind me. His cool breath danced against the nape of my neck. I thrust my hat and scarf at him, wanting to put space between us.

He smelled of pine forest body wash. Mitch seemed to fill the interior of the living space with his broad chest, long legs and head of dark hair. His gaze lingered on me. 'Coffee? Tea?'

My stomach gave a little twist. 'Oh, tea, please. Just milk.'

Kane and Bronte trotted side by side and settled themselves in front of the open fire, so I snatched an opportunity to take a look around.

The interior of the accommodation reminded me of a mobile home – small but cosy. Mitch had put his stamp on the place with heavy, dark walnut furniture, as well as a couple of dramatic seascapes, a red tartan rug and faded maps that wouldn't have looked out of place on a pirate ship.

Mitch's furnishings were more of the classical variety, whereas when Barclay had occupied the bothy, he'd owned more tartan and dark velvet fixtures and fittings.

The air still smelled of the sea though and of fresh, crackling logs that were being swallowed up by amber flames in the grate.

A tiny galley kitchen was off to the right of the sitting room and I caught glimpses of cream, fitted units and red and white fixtures and fittings. It was just the same as when Barclay occupied it.

To the left, the door was ajar. Mitch's bedroom. I caught a brief glimpse of a double bed, with black and white striped bedding and a pile of dog-eared paperbacks on the bedside table.

It was weird being in here and seeing the familiar layout of Barclay's former home swept away and replaced with someone else's. Something told me he would've liked Mitch though.

Moments later, Mitch reappeared and handed me a mug

of steaming tea. I furled my grateful fingers around it. 'Thanks.'

He settled himself down on his two-seater, chocolate brown couch and fired out his legs. 'I'm sorry it's a bit small in here, but it's usually just me and Kane.' He tutted. 'Sorry. You'll be familiar with this place after Barclay.'

'I think it's great. Different from how Barclay had it arranged, of course, but it's snug.' In other circumstances, it could even be romantic.

Mitch grinned. 'Snug is one word for it.' His gaze slid over me. 'So, any ideas about what you'd like to see or have happen on opening night at the art gallery?'

I blinked over at him. God, we really were going to do this. 'How about not get arrested for fraud?'

Mitch pulled a face. 'I'm not even going to dignify that with an answer.' He produced his mobile from his back pocket and tapped at the screen. 'Here. read this.'

I reached over and took his phone. It was an email from Ruth Mangan at the gallery.

Dear Mr Carlisle,

Hope you're well.

13th December is now reserved for your exhibition, so I suggest we start making arrangements.

It was an honour to see your beautiful and enchanting paintings and I can't wait to play a pivotal role in allowing the public to appreciate your talent.

Best wishes and I look forward to hearing from you

shortly with your ideas and suggestions. If you were able to get back to me as soon as possible, it would be much appreciated.

Time is of the essence!
Ruth.

'Good grief,' I ground out, handing Mitch his phone back. I took a considered sip of my tea. 'Funny how Reece and I got the cold shoulder, but send in a good-looking man...' I realised what I'd just said and wished I could evaporate on the spot. *Shit! What was going on with me? What was the matter with my brain today?* I tried to recover myself. My face felt alight. 'What I mean is, send in a *young* man, and she's fawning all over you.'

Eventually, I forced my eyes up to look at Mitch. His mouth hinted at a smile.

Oh bugger.

I buried my face in my mug for what seemed like ten minutes. 'Anyway, my grandma loved the likes of Neil Diamond and folk music, so I wondered if we could get a fiddler to play a mixture of both and welcome guests as they arrive?'

'Okay.'

'And if we could incorporate butterflies in some capacity as well. She adored them and collected ornaments of them.'

'Oh yes. I remember seeing some in her studio, and of course, she uses a butterfly as her painting signature.'

I turned over images of my grandma's paintings in my

mind. 'Maybe we should go for a theme with her paintings; perhaps just have her seascapes or ones of her nature-related pictures, still life's, and her flowers?'

Mitch nodded. 'It's your call.' He looked thoughtful. 'Did Tilda have a favourite tipple?'

My face split into a sudden, wide smile at the memory. 'She used to enjoy a glass of Talisker.'

Mitch's eyes twinkled. 'She had great taste.'

'You like it too?'

'I do. Peat, barley and the seaside influence of the Isle of Skye. Can't beat it. Do you like it?'

I shrugged. 'I've never tried it.'

Mitch looked affronted. 'Oh, we have to remedy that then. I expect you won't be heading out in the car in that weather?'

'No plans to, no.'

'Good. Actually, that was an order, not a request. Don't want you getting caught up in a white-out or stuck somewhere.'

I realised I was touched again by his concern.

Mitch got up and went over to a small, stout cupboard behind his sofa. He pulled out a bottle of Talisker whiskey, containing the warm amber liquid. He fetched two whiskey glasses and poured me one. 'Here's to Tilda's exhibition.'

We clinked glasses and I took a sip. Wow. The single malt whiskey hit the back of my throat, but it was earthy and warming. 'I can't believe I never tried this before.'

He set the bottle down on the table in front of us. 'It's something else, isn't it?' Mitch took a mouthful and savoured it. 'Did your grandma have a favourite food? This exhibition is all about her and her paintings, and it needs to reflect her. Nice touch as it happens to be falling on her birthday, too.'

I could taste the remnants of the delicious whiskey. As I savoured the Talisker, I watched him. Mitch was kind, thoughtful, and good-looking with a dry sense of humour, a mystery wrapped up in a mystery, but considerate nonetheless. No harm in admiring Mitch, but that was as far as I'd allow things to go. It would be best for everyone, especially me; I had already proved myself to be a bad judge of men. My mouth flatlined into a sad smile as I pushed my thoughts back to my grandma. 'Yes, it should be all about her. She would've loved that.'

I felt warm and fuzzy from the whiskey hit. I eyed the bottle.

'Like another one?' he asked. 'I will if you do.'

'Yes, please.'

This time, I downed it like a pro.

'Hey, slow down there, Rosie!'

I pulled a comical face. 'I'm fine, don't worry about me.' This time, the whiskey fuzzed me inside and I found myself smiling. An actual, genuine, big smile. Not forced. Not contrived. Not one that was trying to conceal the pain of having found out my dead husband had been cheating on me.

Here I was, with the snow swirling outside, sitting in a cosy bothy, with a tall, dark and very good-looking lighthouse keeper. Not that I had any feelings or attraction for Mitch at all, I insisted over and over. I was just making an internal observation. Had I been still writing, it could almost have been the plot of a book.

I leant forward and glugged another shot of the whiskey into my drained glass before snatching up Mitch's and topping his up. Mitch gave me a jokey look and removed the bottle.

'I know I've mentioned this before,' I began, the alcohol delivering a sense of bravery, 'but why, Mitch?'

'Why what?'

'Why are you doing this?'

'Och, not this again!' he groaned. He sat back on his sofa and pushed out his legs. 'Because I'm an amazing person with a wonderful sense of community spirit.' He avoided eye contact with me for a few moments. 'Now, back to arrangements and ideas for the exhibition.'

Mitch was doing it again. He was dodging and weaving like one of the seagulls over the harbour. Undeterred, I carried on. 'So, tell me a bit about yourself,' I persisted. 'What did you do before becoming a lighthouse keeper?'

His face closed down. 'We're not here to talk about me. This is about your grandmother.' What was he hiding? I was sure there was something. He was refusing to talk about himself.

I decided to try again later and returned to the subject of my grandma's likes and dislikes. 'She was a fan of Scottish cheeses and Cullen skink. We could arrange for a buffet of a few of her favourite dishes like that.'

'Sounds good.'

Once I polished off the remainder of the whiskey, I stood up. 'Right. Time to go. Whoa...' The room began to tilt on its axis. The Talisker had hit the spot. I tried to gather myself. I should've eaten a proper lunch, not nibbled on an apple and a bloody protein bar. What with that and not sleeping well last night, the alcohol was charging through me.

Nevertheless, I tried to walk in a straight line. Bronte saw me move to leave and departed from Kane's side by the fire.

Mitch was unaware of my watery limbs. He'd been looking at his phone. 'If you're happy, Rosie, I'll pull together a draft email for Ruth Mangan and send it to you to check it over?'

'That'd be great. Thanks.'

Mitch fetched my coat, scarf and hat from the hallway and I started to get ready.

But as soon as he tugged open the door, we were greeted by what looked like a life-size shaken snow globe.

It was a white out.

The sky was a blank, solid block of white, with snow whirling in every direction. What had already landed was banking up in solid clumps, swallowing everything, from the cliffs to the cottage roof. The trees down in the woodland were hanging heavy under the growing weight of the snow bearing down on them. You couldn't even see the line of the water on the wintry horizon. Even the lighthouse was a faint outline across the way, drowning in swirls of white.

Everything was vanishing in a snowy onslaught. A glittering Christmas card sprung to life.

As I stared down in disbelief at my grandparents' cottage, all I could make out of it was the odd roof slate and the peeking chimney pot.

A huge blast of freezing air hit me in the face and I found myself starting to sway on the spot. I fought to steady my feet. Bloody insomnia and bloody whiskey!

I made a move to leave, but Mitch closed the door shut. 'You aren't heading back home in that and certainly not when you're tipsy.'

I whirled round to look at him and wished I hadn't. Shit! It was as if I was stuck on a carousel and couldn't jump off. 'I'm not tipsy! And anyway, the weather isn't that bad.'

'Did you just see what I did?'

I bristled under my coat. I don't know why, but I suddenly didn't want to be here anymore. Mitch was making me feel self-conscious and vulnerable, and I'd had enough of it. I wanted to be back with Bronte in the cottage.

'I suggest you wait it out,' said Mitch calmly. He eyed me. 'It's not that terrible here, is it? Not as bad as venturing out there after a few drinks and having an accident.'

I jutted my chin out in defiance. 'I wish you'd stop going on about me being tipsy. I'm perfectly fine, thank you very much.' I realised I was wobbling again on my legs and made a point of standing to attention.

Mitch's lips carried an echo of an amused smile.

'Are you always so bossy?' I asked in an accusing tone.

'When I have to be.'

My stomach did another weird, twisty thing as he continued to stare at me. It almost stole the breath from me.

I fixed my attention back out of the hallway window. The snow would subside soon, wouldn't it? Of course it would.

Mitch let out an exasperated sigh and gestured for me to hand over my coat, hat and scarf. 'Is it so bad here that you can't wait it out?' he repeated.

I swallowed, feeling fuzzy at the edges. The whiskey was heating up my veins. With an exasperated groan, I began to snatch off my hat. It looked like Bronte and I wouldn't be going anywhere for the time being.

Chapter Twenty-Three

When would this bloody snow stop?

I glowered out of Mitch's sitting room window.

If anything, the flakes were pirouetting even heavier now.

It was as though a giant had tossed his huge, white duvet cover over everything in sight, smothering the roads, trees, roofs, the harbour cliffs.

I wanted to get back to the cottage. I'd been so stupid, downing those three glasses of whiskey the way I had, especially after not having eaten a proper lunch.

'You're pacing up and down like a caged tiger, Rosie. Well, when I say pacing, it's more of an unsteady wobble. Let me make you a coffee.'

'I'm fine, thanks,' I sing-songed. I knew I wasn't and a strong coffee would've been welcome, but I wasn't about to admit to Mitch that I was almost pissed. He'd think I was a pathetic lightweight.

I flopped onto his sofa. Oooh, I shouldn't have done that. My head felt swimmy.

Mitch gave me a doubtful look. He fetched his black digital radio from the shelf behind him, set it on the table in front of us and clicked it on.

The local radio station, Rowan Bay Today, was emphasising the scale of the snowfall, and its persistence, in an extra-long weather report.

'We're safe in here,' assured Mitch. 'Lots of logs for the fire, the fridge is stocked, and there's plenty of hot water.'

I gawped over at him, trying not to look horrified. I couldn't stay here in this little box with Mitch for longer than I had to. I just couldn't. In such close proximity. Yes, it was very cosy and warm, but … it just didn't seem like a good idea at all.

And why's that? teased a voice inside my head. *Why can't you stay here? You're prepared to risk your safety by trying to get back to the cottage? What are you scared of?*

I ignored it. 'As soon as the weather improves, Bronte and I will be off home.'

'Aye, you mentioned that before.' Mitch eyed me. There was a charged silence. 'Rhea in the corner shop said you're an author. You never talk about it.'

I squirmed. That bloody woman! I didn't think Mitch knew I was a writer. I suspected he wasn't an avid romance reader. 'I *was* an author,' I corrected.

Mitch's brows rocketed with admiration. 'Oh wow. What genre do you write?'

'Did,' I murmured, hoping my voice stayed on an even keel. 'I used to write feel-good romance.'

'But you don't now?'

I fiddled with my hair, hating this interrogation. 'No.'

'May I ask why?'

I hoped my chin wouldn't wobble. 'Personal reasons,' I snapped, not looking at him. I realised I'd been short with him. 'Sorry. I didn't mean to sound rude.'

Mitch held up one hand as the flames weaved in the grate. 'No, I'm sorry. I shouldn't have asked.'

I shrugged my shoulders. 'It's fine. It's in the past now. My writing, I mean.'

The weather outside was like someone had picked up a snow globe and given it a good shake. I flashed Mitch a look from under my lashes. The whiskey was still coursing through me and my body felt like liquid. Whether it was the alcohol, Mitch's hypnotic gaze or a mix of the two, I don't know.

I slumped back on the sofa and let out a resigned sigh. My tongue was loosening and I found I wasn't scared about possibly saying more than I should. That took me by surprise. Up until now, I'd been reluctant to tell people the time, let alone be in their company.

Mitch was sitting across from me, looking dark and mysterious, and the snow was whizzing past the windows. I felt languid, able to trust him, to tell him about what had happened. *Okay, Rosie. Go for it.* After all, he was helping with Grandma's art exhibition and he'd gone out of his way to find Bronte for me.

I blew out a cloud of air and hoped I could keep my voice from cracking. 'I can't write anymore,' I faltered, picking my words.

'Because of losing your husband?'

I pressed my lips together. 'Kind of.' I threw my head back. Snowflakes rocked past the windows. 'Joe was running late. He always was. Didn't matter what the appointment was.' I cleared my throat. 'Anyway, I was waiting for him to join me at my book launch, and after an hour, he still hadn't appeared. He'd got caught up in the office. Well, that's what he led me to believe.' The memories of that evening darkened my mind. I took a moment. 'Anyway, I was starting to get quite upset that he still hadn't arrived, so I called him on his mobile and he answered.'

Mitch didn't say anything.

I rubbed my hands together as I sat there. The only sound was our two slumbering dogs and the spitting fire. 'I told him to hurry up, Mitch. I told him that I was waiting for him. So, he put on a spurt, dashed across the road and a lorry was coming the other way.' I tried to bite back a gulp in my throat. 'The driver couldn't stop. Joe was killed instantly.'

Mitch sighed long and low. 'Oh, Rosie. I'm so sorry.'

'Thank you.'

Mitch looked pensive. 'But it's not your fault Joe died. It's circumstances. A tragic accident, whatever you want to call it, but you're not responsible for what happened.'

'I thought I was. I was carrying around all this guilt.' I pushed my hair from my face. 'I tortured myself. I took on all the blame.' I cleared my throat. 'That was until I found out what he'd been doing.'

I sucked in some air. The whiskey was swimming inside me and Mitch's big, silent support was encouraging me to carry on. I couldn't believe I was opening up to him like this, but I decided not to question it, otherwise I'd clam up. I spoke again. 'It turns out he was dashing to see me after having been in bed with another woman who he'd been having an affair with for three years.'

Mitch's expression collapsed. 'Jesus.' He dragged a hand over his curls. 'I don't know what to say, except that he must've been an utter prick to cheat on someone like you.'

The snow continued to patter against the bothy's windows. Our eyes sought out one another. I snapped mine away first. 'Anyway, sometimes you just fall out of love with something and it takes time to readjust to life without it. That's how I feel about my writing.'

He nodded, a knowing glint flashing through his eyes. 'I understand that, but if you don't mind me saying, I get the impression you haven't fallen out of love with being an author. You just think you should because of what happened, because of how he treated you.' Mitch flicked me a glance. 'You didn't deserve that.'

My head was stuffed with tiredness and whiskey, but my body was trying to fight it. I veered the subject away and onto safer ground. 'Nobody knows I'm here, apart from my literary agent and my editor. Not my in-laws, other author friends…' I raised my chin. 'It's what I wanted. To just escape and leave everything behind. I didn't want to be answerable to anyone after what happened. It's just Bronte and me against the world.'

'I appreciate that, believe me.' Mitch's gaze was earnest. 'And your parents?'

'Both gone. Mum passed away two years ago and I lost my dad when I was ten.'

Mitch pulled a pained face. 'I'm sorry.' He sat up a little straighter. 'Both my parents passed away years ago, too.'

'I'm so sorry.'

His chest lifted. 'Life ain't easy sometimes, is it? In fact, it can very often be a pile of shit.'

I made a sound that was something between a laugh and a cough. 'You said it. You think you've got everything sorted out and then it implodes.'

Mitch gave me a thoughtful look. 'What did Joe do?'

'He worked in the legal department of my publishers, Jarred Roberts Publishing. That's where I met him.'

I found the whiskey had really prised opened the gate to my pent-up frustrations, despite my protestations to the contrary. 'So now you know why I feel it would be hypocritical of me to write about something that I no longer believe in.'

Mitch shook his head and gave me a prolonged look that made my heart give an odd jolt. 'You don't believe in romance and love anymore?'

I reddened. 'Nope.'

'Why don't I believe you, Rosie?'

Mitch's directness, with the slumbering flames in the grate and the soft falling of the snow outside, made me swallow hard.

Feeling temporarily a little more sober, I straightened my back. 'It's true. I don't. Not anymore. I did, but I'm done with it. I won't be putting myself and my feelings on the line again.' My voice disappeared. I was gazing across at him. I pushed myself more upright on the sofa. 'So, enough about me. What about you? How did you end up here?' I asked him, veering anyway from his line of questioning. I suddenly felt like my armour was being stripped away too fast, too quickly, and I wasn't ready for it. I was being exposed far more than I'd intended.

A strange expression gripped his face. 'Oh, I'm quite boring.'

I arched my brows. 'I find that hard to believe.'

Mitch called Kane over from where he was nestled beside Bronte and made a fuss of him. 'The fire needs a few more logs,' he insisted, before vanishing out of the sitting room. 'I keep a stock of them in a bucket out in the hall.'

Wow. Well, that was an abrupt end to that conversation. What was going on with Mitch? He seemed to go out of his way not to talk about himself. I mean, I could relate to that, especially lately, but his secretiveness was on another level.

He returned a few moments later with more logs than were needed. He cradled them in his arms and crouched down in front of the open fire. The russet flames lit up the contours of his angular face. 'Still wild out there,' he remarked, giving the logs a good prod with an iron he picked up from beside the fireplace.

Mitch returned to his armchair and sank back down on it. He pushed a frustrated hand through his dark hair.

I didn't think he was about to say anything else, judging by the guarded expression in his eyes.

'That's not fair,' I blurted, the Talisker firing up my assertiveness. 'I just opened up to you and answered your questions, and now you've gone all moody on me.'

'No, I haven't.'

I nodded so hard I thought my alcohol-induced brain would rattle. I stopped. 'You cut my questions dead then and went to collect logs you didn't need.' I could hear my voice. It sounded husky and a little slurry. Not like me at all.

Mitch muttered something under his breath. Conflicted emotions took hold of his dark features. 'Okay. Okay.' He ground his teeth together and stared down at the red patterned rug. Then his deep, Scottish accent broke through the quiet. 'If you must know, I used to own an outdoor activity centre in the Lake District.'

'Okay. That sounds great.' I angled my head. 'Is that when you were doing a lot of pitches?'

Mitch looked discomfited. 'Aye. Pitching to potential clients, sponsors, that kind of thing. And it was great. I loved what I did until...' His voice vanished.

'Until?' I prompted.

He stayed quiet for a few moments, as though gathering himself. 'Until there was an accident.'

'What? You had an accident?'

Mitch swallowed. 'Not me.' There was another agonising pause. 'It was the son of a wealthy businessman from New York; the father made his money in real estate.' He paused and then carried on. 'The lad was larking about out on a rock climb with a couple of friends. One of my instructors and I were accompanying them. We told the lad to stop, but he didn't take any notice. He was too busy showing off.'

'What happened?'

Mitch bit his bottom lip. 'He fell and suffered serious injuries. It took him a long time to get back on his feet again. He had to have a lot of rehab.'

I gasped. 'That's awful. But it wasn't your fault, Mitch.'

'His father didn't see it that way.'

'Why? What did he do?'

Mitch glanced down at a slumbering Kane. 'The father hired a couple of hotshot lawyers. I think he saw himself on some sort of crusade. Despite it being the boy's fault and witnesses there corroborating what had happened, he successfully sued me for negligence and I had to close the doors on my business, make people redundant, the whole nine yards.' Mitch's face paled at the painful memories. 'I had such a good thing going on there, but in one fell swoop, I was ruined.'

My chest ached for him. 'I'm so sorry. When did this happen?'

'Four years ago now.' Mitch clicked his tongue as he dredged it all back up again. 'The boy's father –

Don Colton – wanted money and was determined to ruin me, but he didn't want the story being splashed across the newspapers, as he was rumoured to be involved with some dodgy office block scam in New Jersey.'

'So, what happened?'

Mitch looked resigned. 'Don Colton took out a civil action against me. That's when I lost everything.'

I shook my head. 'You mustn't take the blame.'

Mitch cut me off. 'The lad in question was only twenty, Rosie. He had such a bright future ahead of him.' He focused on the coffee table in front of us. 'Noah – that's the boy's name – was a promising artist. A painter. He'd been accepted by the Glasgow School of Art.' He stopped talking, regrouped and then picked up the story again. 'I hear he suffers from bouts of depression and anxiety now and he's struggling to drum up any enthusiasm for his painting.'

It took me a moment to unscramble what Mitch had just told me. This young lad, Noah, was going to study art. He'd been a promising painter. The young man had been close to his dreams. Then the accident happened; Mitch took the blame on his shoulders for the terrible incident, and as far as he was concerned, Noah losing out on a career in art was down to him.

Things began to slot into place.

Maybe that was why Mitch had insisted on trying to help secure an exhibition of my grandma's work. He felt responsible for what had happened to this young man and saw it as a way to make amends. Was he trying to appease his own guilt? He was doing this in order to deal with his emotions over the accident. He was trying to right a wrong in his conscience. 'That's why you're so keen to help with my grandma's paintings,' I said softly.

Mitch didn't answer. He just stared past Kane and Bronte slumbering on the rug in front of the fire as the snowflakes danced outside.

I then leant forward far quicker than I should have and then wished I hadn't. Whoa! That whiskey was gorgeous, but it was making my head float. I slowly lowered myself back against the sofa cushions.

'I tried to tell Noah what he was doing was stupid,' carried on Mitch, seemingly oblivious to my increasingly delicate state. 'I shouted at him and so did Tim, the other instructor. From the moment Noah arrived at the centre, he was larking around. He was always acting the clown, being sarcastic and taking the mickey out of our authority.' Mitch's voice carried an element of anger. 'I got the impression that he was used to being surrounded by money and didn't hear the word "no" very often.'

'But you can't keep punishing yourself over what happened. You lost your business.' I pressed my lips together in thought. 'Why don't you just admit it? That's the reason why you're doing what you're doing with Tilda's work.'

Mitch looked awkward. He shook his head. 'No.' His voice was steely. After a few moments, he rubbed at his stubbly chin. 'Okay, maybe a bit.'

He sank back against a cushion. 'I bet this all sounds really pathetic to you.'

I took in the way his curls were falling messily forward onto his brow. A deep ripple of something shot through me. 'No. Not at all. I get it.'

Mitch gave a wry smile. 'It wasn't just my business I lost. That was just the start of it. After what happened with Noah, my marriage collapsed.'

I let out a shocked gasp. 'Your wife didn't stand by you after what happened?'

'Not long after I lost the business, Romilly left me. She said she couldn't cope with the fallout from everything. She blamed me for the financial predicament we found ourselves in at the time. We had to sell our house and cars to stay above water and pay the compensation to Noah's father.'

I rubbed my neck. Poor Mitch. 'I'm sorry.' I paused before asking him another question. 'Do you have children?'

'No, Romilly never wanted them. She was always a career girl.' Mitch shrugged. 'If she'd really loved me, she'd have stuck by me. That's what I soon came to realise. We've been separated two years now. She moved away to London.'

I took a side glance out of the sitting room window. The snow was still falling, swamping everything in thick, white layers of icing that looked impenetrable.

'How about you?' he asked. 'Do you have kids?'

I blinked back my intended plan of starting a family with Joe, once I'd got my next book written and out of the way. 'No. No children either.'

We both sat there, studying one another. The atmosphere had changed. Now I understood what that journalist had wanted to speak to Mitch about. No wonder he wanted to seclude himself in this remote location. There was an understanding, charged with something else that I couldn't quite decipher. It was as if an electric current was sparking between the two of us, illuminating the room. I couldn't believe I'd just told Mitch about what Joe had done and the guilt that I'd been carrying around, like some lead weight, before Greta's letter and photographs arrived. I hadn't intended on telling Mitch as much as I had – if anything – but he'd teased it out of me.

Time seemed to drift like the snow outside.

'And that's when you decided to become a lighthouse keeper?' I asked him. 'After what happened?'

Mitch stretched his legs out further across the rug. 'After Romilly and I split up, I wondered what the hell I was going to do next. My life felt like it had shattered in front of my eyes.' He shrugged. 'I'd always wanted to study outdoor education and did a degree at Stirling University when I was seventeen. I graduated when I was twenty-two, worked for six years in the States at a couple of centres, then came back to the UK and finally opened up Rock 'n' Ramble six years ago.' He shook his head in disbelief. 'Everything was going great. I met Romilly when her agency started work on a PR campaign for us and we got married soon after.'

'And the decision to become a lighthouse keeper?'

'Solitude, the sea, the challenge, the change in lifestyle, helping people.' He gave a slight nod of confirmation as he spoke. 'I happened to spot an advert for Barclay's vacancy online, and I thought, why not? They wanted someone quickly and I was desperate to just leave everything behind.' He shrugged. 'The advert listed the sort of attributes they were looking for – good communication skills, fitness, organisational abilities – and as I wanted away from everyone and everything after what happened with Noah Colton, I thought living in the Scottish Highlands, looking after a lighthouse, was the perfect solution.' Mitch almost smiled. 'I'd been working as a forestry guide in the Lake District after Noah's accident, but I knew it wasn't for me. I was craving somewhere where I could try and come to terms with everything and the people I'd let down. I didn't want to be around anyone.' Kane raised his big, beige and black head at his master. Mitch gave Kane an affectionate rub. 'Aye, apart from you, you big lump.'

Mitch stood up and clicked on a couple of lamps. 'Being a lighthouse keeper isn't just a job, though. I've learnt that very quickly. It's a way of life.'

'Barclay used to say that. His father, grandfather and great-grandfather were all keepers of the same lighthouse here.'

'Aye. So I read. Albert, John and Nathaniel Hogan

respectively. The Hogan lighthouse legacy around these parts is one hell of a responsibility to live up to. I intend to do them justice.'

I glanced towards the sitting room window, the curtain of white disappearing into the dark. In the distance, the silhouettes of snow suspended from the cliff face and the rooftops look like ghostly apparitions.

Mitch had resumed his seat in his armchair. 'Do you know that one of the definitions of a lighthouse is "a beacon of light providing a sense of direction, safety and hope"?'

Even though my eyes were growing heavy, his words clutched at my heart. We all needed that.

I blinked across at him. Barclay would've approved of Mitch's appointment. He was hard-working and dedicated. Good grief. How could Romilly have abandoned him like that? Just when he needed her more than ever? She must've been crazy. His serious face was beginning to waver in front of my eyes. I was struggling to focus.

A cosy, muzzy feeling wrapped itself around me and wouldn't let go. It was like we were snug in this glowing, private little haven, with the snow whirling outside. The fire popped and cracked.

Mitch was sitting there, looking delectably dishevelled, and our two dogs were snuggled side by side.

It was the safest, most contented and relaxed I could remember feeling for a long while.

I offered Mitch a lazy, tipsy flicker of a smile and I saw him roll his eyes. Then he grinned back. He had that sort of smile that made you want to smile back at him.

God, he was very handsome. There. I admitted it to myself. Again. But that didn't mean I was attracted to him; I struggled to reason in my addled head. Of course, it didn't. Gorgeous though Mitch was, I would implement iron restraint. My heart couldn't and wouldn't take any more.

He'd ordered me not to go out in the car because he was worried about my safety in the snow. He'd checked up on me, to make sure I was alright when Rhea Stafford said she'd seen a stranger near the cottage. Yes, gratitude. I was grateful to him.

My eyelids were fluttering closed. I forced myself to sit up straighter. I must've looked like a struggling tortoise.

'No more Talisker for you tonight, young lady,' wafted Mitch's deep, Scottish accent.

'Spoilsport,' I mumbled, grabbing one of the cushions behind me and wrapping my arms around it.

'Now, I'm going to make you a coffee whether you like it or not.'

I let out a snort. 'Okay, Mr Lighthouse Man.' I gripped the cushion and my mouth went into overdrive. 'I hate to burst your bubble but I have to tell you, I don't find you in the slightest bit attractive.' My face blossomed with colour when I said it.

Mitch erupted with laughter. 'Yeah, right.'

An indignant gasp shot out of me. Then Mitch threw me a jokey wink over his shoulder and vanished into his kitchen area. I heard him put the kettle on.

The arrogance of the man! He just laughed at me, as

though me not finding him attractive was incomprehensible.

I conjured up in my head pictures of Mitch's sea-coloured eyes and the way his mouth hitched up at one corner when he smiled.

Oh boy, I was struggling to keep my eyes open...

Chapter Twenty-Four

I let out an agonised groan.

Where was I?

I pushed myself upright, realising I'd been lying under a thick, black and white stripey duvet.

I swiped at my gritty eyes with the back of my hand. My head felt as though it were stuffed with balls of cotton wool.

It was only when my eyes prised themselves open that I realised I was in a bedroom. There were closed charcoal cotton curtains at the window opposite and a table underneath it stacked with several glossy coffee table books about Scottish mountains. Beside those were a couple of framed dramatic photographs of Lake Windermere and Coniston.

My head unscrambled. The memory of yesterday flooded my brain. Shit! I'd fallen asleep on Mitch's couch. I must still be in his bothy. Hold on. I peered around again, my red curls exploding out and around my head. This was Mitch's bedroom.

I stared down at myself, still dressed in my jeans and chunky pink jumper.

There was an armchair in the corner with a pillow and another duvet draped over it. It looked rumpled, as though someone had been sleeping in it.

I pushed off the duvet and crawled to the end of the bed. Bronte was snoozing on a cream rug, but there was no sign of Kane.

I heard noises coming from the kitchen through the slim crack in the bedroom door.

Bronte heard me throw my legs out of the bed and trotted round to see me. Her tail thrashed with delight.

I didn't remember clambering into bed. In fact, I didn't remember anything beyond Mitch and I having our heart-to-heart, me telling him all about Joe and then Mitch confiding in me about the young lad's accident, him harbouring guilt over that and the fallout from it that he experienced, both personally and professionally.

Realising there was a small ensuite bathroom off to the right, I padded through in my socks, with Bronte tapping her way behind me. I slipped in as quietly as I could manage, did a wee, washed my hands, splashed my face with cold water and tidied my curls the best I could.

Coming out of the bathroom, I could hear the muzzy sound of a radio in the kitchen. There was the smoky scent of bacon being cooked and the sizzle of frying eggs. My stomach let out an appreciative groan.

Feeling self-conscious, I edged into the kitchen.

Mitch was standing with his back to me, turning over the bacon in a frying pan.

Kane was lingering nearby for scraps and when he saw me and Bronte, he wagged his tail and ambled over.

Mitch turned around. 'Good morning. Sleep well?'

I clasped and unclasped my hands in front of me in want of something to do. 'Yes, I did thanks.' I felt like I was all fingers and thumbs. 'I bet you didn't. You slept in that chair all night?'

'Don't worry. I'm used to camping and sleeping outside, so that's a comparative luxury. Hungry?'

I opened and closed my mouth, taken aback by his kindness, not to mention how delectable he looked, even though it was still early in the morning. His dark curls were still glistening with dampness from his shower. 'Look, I'm really sorry I fell asleep on you like that. Well, when I say fell asleep on you, I don't mean physically falling asleep on top of you.'

Mitch's eyes danced. 'Always a compliment when a woman nods off in your company.'

When I moved to explain, he shook his head. 'It was the whiskey.'

'It was,' I rushed. 'I hardly ate anything before coming over here and I didn't sleep much the night before.' I pushed a hand through my hair. 'I don't even remember getting into bed.'

'That's because I carried you through to my bedroom.'

Mitch's gaze locked with mine. My stomach performed a back flip. Jesus. Where was all this coming from? It was like my insides and heart were stirring. The way he'd said it, in that gruff Scottish brogue of his. 'I was going to leave you to sleep on the couch, but you made a move to get up and almost toppled backwards.' Mitch's small, quirky smile made my stomach swoop. 'But I managed to catch you and stop you from falling. I decided it would be best to pick you up and put you to bed.' He gave the bacon another prod in the frying pan and then turned back to look at me. 'I decided to sleep in the chair, just to keep an eye on you. In case you were sick.'

A rush of something almost winded me, as I stood there, looking at this man. 'Oh. Right. Well, I really do appreciate it. Thank you.'

Mitch was staring at me, an indecipherable look in his eyes. He turned away.

I cleared my throat. 'Can I help?'

'Och, no, thanks, it's all under control. Feel free to go and grab a quick shower before I serve this up. The towel cupboard is right next to my bedroom. Help yourself.'

'Oh, okay. Thanks.'

Outside the bathroom window, the weather was still angry, and snow was swirling as though a giant egg whisk was sending it everywhere.

I peeled off my clothes, set them on top of an Alibaba style washing basket in the corner of the bathroom and switched on the shower. It rushed out in a silvery, hot gush behind the semi-circular screen. There were black and white tiles on the floor and a small, square, shiny mirror above the sink.

I let out a groan of appreciation as the water coursed over me.

Mitch had a bottle of zesty-smelling shower gel, so I lathered myself in that, before washing my hair with a dollop of his woodland-scented shampoo.

Once I'd patted myself dry with the stripey beach-style towel I'd fetched from the linen cupboard, I wrapped it around my wet hair for a few moments. My face was red and glowing.

There was a tube of toothpaste beside Mitch's electric toothbrush on the shelf below the mirror, so I squeezed some onto my right middle finger and proceeded to give my teeth a DIY clean.

I'd just finished throwing my clothes back on and was about to leave his bedroom when I noticed a couple of glossy art books lying at the back of the chair where he'd been sleeping last night.

Curious, I flashed a look over my shoulder to make sure he didn't spot me being nosey and crept over. I picked the first one up. It was all about the techniques involved when painting with watercolours. There were sheaves of scrap paper bookmarking certain pages, and on them were scribbled random notes, presumably in Mitch's bold, sweeping handwriting.

Dry, flat brushes — blend paint and create smooth transitions; Sgraffito — technique used to remove paint while wet, to expose underpainting; Glazing — layering a coat of transparent paint over a dry paint to intensify shadows and modulate colour.

Mitch was researching painting techniques, so he'd be prepared if he was asked any questions about the methods my grandma had used in her artwork.

My heart gave a swoosh. I couldn't believe he was doing this; devoting himself to help achieve Grandma's dream, to help me. And going to such conscientious lengths too.

Overcome with gratitude and emotion, I set down the book where I found it and picked up the other one, which was all about chalk drawing. Mitch had undertaken the same system with this one, too, scraps of paper marking certain pages and his handwritten notes.

Wet chalk creates smoother lines; Feathering — taking pastel chalk strokes longer and working more quickly; Scumbling — creates a soft and velvety effect, by gently layering and blending colours.

I stroked the book in my hand. Okay, so I still strongly suspected that the main reason Mitch had been so keen to help me out with securing an exhibition of Grandma's work was because of the guilt he was carrying about Noah (despite him refusing to openly admit that last night), but that didn't take away from the fact that he'd gone to the trouble of reading up about art techniques.

I put the art book back beside the other one and gave a small, dreamy smile.

Looking after me when I nodded off in a drunken stupor, staying with me all night and sleeping in a chair, doing research like this and now cooking me breakfast.

He really was something else, I concluded with an odd jolt in my chest.

I busied myself and snatched up my wet towel, which I'd draped over the chair to look at the art books.

When I returned to the kitchen, Mitch was shovelling eggs, bacon, fried tomatoes and baked beans onto two warm plates. 'I hope this is as good as it smells,' he joked.

'I've no doubt about that.'

He fetched a large brown ceramic teapot and set it on the kitchen table, together with a bottle of brown sauce and ketchup.

He eyed my wet towel draped over my arm. 'Just dump that in the laundry basket if you like.'

I darted back to the bathroom, deposited the towel in the basket and came back to Mitch pouring out two mugs of tea.

'Take a seat.'

'Thank you.'

I sat down opposite Mitch at the oval, wooden table and set my mobile down beside me. I wanted to thank him for going to so much trouble with the art books and taking notes, but what if he thought I'd been snooping around his room? The last thing I wanted was for Mitch to think less of me or for me to embarrass him. I decided not to say anything for now.

I'd just taken a mouthful of crispy juicy bacon when my mobile rang. Reece's name flashed up on the screen. 'It's Reece,' I explained to Mitch. 'He's probably checking up on me after the snow last night.'

I answered the call and sure enough, that's what it was. 'I just wanted to check you were okay,' he said. 'That weather yesterday was terrifying! I did try to call you last night, but was struggling to connect.'

'I'm fine, thanks. I hope you are, too.'

'Aye, this old codger is managing. I just wanted to make sure you and the cottage withstood it all last night.'

I flicked an embarrassed look over at Mitch, who was supping his tea. His eyes locked with mine over the top of it. I jerked my head away. 'Yes, it looks okay. I didn't actually end up staying in the cottage last night, I ended up having to crash with Mitch in his bothy at the lighthouse.'

'What? With that handsome young fella?'

Mitch had heard Reece's comment. His eyes twinkled across the table at me. His lashes were so long, they were almost casting shadows on his cheekbones. 'Yes. But not … you know…'

Reece let out a chuckle but didn't push the conversation.

I felt self-conscious again and switched the conversation back to Reece. 'Is it bad then where you are?'

'Aye, lass, but don't you go worrying about me. Looks

like there's a slow melt on the way soon, according to the forecast.' He began to wind up the call. 'Once the road conditions improve, I'll drop by, probably in a day or two.'

'I'd like that.'

Reece rounded off the call and I set my phone back down by my plate. I felt fortunate right now; warm and swirling with gratitude. I had two people who were actually, genuinely concerned about me, who were looking out for me. I wasn't as alone as I'd thought I was. This was the least lonely I'd felt since Joe had died, and his other life had been exposed.

I offered Mitch an appreciative blush. Enjoying a delicious breakfast with Mitch, who'd put me to bed when I'd got tipsy and watched over me through the night felt so strange, yet comforting at the same time.

If I were to tell Mia and Lola about him, they'd suggest I get him stuffed and put in a museum.

Had I been still writing, I concluded to myself, Mitch would have made the most wonderful book hero. My readers would've been swooning over him. The thought pricked me. Up until his death, I'd only ever thought of Joe as my muse for my book heroes. No one else could or would ever have been able to replace him. But now I knew of his betrayal, that had changed.

I inwardly cringed as I picked up my knife and fork again and cut a section of egg white. What was going on in my head? Was it the lingering effects of the whiskey from last night? If someone had said to me even a couple of weeks ago, that I'd be sharing breakfast with a delectable lighthouse keeper, I'd have told them they were crazy.

Was I thinking straight? Was I enjoying myself? I weighed up these two questions as I sipped my tea and glanced across the rim of the mug at Mitch. Yes, was the answer to both, I realised.

I found myself studying Mitch again across the breakfast table.

My mug stilled halfway to my mouth. Wait a minute. What was I doing? What was I thinking? I swore I wouldn't get involved with anyone else. No more being let down. I wouldn't allow myself to be treated like a fool ever again. After what happened with Joe, I'd learnt my lesson – or so I thought. And yet, look what I was doing right now, how I was beginning to feel… 'Bronte and I will head back home soon,' I rushed. 'We've taken up too much of your time already.'

I didn't want to come across as some vulnerable, stupid woman in need of help. I was beginning to slowly realise I was perfectly capable of taking care of myself.

'You don't have to rush off,' said Mitch.

I picked up my mug of tea and cradled it in my hands again, for something to do. 'That's very kind of you, but I really should head back.' I glanced out of the kitchen window. The snowfall had stopped and there was the faint trace of rose-gold sunshine.

Mitch polished off the last of his bacon and picked up a slice of toast from the silver toast rack in the centre of the table. 'Kane and I will accompany you and Bronte back home.'

'There's no need. You've done more than enough already. It's very kind of you, but I only have to walk back down the cliff path.'

'And the snow is still thick out there and slippy underfoot.'

I frowned.

Mitch's brows knitted at me over the table. They brooked no argument. 'Look, Rosie, just accept my offer to see you back to the cottage safely. It'll make me feel better, if not you.'

I ground my teeth in frustration before realising my pig-headedness was beginning to melt under those eyes of his. 'Alright. That's very kind of you.'

'You're welcome.'

Mitch returned to sipping his tea.

'Mitch?'

His gaze bored into me. My heart gave an odd jitter. 'Thank you. For taking care of me, for last night and for this morning. I do appreciate it.'

His eyes twinkled across the table at me. 'You're welcome.'

Mitch and I scrunched over the melting, sandwiched layers of crunchy snow, while Kane and Bronte whirled around us, chasing each other and letting out delighted barks.

Behind us, the lighthouse glowed in the early-December sunlight, like a Christmas decoration.

I was filled with thoughts of Mitch, what he'd told me, the way he'd confided in me, his haunting guilt at what had happened to Noah, the way he'd talked about his wife abandoning him when the going got tough, him seeking penance to put something right, his chivalrous, caring attitude towards me and then him sleeping in that chair with a pillow and duvet all night… Everything was wafting through my brain and refusing to leave. The lone wolf, Mitch Carlisle, with eyes as deep and blue-green as the sea.

I batted the thoughts away, fetched my front door key out of my coat pocket and slid it into the lock. I crouched down and gave Kane a rub behind the ears. He rewarded me with a sloppy lick to the face. 'And thank you too, handsome.'

'Oh, so he gets called handsome and I don't?'

I stood up and laughed. 'I mean it. Thank you for last night.'

Mitch flapped one gloved hand. 'I didn't do anything.'

'Yes, you did. You made sure Bronte and I were safe and looked after.' I hesitated. 'Just when I needed it, too.'

'Well, you fell asleep on my couch and I'm not such a heartless rogue that I'd cast you and your pup out in the snow.'

Now it was my turn to flap my hand. 'Are you fishing for compliments?'

Mitch's mouth flickered with a smile.

I eased the cottage front door open, and Bronte shot

inside. I turned in the doorway. 'You can't blame yourself for what happened to Noah.'

Mitch bristled. 'You're trying to psychoanalyse me.'

'Sorry. I didn't mean to.'

'It's okay. I'm sorry I'm a grumpy bugger.'

There was the sound of plopping and dripping around us as the snow continued its slow melt.

I fidgeted in the doorway.

Mitch continued, 'You have to move on at some point. We both do.'

I could feel hot tears jabbing at the corners of my eyes. I nodded.

Mitch frowned under his dark, woolly hat. 'I can't quite believe I told you as much as I did last night. I'm not normally so talkative. You must've cast your spell on me.'

'I'm a good listener.'

There was that irresistible, quirky angle to his mouth again. 'That's one way of putting it.'

Down in the harbour, the water swished under the rose-tipped morning sky. 'Whatever the reasons, I want you to know that I do appreciate your help with this exhibition and getting my grandma's work out there.' I realised my hands were playing with the zipper on my coat.

I couldn't believe what I said next. The words flowed out of my mouth, as though they had a life of their own. 'If you're at a loose end tomorrow, maybe you could drop in for a coffee?' I took a breath. 'I mean, as a way of me saying thank you for last night.'

When Mitch's attention lingered on my face, I coughed. 'I mean, we need to get all our ducks in a row for this exhibition, don't we?'

Mitch's expression remained impassive. 'Of course we do. That sounds sensible.'

He continued to linger there on the step, with me framing the doorway. Mitch gave the back of his neck an absent rub with his gloved hand and I twizzled a curl around one finger. We both looked back at one another at the same time. I wasn't imagining it. I could feel it: a swirling, charged electrical current bolting between the two of us.

Mitch's attention rested on my mouth. Then he performed a little mock salute. 'Bye, Rosie.' Kane followed up behind as Mitch walked away.

Disappointment registered in my chest. Had he been debating whether to kiss me? The truth hit me like an out-of-control express train. Oh God. I'd actually wanted him to. I'd wanted him to kiss me. So much.

I quickly shut the front door and pressed my back against it. My breathing was galloping. What was going on? What was happening between Mitch and me? My emotions were all over the place. I mean, I'd just invited him over for coffee to say thanks for taking care of me. Hadn't I?

Talk about a myriad of contradictions. Mitch was a walking enigma of attraction, with so much depth, but he was also a troubled soul, always striving to do the right thing.

Irritation pulled at me again. I didn't want to be intrigued by him. I didn't want to be fascinated by his looks, personality, his kindness and his insistence that he'd done wrong and that was why Noah's life had taken such a tragic direction. I didn't want to be standing there now, with my heart thudding against my ribs, imagining what it would be like to kiss him.

A game of push and pull was playing out inside of me.

I removed my coat and hung it up on one of the hallway pegs together with my hat and scarf. I peeled off my gloves next. *Think about something else, Rosie,* instructed my inner voice. *Start making more plans for the exhibition. Focus on plans for the Lumiere Gallery.*

Ruth Mangan nudged again at the corners of my mind. What the hell was her issue with my grandma? She definitely gave the impression she had one. All nicey-nicey to us and gushing over the idea of Grandma's paintings one minute and then throwing me, Reece and the artwork out of her gallery the next.

I set my shoulders.

Right.

I'd dump the clothes I was still wearing from yesterday in the washing basket and put a load on. Then I'd throw on clean underwear, jumper and jeans and start some detective work on our Ms Mangan.

But it seemed that today had other ideas.

As I was about to head to my bedroom to put on clean clothes, I glanced out of my window.

Mitch was standing outside the lighthouse, scanning his

surroundings. He spotted me at the bedroom window and began gesticulating wildly at the top of the cliff path. What was going on?

I grabbed a fresh jumper, jeans, socks and underwear and threw them on. Then I hurried back to the front door and opened it. Mitch was scrambling his way through the melting snow towards the cottage fence. I stuck my head out. 'Everything okay?'

Mitch looked grim. 'It looks like someone's in trouble in the bay.'

And then he was off, slipping and sliding down the wet, slushy path to help whoever it was in difficulty.

My heart lurched. Christ, that water would be freezing! Was Mitch going to tear into the water and conduct a one-man rescue?

I didn't know what to do. But I had to do something. Racing to my grandma's linen cupboard, I grabbed some clean, fresh towels and a couple of thick picnic-style rugs. 'I won't be long,' I called out to a confused Bronte.

I dropped them to the floor, pulled my coat, hat and scarf back on, laced up my walking boots and bundled the towels and blankets back up in my arms. I locked the cottage door behind me and made my way down the path to the bay.

My heart stilled in my chest, as I took tentative steps on the slick, wet stones. I could see that Mitch had made his way to the bottom of the path. There was somebody thrashing about in the water sending chilled, grey spray up into the air. Mitch was shouting to them.

I watched with an increasing sense of dread as Mitch tugged off his coat, jumper and boots. 'I don't have time to go and get my boat.' He threw his clothes onto the sand and then charged towards the water and dived in. It closed over his head. Panic and horror gripped me. 'Shit! Mitch! What are you doing? No! Don't!'

Hanging on to my armful of blankets and towels as though my life depended on it, I managed to keep myself upright on the thick, melting snow. When I got to the bottom of the path, I staggered towards the shoreline and dumped my armful of linen on top of a nearby rock.

Worry rattling through me, I squinted out towards the water. The person who had been bobbing up and down in the water like a spinning top was still there but there was no sign of Mitch. I swallowed. Where the hell was he? Why did he have to try and be bloody Action Man all the time? Why did he insist that he had to try and help everyone, and put himself at risk?

Bile rose up in my throat. Don't tell me I was on the brink of losing someone else that I cared about.

Oh, thank God! Relief charged through me as Mitch's head forced its way out of the water beside the struggling person. He took them in his arms and began making his way back to the shore.

Under the churning winter sky, time seemed to slow down. The water was strong and resistant, disturbed waves slapping against each other, but Mitch ploughed on with his swim, kicking his legs as he guided the person in his arms back to shore.

I watched him, with burning admiration, awe – and irritation. What if he'd got into difficulties?

I reached for the towels and blankets I'd brought and rushed towards Mitch and the bedraggled figure he was carrying out of the water. Her sodden clothes were clinging to her like a shiny second skin and her mascara was trailing down her face in black streams.

It was only when Mitch set her safely on a rock and I bundled her into one of the thick blankets that I recognised her. Her burgundy hair was stuck to her face. It was Rhea Stafford. What the hell had she been doing that she'd fallen in the sea?

Rhea gazed up at Mitch and me with big sorrowful eyes. She gulped in some of the tangy sea air before dissolving into tears. 'Thank you,' she managed in racking sobs to Mitch. 'Thank you.'

I crouched down in front of her.

'You need to get checked over by a doctor,' said Mitch through jittery teeth. He grasped another blanket and whirled it around himself, like a superhero.

'Here's my phone,' I said, plucking it from my jeans' back pocket and handing it to him. Mitch was towel-drying his hair with one of my spare towels. He was standing there like some topless, sinewy male model.

I jerked my eyes away and focused all my attention on poor Rhea. From wanting to bop her on the nose, I now felt sorry for her. 'Rhea, what are you doing out here after the weather we've had? It's freezing.'

She was fighting to look me in the eyes from under her

straggling fringe. She clung to the blanket around her. 'I took a boat out.'

She shot Mitch a fearful glance, but he was too busy speaking on the phone asking for an ambulance.

'In this weather? Whatever for?'

She rubbed the seawater from her face. 'I wanted to say goodbye to him properly. You know, just me, on my own, privately…'

'Say goodbye to who?'

'Freddie' she struggled. 'My husband. He died ten years ago today. He loved coming out here to fish.' She took a breath. 'So, I pinched one of the boats that was tied up further along the shore and took it out with some flowers to throw in the water. But I lost control.' Her voice caught. 'Och, I'm just a stupid, old woman!'

Rhea's grief, and her actions because of it, swam through me. It resonated. Emotions can do that to you, make you do things that under normal circumstances you would never even consider. I swallowed. 'No, you're not. You're still grieving.'

'I stood up and then toppled into the water. Lord knows what would have happened if your chap hadn't arrived on the scene when he did.'

Poor Rhea. Misery and embarrassment were radiating out of her lined, grey eyes.

Mitch came striding back over. He'd thrown his coat, jumper and boots back on, but his jeans were still sodden. 'Ambulance will be here shortly.'

'Oh no!' groaned Rhea. 'I don't need a doctor or the hospital.'

'Just get checked over,' ordered Mitch. 'Best to be careful.'

Moments later, the zingy yellow sight of the ambulance appeared at the top of the footpath and two paramedics made their way down to us.

While they attended to Rhea, I cornered Mitch. 'You need to get home and get those wet clothes off.'

Mitch arched a brow. 'Only if you promise to help me.'

I became flustered. 'I mean, get dry clothes on after your Aqua man stint.'

Mitch nodded his head towards Rhea. 'Has she told you what happened?'

'Yes. She borrowed a boat and went out on the water to leave some flowers for Freddie, her late husband, but she got into difficulties.'

Mitch tutted. 'Fancy going out after that storm last night.'

Defence of Rhea and her emotional, impulsive actions kicked in. 'Grief can do funny things to people.'

'And who the hell let her borrow a boat? That's just irresponsible.'

A blush stung my cheeks. 'Well, Rhea didn't actually borrow it.'

'What do you mean?'

I shuffled on the spot, then started moving around, gathering up the remaining wet towels and blankets. 'She took it.'

'You mean stole it?'

'She was going to return it,' I insisted. 'Her head is all over the place right now, Mitch. She's upset and embarrassed. It's the tenth anniversary of losing her husband.'

I gazed up at him, my eyes imploring. 'Please don't report her. She didn't mean to cause any trouble. She wasn't thinking.'

'Rosie, I'm the local lighthouse keeper.'

'And I know there's a heart beating in there, otherwise you wouldn't have thrown yourself into the water to save her.' Without thinking, I pushed out one hand, thrust it under his open coat and rested it on his chest. I could feel his warm skin through his jumper and the throb of his heart. 'And you are a selfless, kind man who thinks of others. Just look at all the things you've done for me.'

Mitch's gaze followed my hand and rested on it.

My eyes drifted to where my hand was on his chest. Oh shit! What was I doing?

I yanked it away as though I'd just received a third-degree burn. 'Come on, Mitch.'

He pushed a hand through his wet black curls. 'Do you know where the boat she purloined is now?'

Rhea had heard. The two paramedics were gathering up their equipment and about to escort her back up towards the ambulance and to hospital. 'It's just past Raven's Rock, so not far.'

Mitch sighed, defeated. He gazed down at me from

under his wet curls and nodded. 'Okay. I'll jump in my boat now and go and retrieve it.'

Rhea let out a relieved breath. She took Mitch's hand and clasped it in her freckled one. 'Thank you. The next time you come into the corner shop, you get your stubby beers on the house.'

Mitch dismissed the paramedics' requests to check him over. I insisted that I'd return him to his accommodation and make sure he had a hot shower and thawed out.

We watched the three figures of Rhea and the two paramedics in their dark green outfits make their way back up the path and to the ambulance. 'Thank you,' I smiled up at him.

'For what?'

'For not dobbing her in it.'

Mitch shook his head, exasperated. 'I must be losing my mind.'

I took a long look at him. I think I was too.

———

Mitch took his boat, went to retrieve the one Rhea had borrowed, and brought it back to the bay.

As soon as he left the snow-battered bay behind and returned to the warmth of his accommodation, he thawed himself out for a few minutes in front of the orange, crackling fire. 'I'll go grab a shower in a minute and put on some fresh, dry clothes.'

I promised myself I wouldn't dwell on images of Mitch in the shower. 'And I've just made a fresh pot of tea.'

Mitch's features were bathed in the warm crackle from his fire.

'So, you managed to locate the boat that Rhea borrowed?'

'Aye. It wasn't that far out and was floating just a few feet away from Raven's Rock, like she said. I tied it to mine and brought it back to the harbour.'

'Thank you,' I smiled gratefully at him. 'What about the boat's owner?'

'He had no idea it had gone missing.' He flicked me a look. 'Old Arty, one of the fishing guys, told me who owned it. Some guy called Tam Love. Told him I'd spotted it floating. Must've got free in the storm.'

'Thank you again,' I said. 'Really.' I blushed. 'You gave me such a scare,' I told him, as we studied one another.

'Why was that?'

'Because you charged off into the water and I didn't know what had happened to you.'

'All part of the job, ma'am,' he joked.

'Please don't be flippant.' I heard my voice crack.

'Rosie. What is it?' His face was brimming with concern.

The thought came to me in a blinding panic that something could have happened to Mitch today, someone else I cared about. I couldn't go through that again. I'd had enough of it. Living on a knife edge all over again. Expecting the worst to happen. Waiting for them to be stolen away from me. I realised as I processed these emotions, that I wasn't so much thinking about Joe but about my parents and grandparents.

I shook my head and forced my mouth into a smile. 'Nothing, I'm fine. Just cold.' I was doing it again, allowing my feelings for Mitch to start to bubble. I gestured to his tea. 'Now go grab a shower, enjoy the tea and if you need anything, you know where I am.'

Then I grabbed my coat and left.

Chapter Twenty-Five

I was still full after Mitch's delicious cooked breakfast, so I decided to take a rain check on lunch.

I'd start researching Ruth Mangan now, I decided with a frisson of determination. I wanted to stop thinking about this morning and what had just happened – Mitch ploughing into the stormy sea, not considering his own safety or the risky situation he was putting himself in, Rhea thrashing around in the water, her stricken, tear-riddled face when she spoke about Freddie, my feelings of panic when I couldn't spot Mitch in the water and I thought something had happened to him.

I knew I was being a coward, trying to keep my distance from people in case I lost them. It was inevitable. It would happen one day. But to me, it seemed far more sensible not to risk it in the first place. Joe had proved that. Damage limitation.

I gave my head a wobble and refocused on Ruth

Mangan. Would I discover much about her? Well, there was only one way to find out and that was to try and do a bit of detective work. Some people still seemed to have very little social media footprint, although I think they were in the minority.

I just hoped Ruth wasn't one of them.

Bronte gazed up at me from the sitting room rug.

I frowned.

Bugger. Of course. I hadn't brought my laptop with me. Memories of me dashing around our apartment, grabbing what I could in a whirlwind of tears reared up again.

Maybe I shouldn't have been so hasty, so pig-headed about not bringing my laptop. Okay, so I'd decided my writing career was over, but still, it wouldn't have hurt to bring it just the same. I hadn't been thinking straight. In fact, I hadn't been thinking at all.

I crinkled my nose. I'd just have to use my phone to look up information about Ruth.

Then an idea popped in my head. Hold on. Grandma had her own Lenovo laptop.

I remembered her saying she'd bought it in an online sale last Christmas and that she'd been using it to look up art exhibition information and tips and tricks for her paintings. She'd used it to log onto Facebook to chat to me, too.

Right. Where might it be? Where would she have kept it? And even if I found it, would I be able to guess her password and gain access to it?

Bronte followed me down the hallway with interest as I

made my way into my grandma's art studio and took a look around in the cupboards. I wasn't holding out much hope that it would be in there. I'm sure I would've spotted it when I'd started sorting out some of her clutter and papers.

Once I was satisfied that I'd checked everywhere in there, I headed back up the hallway, the sights and smells of her smudges of paints and her ornamental butterflies lingering at my back.

Bronte was at my heels as I proceeded to check the chest of drawers and wardrobe in my grandparents' bedroom.

Glimpses of her long-fringed skirts and embroidered tops and of Grandpa's favourite white trilby, the one he wore to the local bowling green, poked out of the wardrobe.

Nope. Her laptop wasn't in there either.

With a growing feeling of frustration, I headed back to the sitting room to check in there.

I clicked open the heavy, maple and glass cabinet by the back wall and crouched down to peer inside. I was beginning to run out of ideas as to where she might've kept it. Grandma Tilda hadn't been the most methodical of people, so it could be stashed anywhere.

There was a pile of creamy lace tablecloths folded up on the left inside the cabinet. On the right-hand side was a stack of green and gold placemats. I was about to close the double cabinet doors when I caught a glimpse of what looked like a sugar-pink leather laptop case. I reached in and angled it out. Yes. This was it.

I took it over to the sofa, slid it out of the zipped-up case and plugged it in at the nearest socket. The screen shimmered into life. It had seventy percent power.

Then it winked at me, demanding I enter in my grandma's password.

I sighed, before tapping in my late grandfather's Christian name, Howard. Nope. Wasn't that. I entered my name. It wasn't that either. I typed in my mum's name, Tessa. No. That wasn't her password. I tried Dad's name next. No, it wasn't Jack. Then I tried the name of Grandma's favourite Van Gogh painting, *Almond Blossoms*, but that wasn't it either.

Frustration gripped me. What the hell could it be?

I tried to slip into my grandma's shoes as I sat there, studying the laptop screen. It must be something that meant a lot to her. But what could that be? The make of one of her favourite paint brushes? The name of one of her favourite artists? Or might it be her favourite species of butterfly? I had no idea but it was worth a try.

My fingers danced over the keys as I typed in 'Swallow tail'.

I held my breath.

The screen winked and then it took me to her home page. It worked!

With a happy 'Yes!' I rattled in the name of Ruth Mangan's art gallery into the search engine. It came up in seconds. The website was a swish affair, with a sliding gallery of various local artists' work.

Under the menu, there was a profile of Ruth Mangan.

Above it, was a dramatic, black and white headshot of her. A slash of lipstick, serious chin and grey bob.

I turned my attention to her bio below her picture.

Ruth Mangan, owner of the prestigious Lumiere Gallery, is a renowned art critic and talented artist, who turned her attention to opening up her own gallery, forty-five years ago.

Ruth has written for a number of well-known and respected art magazines and contributed to a number of newspapers.

Born and bred in Rowan Bay, Ruth strives to encourage other artists and is a fervent supporter of new and up and coming talent.

I pulled a sarcastic face. Yes, but it seemed she was very selective about who she supported.

My attention flitted to the website menu again. It looked like there were a couple of other staff members who worked there. One was a middle-aged, friendly-looking woman with red spectacles called Andrea Thompson, and the other was a delicate-featured younger man going by the name of Kennedy Whitelaw. I wondered whether it might be an idea to try and speak to them about Ruth.

Then again, Ruth was so intimidating, they might not want to talk to me, in case they lost their jobs.

I resumed reading Ruth's bio.

Ruth was the founding member of The Rowan Bay Artists' Society in nineteen eighty-two, which is still running today.

I glanced out of the cottage sitting room window. There had been more rain and the snow was morphing into piles of beige slush. Dripping jewels of water dangled from the bare tree branches and the roofs.

A thought occurred to me. What if I were to try and speak to another member of The Rowan Bay Artists' Society? Might they be able or even agreeable to tell me more about her?

There was a link to The Rowan Bay Artists' Society at the bottom of the art gallery website, so I clicked on that.

Thankfully, they'd moved with the times too and had a modern website to navigate. All past chairs, their photographs and biographies, together with some impressive examples of their own artwork, raced along the screen.

The chairs were listed in chronological order, from when they took up the role to when they handed it over to the next.

Ruth Mangan's name was first on the list, followed by her successor, a woman named Kirsty Ralston, who took over from her in nineteen eighty-nine. She had a bohemian vibe about her, with wild, grey-blue curls and a pair of copper leaf, dangly earrings.

I speed-read Kirsty Ralston's biography. Keen artist of nature and wildlife, born in Shawlands in Glasgow in nineteen fifty-seven, gives evening classes to other nature painting enthusiasts at Rowan Bay Town Hall.

The name was nudging at the corner of my mind. I was sure Grandma had mentioned Kirsty to me before.

I noticed her mobile number and email address were at the bottom of her bio, as well as a link to her website.

I sank back on the sofa for a few moments. Bronte ambled over and jumped up beside me to make herself more comfortable.

I decided to give Kirsty Ralston a call. No time like the present.

It rang out before a recording of a fruity Scottish voice burred down the line and asked me to leave a message.

I took a breath, gave my name and number and asked her to call me back. I decided not to tell her the reason why I was calling. I figured if she thought I might be interested in buying one of her paintings, she would definitely return my call.

The issue that Ruth Mangan seemed to have with my late grandma continued to niggle at me, even when I took a delighted Bronte down to the bay for a scamper in the winter waves.

I was laughing at Bronte jumping backwards and forwards in the surf when she was joined by a little Jack Russell Terrier.

'Teddy! Come here! Oh, I'm so sorry!'

An older lady, cocooned in a bright pink waterproof, came striding over. 'Selective hearing, this one.'

'Oh, don't worry. Believe me, she's the same.'

The lady squinted at me out of friendly, sky-blue, lined eyes. 'Ah. You're Tilda's granddaughter.'

'I am, yes.'

The lady bent down, clipped on Teddy's lead and shook my hand. 'I'm Gwen Montrose. I used to manage the local post office.'

'Rosie Winters.'

She sighed. 'I'm so sorry about your grandma. She was such a sweet woman.'

'Thank you.'

We ambled away together back up towards the path with our dogs snuffling on leads either side.

'And you're staying in their cottage?' She pulled a comical face. 'Sorry, but you can't keep many things secret around here.'

'Yes. For the time being.'

The waves rocked below us as we negotiated our way back up the path.

We reached the top and Gwen nodded over at the cottage. 'They were devoted to each other, your grandparents. Not many marriages like that anymore.'

Joe pinged into my mind. 'No, you can say that again.'

She offered a pleasant smile. 'Well, very nice to meet you, Rosie.'

'And you.' I made to open the garden gate, when a thought made me pause. 'Wait. Sorry. Gwen?'

She spun round and encouraged Teddy back on his navy-blue lead. 'Yes?'

I raised my chin from out of my green scarf. 'I don't suppose you know a woman called Ruth Mangan?'

Gwen's pink waterproof crackled in the stiff wind. I noticed a strange look pass across her face. 'Ruth Mangan?'

'She owns the Lumiere art gallery?'

'Aye. I know who she is.' She paused. 'I was never friendly with the likes of her. Served her in the post office but that was as far as my dealings with her went.' She looked pensive.

The clouds bumped and jostled against each other over the bay.

'She… She blamed your grandma for how things turned out for her, which was ridiculous.'

My eyes popped. 'Why? What happened? What was my grandmother supposed to have done?'

Gwen started to move away in her heavy, black and pink walking boots. 'I'd speak to one of the former members of the local art society if I were you. Your grandma was a member at one time.' She cajoled Teddy away. 'Very unnecessary business, all of it. Your grandma didn't deserve to be treated that way.'

I stood there, with more questions than answers whirling around my head like cartoon canaries, as Gwen and her dog hurried away.

———

While I pottered for the rest of the day, taking Bronte out again, putting on laundry and debating whether to respond to more messages from Mia and Lola, I kept checking my phone. I was even more desperate for Kirsty Ralston to call me back, after Gwen's cryptic conversation down by the bay.

But despite willing my phone to ring, she didn't return my call.

The next morning, I had my breakfast, showered, dressed, and was just slipping on Bronte's lead to take her out on her first walk of the day when my phone jumped in my pocket.

Kirsty Ralston's jolly voice slid into my ear as she introduced herself. 'Tilda's granddaughter! Oh, my word! She was so proud of you! She was always showing me photographs of you.'

I let out a playful groan. 'I hope she didn't bore you too much.' I paused. 'So, you knew my grandma?'

'Aye, I did. She was an amazing lady. So, are you in Rowan Bay at the minute?'

'Yes. I'm currently staying in Grandma's cottage.'

'Well, I hope you can find some solace here. Is there something I can help you with?'

I admitted there was. 'I actually wanted to talk to you about Ruth Mangan, if that's alright?'

'Oh, there's plenty of material there, I can tell you,' she said with a short, dark laugh. 'No wonder you want to talk to me about Ruth.'

My curiosity went into overdrive. 'Sorry? What makes you say that?'

Kirsty hesitated. 'Are you around at all today, Ms Winters?'

'Please call me Rosie. Yes, I am.'

'Excellent. How about I drop by to see you around half past two this afternoon?'

'That's fine by me.'

I could sense her smiling down the line. 'Good. I'll see you then.'

I finished the call and shoved my mobile back in my coat pocket. Bronte peered up at me as if to say, 'Are we finally going out now?!'

I had a feeling that whatever Kirsty Ralston was going to tell me this afternoon about Ruth Mangan, it wasn't going to be favourable if it echoed what Gwen had alluded to.

Chapter Twenty-Six

P romptly at half past two that same afternoon, Kirsty Ralston knocked on the door.

As I opened it, I was greeted by a cheery-faced woman in her late sixties. Her hazel eyes danced.

She was swathed in a long, rainbow-knotted scarf, walking boots and a mohair, beige coat down to her ankles.

She stepped inside, peeled off her stripey gloves, and made a fuss of Bronte.

Her expression faltered a little as she took in my grandma's artwork adorning the hallway. 'I'm so sorry about Tilda. She was a lovely lady.'

I took her coat and scarf from her and hung it up on a peg behind me. 'Thank you. Did you know my grandma well?'

'I like to think I did. We'd been friends ever since she moved here. I bumped into her at the local library while we were both browsing the arts section.' Her shoulders sagged.

'I'm so sorry I missed her funeral. I was away in France teaching at an art school.'

I smiled and encouraged her into the sitting room. 'No need to apologise. Would you like tea or coffee?'

'I wouldn't say no to a cup of tea. Just a dash of milk, please.'

I made a pot of tea as quickly as I could, put some shortbread squares on a plate and carried it all through to the sitting room. Kirsty accepted her floral mug of tea with grateful thanks and clutched it in her ringed fingers.

She gazed around before she began to speak. 'I used to travel a lot in my younger days, but whenever I came back to Rowan Bay, Tilda would tell me what you were up to and show me pictures. She was so proud of your novel writing, too!' A melancholy expression stole over her. 'You look so much like her.'

I took a mouthful of tea and examined her over the rim of my mug. 'I'll take that as a compliment. Thank you. One or two people have told me that.' I paused. 'So, Ruth Mangan?'

Kirsty pulled a dismissive expression. 'Oh aye. That woman. She was always so jealous of your grandma. Everybody in The Rowan Bay Artists' Society said it too. It was common knowledge.'

'But why?'

Kirsty eyed me. 'Two reasons. The first was that Ruth knew she was never as good an artist as Tilda. Don't get me wrong, Ruth's good. Her chalk sketches are wonderful.

But her work never had the individuality and passion that your grandma's did. And she knew it.'

I considered this.

'They were both members of The Rowan Bay Artists' Society, but Ruth went out of her way to make Tilda feel uncomfortable. She allowed her to join – eventually – but didn't welcome her with open arms, so after several months, your grandma left.'

I stared at her. 'When was this?'

'My goodness. It wasn't long after your grandparents moved here, so it must be about forty years ago now.'

I frowned and took another sip of tea. 'And what was the second reason you said Ruth was jealous of my grandma?'

Kirsty drank her tea again. She gave me a meaningful look. 'What would you say if I told you Ruth was in love with your grandfather?'

It took me a few moments to digest this. 'Are you serious?'

'Very much so. Och, your grandfather knew. Apparently, Ruth fell for him not long after they moved here, but he never encouraged her. Howard only ever had eyes for Tilda.'

Bronte sashayed over to me and curled up by my feet. I let my shocked fingers stroke her head. 'How do you know all this?'

Kirsty glanced out at the December clouds buffeting each other. 'Oh, a few people knew, especially us members of the local artists scene. What with your grandma's artistic ability and her being married to the man Ruth wanted; she couldn't contain her jealousy.'

Kirsty tapped her rings against the side of her mug. 'Ruth was always a dissatisfied, unhappy soul.' Kirsty let out a sudden peal of infectious laughter. 'I shouldn't laugh really. You'll know that Tilda got along with everybody, but even she couldn't penetrate Ruth Mangan's heart of stone.'

Kirsty paused before continuing her explanation. 'Your grandma didn't want to cause friction or tension in the community, but she was only too aware that Ruth Mangan didn't like her.'

I turned all these revelations over in my head. It echoed what Gwen had hinted at. No wonder Ruth had become nasty when she'd realised those pictures were the work of my grandma. It must've brought all those feelings of envy and resentment back up to the surface. That explained what Grandma had been referring to in her diary entries: the resentment and frostiness she'd received after arriving here. This must've come from Ruth Mangan. 'Is Ruth married?' I asked.

'She was.' Kirsty lowered her voice even though she didn't need to. 'Her husband was a good-looking chap, but a right big head. Jacob Mangan. He always thought he was meant for better things, had his eye to the main chance.' Kirsty's hands hugged her mug of tea. 'He was an art critic too. Used to make condescending remarks about Ruth's work and then pretend he was joking. You know the type.'

'So, what happened between them?'

'He fell for a ceramic artist he met at her launch show in

Glasgow. The ironic thing was she bore a passing resemblance to your grandmother, the same red curls and smiling eyes.' Kirsty shook her head. 'Well, you can imagine how painful that was for Ruth. Talk about adding insult to injury. She was riddled with jealousy about Tilda as it was, and then her own husband runs off with someone who looks like her.'

Kirsty sighed. 'Your Grandpa Howard was everything Jacob Mangan wasn't, and Ruth knew it. I don't have to tell you what a kind, funny and interesting man he was.' Her eyes sparkled. 'Nobody could wear a kilt like Howard Michaels!'

I grinned and nodded, taken back to years ago and the sound of the photograph album pages being turned by my mum to show me my grandpa done up in his full regalia with those sturdy legs of his, broad shoulders and rocking his kilt like no one else could. No wonder Ruth had reacted the way she had when I told her I was Tilda's granddaughter and that the paintings were her work. I realised that I couldn't confide in Kirsty about Ruth rejecting the idea of exhibiting Grandma's art when she'd discovered that the paintings I'd taken there had been hers. Kirst might accidentally let something slip about what we were doing. One wrong word and it would drop Mitch in it and sabotage any chance we had of Grandma's work being shown in the Lumiere Gallery.

As far as everyone else was concerned, Mitch was the painter of those pictures, not Tilda Michaels. At least not yet.

As though reading my innermost thoughts, Kirsty spoke again, breaking through my deliberations. 'I hear that gorgeous new lighthouse keeper is hiding his light under a bushel.'

'Sorry?'

Kirsty's eyes shone. 'Ruth could barely contain herself. I bumped into her at the hairdresser's last week. She was going on about how talented he is, especially with watercolour.' She sat forward in a confidential style pose in the armchair. 'It's lovely to have new artistic talent here in Rowan Bay!'

I fidgeted on the sofa.

I conjured up images of my late grandparents and Ruth.

A love triangle. Well, I never.

I took a long, slow mouthful of my tea.

It could almost be the plot of one of my novels; that's if I'd still been writing.

Chapter Twenty-Seven

As soon as I'd thanked Kirsty for coming over, she vanished across the patchy remnants of snow.

I closed the door and fetched my mobile from the sitting room table.

I dialled Mitch. 'I need you,' I blurted before realising what I'd said. My cheeks scorched.

'Well, there's an invitation I'm not going to turn down,' teased Mitch.

He made me blush even harder. 'Sorry. I mean, I need you to come over. I've got some rather interesting information about Ruth Mangan.'

'Sure. Give me ten.'

Minutes later, there was a knock on the front door and I moved to open it. I realised I was fluffing out my curls and stopped. Bronte let out a volley of excited barks when she saw it was Mitch.

He sat down on the sofa and began fussing over her, and

I took up a seat opposite. I tried not to register how delicious he looked, with his dark hair windswept and the stubble grazing his chin.

Mitch gave a mock bow of his head. 'So, why did you get me over here?'

I explained about meeting Gwen and then Kirsty and what Kirsty had told me about Ruth's jealousy of my grandma's artistic talents.

'Okay.' Mitch looked at me, waiting for me to explain further.

I sat forward in the armchair, still mulling over what Kirsty had just told me.

I steepled my fingers together.

'But that's not all. It turns out Ruth was in love with my grandfather.'

Mitch's eyes grew. 'Seriously? Wow!'

'It wasn't reciprocated,' I went on. 'Kirsty said my grandma and grandpa knew about Ruth's feelings for him, but my grandfather never encouraged her.'

Mitch's expression was thoughtful. 'It certainly explains a lot, doesn't it? Why she changed her mind about exhibiting the paintings when she found out the name of the artist, and the way she reacted about the whole thing.'

'It does, for sure.'

Bronte slithered over to me for some TLC. 'I know this is going to sound bad, but in a way, I can't wait until Ruth finds out it wasn't you behind those paintings but my grandma.' I realised my jaw was tightening at the unfairness of it all. 'I'm sorry. That must sound so awful and petty.'

Mitch held me to my chair with his tropical sea eyes. 'No, I get it. We're all human after all.'

He was right about that and I so wanted this exhibition to happen for Tilda's sake.

But I didn't want to make Mitch do anything he didn't want to. I knew I was beginning to think too much of him for that. 'Look, Mitch, do you still want to do this? I wouldn't blame you if you didn't.'

Mitch shook his head. 'Rosie, I volunteered.' His lips quirked. 'Well, okay. Ruth assumed I was the artist, and I chose not to correct her. You didn't bully me into it.'

I cringed at the thought.

'Don't look like that,' he insisted with a devastating smile. 'Let's just push on. If Ruth were to find out now, she'd have us both run out of town. More importantly, Tilda's paintings will just continue to languish in her studio without anyone ever having the privilege of seeing them.'

I knew what he was saying was true.

'Our goal is to get those paintings seen and that's what we're going to do. We're so close now.'

Mitch stood up and towered over me. 'I'd better get back. The forecast is looking a bit choppy out at sea, so I'd better be on standby.'

'Sure. Thanks for coming over.'

With Bronte trailing after us, we headed towards the front door. I reached out my hand to turn the door handle, and Mitch did too. But then he brushed my hand with his fingers. He looked at me and then cupped my hand in his. He gave it a comforting, gentle squeeze. 'Everything's going to be okay.'

I struggled to bury a breathy gasp; the sensation of his fingers caressing mine was sending sparks of fire through my body.

Our eyes met.

I admired the generous angle of his mouth. Our hands were still touching.

Then Bronte let out another bark, yanking me back from my churning thoughts.

I tugged my hand away first.

What was I thinking? This was a mistake. I was good at creating all this heart-stopping romance on a page – or at least, I used to be – but making it real, having it in my life, keeping it – it wasn't to be. What Joe had done, was proof enough.

I wasn't going to make a fool of myself over a pair of Mediterranean blue eyes.

And yet … this man… He wasn't Joe.

I swallowed.

Mitch was still looking at me. A myriad of emotions were crossing his face. 'Rosie…' He took a step closer. His gorgeous mouth was inches from mine. My heart was screaming for him, while my head was telling me to pull back.

The zinging, charged silence was broken by an abrupt knock on the door. Bronte barked again.

Part of me was relieved at the interruption. The other

part was not. 'I bet it's Reece,' I flustered, reaching for the handle. 'I'll tell him everything that Kirsty has told me.'

I tugged open the door.

But it wasn't Reece standing there on the step.

It was a woman.

She had shiny, dark brown hair bouncing past her shoulders, and bold, red lipstick.

A Breton striped blue and white jumper was peeping out from under her fitted woollen coat. She was very striking.

I was about to ask her if I could help or if she was looking for someone, but Mitch's stunned voice carried over my shoulder. 'Romilly?'

My head jerked round to look at Mitch. I knew who this woman was; I wouldn't forget that name.

Mitch's estranged wife.

Chapter Twenty-Eight

My head kept snapping round to look at Mitch and then back at Romilly.

She reminded me of one of those louche, French fashion models with killer cheekbones and a bored air. I suddenly felt rather scruffy.

'Hey, Mitch,' she drawled, sliding me a bemused look. Her voice was anglified and soft. She turned to me again, her cool, navy eyes appraising me. She attempted a smile.

Mitch pushed a confused hand through his hair. His voice was disjointed. Puzzled. 'Romilly. Hi. What are you doing here?'

'I thought I'd drop by and see where you were hiding out nowadays,' she purred.

Mitch looked thrown. 'What brought you here? I mean, why didn't you go up to the lighthouse?'

'I did but there was no answer. I went to your

accommodation but there was no sign of you there either. Then I saw this place and thought a neighbour might know where you'd got to.' She flicked me a cool look. 'It seems I was right.'

She huddled deeper into her coat. 'Couldn't you have chosen anywhere more remote to live than this place? It's the back of beyond!' She performed a theatrical shudder. 'It's taken me hours to get here!'

'It's not that remote,' argued Mitch, jumping to the defence of Rowan Bay. He gestured to me. 'Sorry. This is Rosie Winters. Rosie, this is my … wife … Romilly.'

'Hi,' I said, managing somehow to dredge up a friendly smile.

She nodded. 'Hi.' She swung away from me and drilled all her attention back into Mitch. 'Can we talk? I could murder a drink after all this bloody travelling.'

Mitch looked like he'd stood on something painful. 'Aye. Okay.'

He moved out onto the top step, with the cold, mushy snow behind him. 'I'll catch up with you later, Rosie.'

'Fine. Sure.' I hoped I sounded casual enough. 'Nice to meet you, Romilly.'

She pushed some of her hair back behind one ear. 'And you.'

Yeah, right, I thought to myself as they made their way up towards the lighthouse, with Romilly bumping her leather wheelie case behind her. As I began to close the front door, I spotted Mitch gallantly take the handle from Romilly's gloved hand and pull it along instead.

I kept my strained smile plastered on until I shut the door.

As soon as I did, a leaden feeling lodged itself in my ribcage. She was very good-looking. Was she hoping for a reconciliation with Mitch? Had she come to realise she'd made a huge mistake in letting him go?

I drew up in the hallway; all these questions tumbled through my head. Why was I dissecting her arrival? What did it matter why she was here? It was none of my business.

But with a hard, shocking stab of reality, I realised it did matter to me. Very much. The thought of Romilly and Mitch all snug in his bothy, just like we'd been during that angry, unforgiving snowstorm, was wounding me.

That intimate moment between us only moments ago, right here in the hallway, the close proximity of him, those sparks of jade in his eyes, the scent of his woody aftershave, that very faint, silvery scar above his top lip I'd never noticed before. God, why was I thinking this way? What was I doing?

Mitch was still married.

Fear crept in.

I widened my eyes at the realisation. But whether I wanted to recognise it or not, I knew I was beginning to harbour feelings for Mitch. They had stealthily crept up on me and caught me off guard.

It was as if my heart was expanding to allow someone else in to take Joe's place. At one time, that idea would have been incomprehensible. There would never have been anyone else for me, apart from Joe. But now … there was Mitch.

His selflessness, his kindness, his altruism, his conscience about Noah and what had happened, not to mention his dark, intense good looks, were beginning to consume me, and I suddenly felt helpless. Now I was the one who felt like I was drowning in the bay.

But Romilly had rocked up here, and I had no idea what was going to happen now. Were these growing feelings I had for him a waste of time? Was I about to put myself through more emotional agony?

The truth reverberated in my head.

More pictures of Mitch tumbled in front of my eyes.

No. I couldn't do it. I couldn't face going through all that again. I couldn't wake up each morning like I had been after Joe's death, turning over my emotions again and again and picking at a wound that I thought was healing, only for it to open and hurt me again. What if I lost Mitch? What if he let me down? I'd be putting myself through the same cycle of hurt and grief again.

When would I ever learn? I'd promised myself I would keep a lid on my feelings for him. I was convinced I could do that. But here I was, allowing my emotions for Mitch to spill over and now look what was happening! His glamorous wife had turned up and they were no doubt cosied up together right now, with the bay romantically serenading them.

I tried to mentally push Mitch back into the recesses of my mind. I had to try and move on.

The words filled my head. If Mitch decided to reunite with his wife, it might be better for me to leave Rowan Bay. I couldn't imagine the awkwardness, living here in the cottage and so close to them.

If they gave their marriage another chance, then selling this cottage would be the best option. I liked living here. It was everything London wasn't: green, peaceful and with the bay swishing like a silver curtain. But staying here, gazing up at the proud, white and blue column of the lighthouse each day, knowing Mitch and Romilly were all loved up together in the bothy, it would be too much.

I gave a tearful blink. Decision made. If Mitch and his wife were reuniting, I'd put the cottage up for sale.

I'd start over with Bronte elsewhere. I'd always carry the memories and my love of Rowan Bay with me, but I'd take them somewhere else. Put all this mess and mayhem behind me.

I forced a jovial smile down at Bronte. 'Come on, sweetheart. Let's go get some air.'

I didn't see Mitch or Romilly for the rest of the day.

That night, I got ready for bed. The beam from the lighthouse cast itself over the top of the choppy harbour water, like liquid gold.

They're up there together, hissed an inner voice. What were they talking about? What were they doing? Were they snuggled up by the fire, with the flames popping?

I hitched the duvet up over my head and clamped my eyes shut.

It was raining the next morning, the raindrops splatting on everything. All but small, irritating patches of snow remained.

As Bronte and I ventured out, swathed in our cosy waterproofs, my eyes insisted on pulling themselves towards the lighthouse. I so wished I could stop looking up there, but I couldn't help myself.

I swore under my breath, cursing my vivid imagination. Were they in bed, having a lie-in? Had they decided to reconcile?

It was like I was deliberately torturing myself. Had I turned into a masochist?

It was only a few weeks now till Christmas. The prospect of that filled me with dread. The scenery had changed here, from a picture-perfect Christmas card, with pretty snowflakes dancing from the sky, to rain-slicked rocks and cliffs, which looked as deflated as I felt.

If I was going to put the cottage on the market, I'd get Christmas and New Year out the way and then hit the ground running with a valuation in early January. There was no point in hanging around Rowan Bay longer than I had to. I'd also tell Reece of my plans, and Barclay, of course.

In the meantime, I could start looking at a few properties

to get a feel for what was out there, although I had no clue where I wanted to go. I'd also have to decide what to do about the flat in Hampstead.

I watched Bronte weave amongst the trees in the woods. If Mitch had experienced a change of heart and decided to get back together with Romilly, then we'd have to tell Ruth Mangan the truth about him not being the artist of my grandma's paintings.

Yes, I wanted to have my grandma's work out there, but I was going to insist to Mitch that we put an end to our plan.

Having to be close to Mitch would be too painful, especially with Romilly around. And Romilly could inadvertently put a spanner in the works by saying the wrong thing. It wouldn't be worth the aggravation. It would be like treading on eggshells the whole time in the run-up to the exhibition, and after everything that had happened, I didn't fancy the stress. The best thing would be to put plenty of space between Mitch and me. It was the only way.

Keeping up this pretence of him as the talented painter would be too protracted and hurtful when I knew he was off to give his marriage another chance.

I'd had enough of mayhem and disorder, but I couldn't turn back time.

It was down to me now to sort out my life and start taking some grown-up decisions.

Bronte and I ambled amongst the wet dankness and moss.

I was glad I'd stopped writing though I reassured myself for the hundredth time. You can't keep flogging a dead horse. How could I ever return to romance writing, when my real-life heroic inspiration had turned out to be a fraud?

I buried my chin deeper into the high collar of my quilted winter coat.

Bronte snuffled ahead, her pert, little black nose skimming across the top of the damp grass of the woodland floor.

We were just about to reach the other side of the woodland and begin the slow journey back when a voice travelled from behind me. 'Rosie. Hey!'

Oh no.

My heart swooped.

I straightened my shoulders and turned around, pinning on a smile.

Mitch had Kane with him. On spotting Bronte, Kane picked up speed and they went careering off ahead together amongst the trees.

'How's things?' I asked, feigning a casual air.

What I really meant was, is your glamorous wife still around? But I held it back with all the force I could muster. It was none of my business if Romilly was waiting to drag him to bed when he got back.

The prospect of that, made my heart shrivel. *Don't Rosie. Just, don't.*

'Aye. Good, thanks,' answered Mitch, oblivious to my emotions throwing themselves around. 'Can we join you on your walk?'

'We?' I asked, glancing around for shiny-haired brunettes with piercing navy-blue eyes, but trying to look like I was just taking in the scenery.

'Kane and me.'

'Oh. Right. Yes, of course.' Where was Romilly?

I swallowed the question, even though it was burning the tip of my tongue. Mitch slid me a prolonged look from under his black brows. Was he psychic? 'Romilly's gone back to London. She set off this morning for her flight.'

I pushed my hands into my coat pockets. 'Oh?'

I refused to entertain any glimmer of optimism. What did that mean? Had she gone back to sort everything out before moving back to Rowan Bay? Was she going back to London to say goodbye to family and friends, and share the good news that she was back with Mitch?

I didn't want to ask Mitch, but not knowing what was happening was eating away at me. Oh, sod it. I couldn't carry on dancing around the topic like this. It was agonising. 'I suppose there's a lot for her to sort out.' There. I'd said it.

'Sorry?'

'If she's moving up here.'

Mitch stared at me, as though I'd just confessed to an armed robbery. 'Why would she do that?'

Was he going to make this any harder for me than it already was? I tried to gather myself. 'Well ... you know ... if you two have got back together...'

Mitch shook his head and let out a shout of laughter. 'Good God, no!'

I blinked across at him. 'No?'

'No. One hundred percent no.'

The rain-tossed sky shifted behind him. 'Romilly only came up here to tell me she's met someone else and wants to get married again. Some financier in the city. She wants a divorce, which is fine by me.'

A strange sensation whipped through me. Was that happiness? Relief?

'She's always been a drama queen. She could've told me all this on the phone, but I think she used it as an excuse to come up and have a nosey at Rowan Bay and see what sort of life her oddball soon-to-be-ex-husband has up here.'

I gazed up at him, admiring his profile. 'You're not an oddball, Mitch.'

He laughed, showing off his white teeth. 'Some may disagree with you on that one.' He hesitated. There was meaning radiating out of his gaze as he drank me in. My heart was fluttering like a wild bird. My attention kept straying to his lips.

'Romilly said you were very pretty.'

It took a few moments for me to realise who Mitch was talking about. 'Me?'

'Well, she wasn't talking about Kane.'

I laughed it off, but my insides were turning to water. This was ridiculous. I'd come here to lick my wounds and vanish into myself. *And how is that working out for you, Rosie?*

We studied each other, oblivious to the fresh squall of winter rain picking up again.

I huddled deeper into my coat. 'I don't want you to feel sorry for me, Mitch.'

Mitch's eyes widened. 'What on earth are you talking about?'

Bronte and Kane were jumping over branches and letting out barks of happiness.

I tugged my gloved hands out of my coat pockets. They flailed around as I spoke. 'Joe, me desperate to make Tilda's dream a reality, me deciding not to write any more books.'

Mitch took me by surprise by moving even closer to me. I could make out the flecks of mint in his eyes. 'You're something else, Rosie.'

'Gee, thanks. I think.'

His attention rested on my mouth. 'When you get nervous, you talk a lot.'

'No, I don't. I just feel like I have to explain the situation and make it clear that...'

'You're doing it now.'

I pulled a face at him. 'Well, what do you want me to do about it?'

Mitch gave me a long, hot look that turned my insides to butter. 'I don't expect you to do anything about it.' He laced his fingers through my hair. 'I'm just going to have to kiss you to shut you up.'

Mitch lowered his mouth onto mine. The realisation that I was being kissed by another man and not Joe made my heart give an odd jump. But Mitch was gentle at first, tasting my lips, caressing them. Then his kisses deepened. I moulded my body against his. I had to. My nerve endings were giving me no choice. I became oblivious to the fresh, darting rain that was splatting against the woodland floor. I clung to him, kissing him back. We pushed ourselves against one another. I felt like all our contours aligned. Excitement raced through me. I didn't want him to stop.

After what seemed like forever, we reluctantly took a step back and clutched each other's hands. The rain continued to come down in sharp, silver arrows, but we didn't care.

The swish of the harbour water in the distance was like a faint lullaby.

'You, okay?' he asked, picking up my hand and caressing it.

I drank him in. 'Yes. I think I am.'

Mitch's gaze was soft. 'Take a chance on me, Rosie. Please. Give romance another go.'

Tears nudged the corners of my eyes.

'I'm not perfect. I talk in my sleep and dump my loose change in the kitchen.' I noticed him lacing and unlacing his gloved hands.

'I'm glad you're you,' I managed, my voice wavering. 'But I'm scared.'

His face adopted a more serious edge. 'Give me a chance, Rosie. I promise that I'd never cheat on you.' He rubbed at his strong chin. 'If I've learnt anything from what happened to Noah and losing my business, it's that we have to be happy when and while we can and not to take anything for granted.' He took my hands in his again and stroked them. 'If someone had said to me two months ago that I'd fall for a widowed, titian-haired romance writer, I'd have laughed.'

He shook his dark head in wonder. 'I came to Rowan Bay to escape from everyone and everything. I thought that if I could be the local lighthouse keeper and save people – give something back for what happened to Noah – then that would be more than enough for me.'

My stomach rocked. 'I've seen first-hand you saving people, remember? When you rescued Rhea?'

Mitch grinned and gave me a sexy wink. Then his expression became more pensive again. 'You're kind, funny, beautiful and thoughtful. Stop putting everyone else first for a change.' He forced a hand through his tangle of curls. 'Let me prove to you that you were wrong about love and being loved.'

I was struggling to speak. My throat was clogged with emotion.

'You deserve to be loved again after Joe. You need to know that you weren't writing about something that doesn't last.' His expression was appealing. 'You know what I think? I think your heart is ready for someone else. And I want that someone else to be me.'

I let out a little sob.

My stomach fluttered at the sight of him standing there, oblivious to the wind and the rain. I was losing myself in his eyes as they swept my face.

'You just have to find the right person, someone who genuinely loves and appreciates you for who you are and what you stand for.'

Mitch's expression was earnest. 'Remember how I gave you a definition before, of what a lighthouse is? Well, I have another one that I read just recently. A lighthouse is a powerful beacon that illuminates a path through darkness and uncertainty, towards the light.' He raised a hand and traced my jaw. 'Let's do that for each other.'

I couldn't speak. I pressed my lips together, not able to swallow back a gulp of emotion.

Mitch threw his hands up in the air. 'And I know you're not Romilly. I got hurt too. But maybe we were meant to find each other.' He grinned. 'Two sarcastic, grumpy, dog-loving lost souls who could make feeling guilty an Olympic sport.'

'Grumpy?!' I struggled, my chest threatening to brim over with happiness. 'You speak for yourself.'

Mitch let out a jokey gasp. 'Oh, come on. When you first arrived here, nobody could say the right thing to you.'

I pulled an agonised face. 'Yeah, you're right. When I got here, I was angry at everyone and everything. I was hurting over Joe's betrayal and missing my grandparents and my parents so much. I didn't think I deserved to be happy.' I gave him a coy glance from under my lashes. 'But you were so patient with me, so kind and helpful, not to mention gorgeous.'

Mitch arched a brow and laughed. 'I'm glad you added gorgeous.'

I laughed again, through some threatening tears. 'I kept telling myself not to fall for you and that it was wrong.'

'And now?' he asked, pulling me towards him.

I lost myself in those captivating ocean-like eyes of his. 'And now, I'm going to grab happiness with both hands.' A watery smile spread across my face.

Mitch tapped the end of my nose with his finger. 'I'm glad to hear it. Me too. I was convinced I didn't need anyone in my life, but then you came along and I knew I'd been lying to myself.' He gave a shy smile.

Oh God. This man. This wonderful, caring man.

His bashful smile deepened. 'I was working up in that lighthouse or sitting in the bothy and finding myself thinking about you non-stop.' He hesitated. 'And while I'm at it, I have another confession to make.' He pulled an embarrassed face. 'I was jealous.'

'Jealous of what? When?'

Mitch cringed at the memory. 'When I thought you had a male visitor to the cottage. Reece.'

I started to laugh through a gauze of tears.

'Please don't tell Reece this, but I imagined him to be some suave, city slicker type in his late thirties. You've no idea how relieved I was when I clapped eyes on him and found out he was over eighty and a retired furniture designer.'

This time, we both laughed together before drawing closer again. I knew now that I'd been trying to fight the inevitable.

And as we kissed over and over, huddled together under the twisted, soaked canopy of trees, I knew that Mitch was my here and now – and my future.

Chapter Twenty-Nine

M itch and I spent the next couple of weeks tangled up in bed in his bijoux little bothy.

We made love, laughed, teased each other, ate stollen and other assorted festive fayre, talked and revealed more of ourselves to each other, took the dogs for long, romantic, wintery walks, and all the while struggling to get bed space with Bronte and Kane!

Thankfully, there weren't too many more dramatic storms for Mitch to contend with in the lighthouse, but I would accompany him up there to watch him guide the fishing boats home as the stars shone like tossed diamonds over our heads and the water glinted blueberry black.

Reece came to visit on numerous occasions, bringing tasty treats for Bronte and Kane, and was delighted about Mitch and me. 'You're a young woman still with your whole life ahead of you,' he smiled kindly at me. 'Love your life and live it to the full.'

Christmas was almost here, and I realised I wasn't dreading it anymore. In fact, I was relishing it and looking forward to turning the page on this year and starting the next with renewed hope and optimism.

With Mitch's help, I'd fetched my grandparents' white six-foot imitation Christmas tree down from the loft and bought a new set of rose-gold fairy lights to decorate it with. Grandpa's old set, a tangled-up ball in a carrier bag, no longer worked. I also bought another two sets – one to lace along the top of the garden fence and another to frame the doorway of the bothy.

Mitch wasn't too convinced by the idea, but once he'd tacked them in place and we had a grand switch on, with both Bronte and Kane sitting there transfixed by the comings and goings, he changed his mind.

We'd been pre-occupied, too, with getting everything ready for Grandma's gallery exhibition.

I'd already contacted my solicitor back in London and asked him to set things in motion regarding putting the Hampstead apartment on the market. I'd also started tying up legal proceedings concerning Joe's will. He'd left everything to me.

I wasn't sure how I felt about that but decided to make a contribution to a few charities with it and start a bursary scheme for writers from disadvantaged backgrounds. At least the money would do something positive.

As soon as I'd made a start, it felt like I'd taken a giant step in carving out a different set of memories for myself.

A pang of sadness hit me nonetheless. As it turned out,

Joe had treated not only me badly, but Greta too. She'd fallen for his charm and his lies every bit as much as I had. After some mental to-ing and fro-ing, I obtained her address from Mia and decided to drop her a line. I said in my letter that I'd moved on from everything and that leaving London and coming to Scotland had helped me to find closure. I also told her that I hoped she was able to do the same and that we shouldn't allow what Joe did to taint our lives and follow us around. We were worth more than that, and how he'd decided to behave had no bearing on either of us.

Just a few days after she'd received the letter, Greta sent a reply to Mia for my attention, thanking me so much for reaching out and saying how grateful she was that I'd said what I had. She said the guilt she'd been carrying around after discovering Joe's lies about his marriage, had been on the verge of breaking her. And even though the remaining words of her letter were still full of apology, I sensed a lifting and relief when she wished me well.

In a whirlwind, the 13th December, my late grandma's birthday and the night of her art exhibition came rushing up to greet us.

I'd chosen the twelve paintings to exhibit, the ones I felt best represented her talent and creativity, as well as her personality and passion. They consisted of a couple of the bay at dawn and dusk, a few of her other still life table arrangements featuring a dressing table with a mirror and hairbrushes, some of her chalk drawings of daffodils and lilies, and three of her portraits works of Rowan Bay fishermen tending to their nets or aboard their boats.

A few days before the exhibition, Mitch, with me secreted in his car, had ferried them up to the Lumiere Gallery, with Ruth enthusing over the artwork choices and extolling again how talented he was. Little did she know, but she'd soon find out.

Christmas had arrived in all its splendour to Rowan Bay, with the centre of the town illuminated by its Norwegian tree. The shop windows sparkled with festive decorations and strung up between the lampposts were Santa and his reindeer shining down on the excited, hyped-up faces of the local children.

Last Christmas had haunted me at first. The memories of twelve months ago with Joe, spending a romantic Christmas Day together with warm croissants and Buck's Fizz had been tarnished by the thought of him making excuses to pop out. Even on Christmas Day he'd dashed somewhere and been gone a couple of hours, citing an emergency at his cousin's. I hadn't questioned it at the time, but now, I knew otherwise.

But Mitch had banished the dread that had been consuming me. He'd revealed hope and ripped up my pessimism. He'd made me realise that I deserved to be happy.

It was almost seven o'clock on the evening of the exhibition and the Lumiere Gallery was lit up every bit as much as the centre of Rowan Bay.

Tasteful white and silver festive lights were laced around its panoramic window glistening against the dark, and more lights were entwined through the bare trees situated at each side of the gallery.

The subtle lighting highlighted my grandma's depiction of the lighthouse during a stormy night and was hanging in the gallery window; her passionate brush strokes of the forceful waves made my spine tingle with pride.

If only she could see this now.

I gave an emotional smile. My insides were tumbling over each other, but I assured myself everything would be okay. If I didn't do this for Grandma while I had the chance, I'd regret it, and I'd had enough of regret.

The air inside the gallery was languid with soft panpipes, and the scent of Scottish salmon and seafood canapés intermingled with expensive perfume.

Elegant flutes of champagne were being whirled around on trays by a couple of students suited and booted in black waistcoats, trousers and fitted white shirts.

Exhibition guests ranged from a couple of newspaper reporters and art critics to local dignitaries, councillors and other artists.

There was a rather bored-looking young man checking off names at the door. Getting me inside as Mitch's plus one had been fine, but gaining Reece access had meant conducting a bit of a distraction. We wanted to keep our heads down until we revealed who the real artist of the paintings was.

I'd pretended to lose a contact lens at the entrance and

asked the young man in question to help me look for it. While he'd been stooped over, peering at the snowy step, Mitch had managed to slip Reece inside.

Once the coast was clear and I knew Reece was safely ensconced in the gallery, I'd let out a tinkly laugh. 'Oh, silly me! I'm so sorry! I've just found my lens on my coat collar.' I pretended to angle the non-existent lens into my right eye. A mime artist would've been impressed.

The man at the door pushed out a strained smile. 'At least you found it, miss.'

'How are you feeling?' I hissed out of the corner of my mouth at Mitch, once the three of us had deposited our coats with the cloakroom attendant, a welcoming young woman in glittery eye make-up.

'I've felt better,' he answered with a rueful look.

'To be honest, me too,' I confessed. 'I know all this was my idea, but I'm still nervous.'

'I hope you're not having second thoughts, Rosie.'

'No.'

Mitch attempted to make me laugh. 'I just hope someone doesn't ask me anything too intricate about my artistic technique.' He waggled one brow suggestively.

I grinned up at him. 'Well, I know for a fact that you've been a bit of a swot.'

'What?'

I offered him a knowing look. 'I didn't tell you at the time, but the morning after I got plastered and fell asleep at yours I spotted two art books in your bedroom. You've been reading up and making notes.'

Mitch looked coy. 'Ah.'

I slipped my hand in his and leant up to deliver a kiss on his mouth. 'Just when I think I can't fall for you anymore.'

He smiled playfully against my lips. 'Just keep the kisses coming, Red.'

Red. By coincidence, he'd started using the nickname Barclay had for me since I was a kid. I mentally toasted Barclay and Mags and took a sip of my champagne.

Ruth was holding court on the gallery floor, clutching her champagne glass as she chatted to a couple of older men. One was sporting a pair of round, pillar box red spectacles and the other was dressed in a lime-green waistcoat.

She was decked out in a sharp trouser suit in dove grey.

I kept myself concealed behind Mitch for the time being, while Reece also tried to remain in the background, flitting here and there and helping himself to the canapés.

I didn't want Ruth clocking me as soon as we'd arrived. She would rumble us in no time.

While Mitch shook hands with a couple of the local councillors who congratulated him on his stunning art, I gazed around at my grandma's pieces adorning the claret walls of the gallery.

It was as if the paintings were looking right at me. They were bursting with colour and life, enhanced by the discreet spotlights above them.

My mouth flipped into a smile. What a woman she'd been. So full of creativity and joy, despite her engagement to Reece coming to an abrupt end. Then she'd met my grandfather, devoted herself to him and my mum and allowed her artistic ambitions to slide into more of a hobby.

Now, all these years later, her dreams of having her work exhibited had finally happened – albeit posthumously. I thought about her portraits of her ex-fiancée and her husband. I buried an admiring chuckle.

What a woman!

I just hoped that she was looking down out of that tumble of hair of hers and smiling with pride. She deserved this.

As I'd suggested, there was a nod to her love of butterflies, with tea and coffee being served from butterfly-sprigged crockery.

There were also glasses of Talisker on offer. Tonight was all about my much-loved and much-missed grandma.

I glanced up and noticed that Mitch was watching me. He looked so dashing in his three-piece charcoal suit, grey shirt and lavender tie. A journalist was asking him about his artwork. 'I just follow where my inspiration takes me,' he answered smoothly. 'Now, if you'll excuse me.' He made a beeline for me through the body of people. He whispered into my ear. 'I'm hoping I don't have to bullshit my way through any more questions. I've managed to draw on what I've read up about, on the technique side of things, but I'd prefer if we didn't have to keep this up for much longer.'

I nodded emphatically up at him. 'As soon as Ruth is about to introduce you, that's when we'll come clean.'

My attention lingered on his chiselled, dark looks. Mitch gazed down at me. 'You behave yourself, Ms Winters, otherwise I'll have no alternative but to throw you over my shoulder and take you straight home.'

A frisson of anticipation rocketed through me at one hundred miles an hour. 'Promises, promises.'

Mitch allowed his gaze to rake my piled-up curls and then my knee-length, mint green woollen dress. 'It's not a promise. It's a fact.'

Reece, also looking very dapper in a pin-striped suit, blue shirt, and silver tie, materialised beside us. 'I don't think Cruella de Vil has spotted either of us yet, Rosie.' He took a swig from his flute.

'No, she can't have done, otherwise she would've been straight over, asking what the hell we're doing here. She's too busy schmoozing.'

Despite my nibbling nerves about what would happen this evening and Ruth's reaction to our revelations about the artwork, I was also experiencing bubbles of happiness exploding inside me whenever I looked at Mitch.

And because of that, what happened next was my own fault. I'd been too busy mooning over him and not concentrating on what was happening around me.

I'd allowed myself to drift within Ruth's line of sight without realising I had done so. I'd been too preoccupied making plans for the future. Everything seemed to be slowly slotting into place now, but what about my writing? I hadn't really thought about what I intended to do in the future. My confidence had taken such a devastating knock ever since Joe. I'd had the courage to admit my feelings for

Mitch, but what about my novels? Did I feel brave enough to reconsider that too?

Whilst I was mulling all this over, I inadvertently glanced across and realised with a jolt of horror, that I was in Ruth's eyeline. I moved to duck behind a tall, thin couple who were engaged in animated conversation, but it was too late. Ruth had spotted me. Her smile collapsed.

The woman she'd been chatting to, who I realised was Kirsty Ralston, watched in bemusement as Ruth stalked rudely away from her, mid-conversation.

Shit.

She came storming towards me. 'What are you doing here?' she snapped, her red mouth contorting into a grimace. 'I don't remember you being invited.'

I should've been careful for a little bit longer.

I opened my mouth, willing my brain to come up with something fast, when Mitch emerged at my side. 'Rosie's with me.' He allowed his simple explanation to hang in the air. His expression brooked no argument. 'You said I could bring a plus one on the invitation. Well, Rosie is my plus one.'

There was an embarrassing silence. Ruth's hard eyes scorched into me. 'Oh. I see. Right.'

I noticed out of the corner of my eye, that Reece had spotted what was happening and had managed to dart behind a gentleman in a checked cap who was admiring my grandma's painting of the dressing table still life.

'Hello again,' I said, conjuring up a cool smile for Ruth. She didn't reply.

'So, this is the talented artist?'

The icy exchanges were broken by the man in the red spectacles. He cut through our threesome and shot out one hand towards Mitch. 'Your work really is sublime, Mr Carlisle. It has an old worldly feel about it, which I love.'

Mitch remained unflustered. 'I appreciate that. Thank you.'

The man in the spectacles let out a chuckle. 'Oh, forgive me. I didn't introduce myself. I'm Grant Hefton, art critic for *The Review* magazine.' He gestured at the paintings. 'What art techniques do you prefer to use in your work?'

Mitch carried on. 'Very nice to meet you, Mr Hefton. Well, I tend to enjoy dry brushing. It gives me that scratchy, textured finish when I'm trying to capture the essence and texture of nature: trees, clouds and hedgerows in particular.'

I gazed at him. He really was something special.

But he wasn't finished yet. 'And then, of course, there's gestural painting, where I apply the paint in a series of free, sweeping gestures. It's a great way to show your emotion on the canvas. Jackson Pollock was an advocate.'

Grant Hefton nodded vigorously as he plucked a notebook from his trouser pocket and started jotting down notes.

Mitch gave me a discreet wink.

My heart inflated. God, Grandma Tilda would've fallen in love with Mitch almost as much as I had.

Grant Hefton looked up from his spidery scrawl and was on the point of asking Mitch another question, when a woman with candy-pink hair, wearing a long, fringed, patterned skirt, appeared at Ruth's elbow. She angled her way into the semi-circle. 'Excuse me. Aren't you Ruth Mangan?'

Ruth bathed her in a mega-watt smile. 'Yes, I am. And you are…?'

'Becky Hollis. I'm a journalist with *The Tribune* newspaper.' She offered Ruth a smile that didn't reach her eyes. 'I understand you were an artist yourself back in the day.'

Ruth's expression pinched under her powder. Her demeanour changed in an instant. She started to angle her body away from the journalist. 'Yes, that's right, I was. Now if you'll excuse me.'

But Becky Hollis had Ruth in her sights. Her pixie face morphed into a frowning expression. 'Weren't you accused of trying to take credit for another artist's piece of work?'

The reporter had raised her voice an octave. The thrum of conversation lowered in the gallery and clinking glasses stilled. There were still the panpipes playing, but even they seemed to lower in volume so they could hear what was going on.

One of Ruth's manicured, pale hands flew to her throat. 'I… I don't know what you mean. I… I would never do anything like that.'

Undeterred, Becky continued with her barrage of questions. 'The artist in question decided not to proceed with any legal prosecution, didn't they, Ms Mangan? You were very fortunate.'

Mitch and I stared at one another.

'It was all an unfortunate misunderstanding,' struggled Ruth. 'I explained all this at the time. Now, I really must...'

Becky Hollis was unrepentant. 'Is that why you felt you had no option but to stop painting, Ms Mangan?'

The reporter pinned her to the gallery's shiny, wooden floor with her relentless, kohl-lined, light eyes. 'Because of what you did to sabotage...' She rifled in her bag and pulled out her notebook. She flicked over a few pages. 'Ah. Here it is. Tilda Michaels. You tried to pass off one of her paintings as your own, isn't that right?'

I spun round to look at Becky Hollis. Ruth was struggling to look at me or at the other guests, who were all murmuring amongst themselves. Stunned, I managed to find my voice. 'Did you say Tilda Michaels?'

Becky gave me a quizzical look, as though she'd only just spotted me standing there. 'Yes. Why?'

My eyes blazed at Ruth. What on earth had been going on here? What had this woman done to my grandmother, out of pure jealousy and spite?

It was then that Ruth's hand settled on her chest, like a speckled starfish. The colour seeped out of her cheeks, and as if in slow motion, she began to crumple.

'Ruth!' called out Mitch, dashing forward and catching the fainting woman in his capable arms. 'Quick! Someone grab that chair, please.'

I wanted to drill Ruth Mangan with questions, make her realise that she hadn't achieved anything by being so spiteful; I wanted to reveal to these people what this woman, with the perfect, shimmery, grey bob and husky laugh, was really like, what she was capable of.

And yet, staring at her now, gulping a glass of water in her trembling hands, flopped in a chair like a ragdoll, I knew I couldn't do it. At least not publicly. Everyone was examining her as it was, like something that had been dug up during an archaeological find.

It didn't seem right. I wanted to know the truth. I wanted her to know what I'd discovered about her. But looking at her now, hunched over and taking deep breaths, she appeared old and fragile. What would my grandma do in this situation? I really didn't need to ask myself that question.

'I'm fine,' bleated Ruth to a concerned woman, who was wrapped in a fancy shawl. 'It's just a little warm in here, that's all.'

Becky Hollis sidled up to me. 'Why did you just ask me about Tilda Michaels? Did you know her?'

She seemed oblivious to the wan figure of the older woman in the chair in front of her.

My attention travelled from Mitch, who was now standing talking to Reece, to the puzzled guests. I turned my gaze to my grandma's paintings observing everything from the four walls of the gallery, and then back to a shaken Ruth. She was gripping her glass of water. She raised her sunken eyes and they looked into mine.

The resentment and dislike had gone from them. Her gaze was wide, pleading, vulnerable.

I couldn't do this. I didn't like Ruth and I detested the

way she'd treated my grandmother, but spilling everything out to this journalist, especially one who was showing no guilt or regard for triggering Ruth to faint. Well, it wasn't right.

I attracted Mitch's attention. He muttered something to Reece who nodded.

'Sorry, I was mistaken,' I said to an eager-faced Becky Hollis. I shot Ruth a brief look. 'I thought I recognised the name of the artist you mentioned, but I've just realised I don't.'

The reporter's expression, like an eager bloodhound, faltered. 'But... But you seemed to know her name.'

I shrugged. 'Must have misheard. Sorry.'

She glowered at me from under her pink fringe before snatching up a canapé from a passing waiter and popping it in her mouth. 'I'm not done yet. I want to talk again to Ms Mangan.'

'I think it would be better if you left.' Mitch reappeared beside me. His voice was composed but carried an element of steel.

Becky Hollis's chin jutted out in defiance. 'I'm not leaving until... Hey!' But Mitch had grasped her by the elbow and was steering her through the guests towards the gallery door. He unlocked it and angled her outside. He closed it on her protesting face. 'I'm going to write about you, Mr Carlisle. You won't sell many of your paintings then, I can assure you.'

Mitch shrugged. 'Please feel free to write about me all you want, Ms Hollis. But you need to get your facts straight first. You see, I'm not the artist who painted these pictures.'

She glowered through the glass and wrapped her arms around herself. She looked like a furious fairy in her long, suede, winter coat. 'What are you going on about?'

Mitch pushed his face closer to the door and dropped his voice. 'I'm a lighthouse keeper, not a painter. And I didn't paint those pictures.' Then he gave her a dazzling smile and hauled the long, beige and chocolate curtain over the door to obscure her view.

After a few agitated thumps and kicks of the door from the other side, we heard Becky Hollis squeal away in her car.

Mitch and Reece wandered back over to me.

Ruth stared up at Mitch, a look of confusion rearing in her eyes. 'Thank you. For getting rid of her just now.' She took another gulp of water and rested the glass on her lap.

I turned my head away to talk to Mitch and Reece and lowered my voice. 'I couldn't humiliate her after what just happened. But I do still want to speak to her about Tilda.'

'In private,' nodded Mitch.

'Yes.'

He slid his hand into mine and caressed my fingers. A wave of love gripped me. 'What you did just now – getting rid of that horrible reporter – that was very kind of you,' I said.

Mitch smiled. 'And you could've blabbed to that journalist and really humiliated Ruth. But you didn't.' He gestured his head in Ruth's direction. 'Let's give her a few more minutes to recover and then we could try and speak to her in her office.'

After a few moments, streaks of colour were returning to Ruth's cheeks.

I studied her. 'Are you alright?'

She raised her grey bob. It was flapping onto her face. 'Yes. Thank you.'

I knelt down in front of her, my woollen dress fanning out over my knees. 'Do you feel up to speaking to us? In private? It won't take long.'

Her forlorn eyes felt like they were processing every inch of me. 'Yes. Of course.' Her cheeks blossomed with colour. 'It's the least I can do.'

She rose from her chair and Mitch walked beside her, just in case she felt faint again, although she looked much steadier on her feet now. 'Nothing to see here,' she joked to the faces of the concerned guests watching her. 'Please continue to avail yourselves of the hospitality on offer.'

Taking her at her word, Reece gleefully helped himself to another flute of champagne.

Meanwhile, Mitch, Ruth and I headed to the back of the gallery floor. Ruth encouraged us into her office and clicked the door shut behind her.

Her office was a white affair, with an oval-shaped glass desk, dry reed plants and obscure black-and-white framed paintings of triangles and squares on its walls.

No sooner had Ruth taken up her seat behind her desk and Mitch and I had sat down in the two white leather chairs than I spoke. 'Mitch didn't paint those pictures, Ruth. He's not the artist.'

Her attention pinged from me to Mitch and back again. 'Sorry?'

'It's true,' admitted Mitch. 'I don't paint. Well, a lick of emulsion in the lighthouse.'

Ruth's mouth popped open. She looked from me to Mitch and back again as though struggling to understand what was playing out here. 'Then if you didn't paint those pictures, who did?'

I levelled my gaze at her. 'My grandmother.'

Ruth's red lipstick, which had faded somewhat, twisted into a stricken O shape. 'But... But ... Mitch ... you said...'

'No, I didn't say anything. You just assumed I painted them.'

She started to clasp and unclasp her hands. Her shoulders sank under her well-cut suit.

Through her office door, I could hear fervent murmurs of conversation and the tinkling of champagne glasses.

'I don't believe you,' she insisted, though the tremble in her voice was telling us otherwise.

'What's my grandmother's art signature?' I asked.

Ruth blinked at me.

'She never autographed her work in the usual way, but she did always paint a tiny image of something somewhere obscure in all of her pieces. What was it?'

Ruth pressed her lips together. She shuffled in her office chair. 'A butterfly. A small, yellow one.'

Mitch jerked his head. 'Go and take a look at her

paintings, if you don't believe us. In fact, go and check the front right table leg of the French-themed breakfast watercolour that's on display just outside this office.'

Ruth rose up from behind her desk and straightened the hem of her jacket.

She stalked past us and opened her office door, letting in bursts of laughter and conversation. She was only gone a matter of seconds.

Ruth returned and clicked the door closed again behind her. She was having difficulty looking at either Mitch or me. She resumed her seat and hooked some hair back behind her right ear. 'I just saw it,' she managed. 'The butterfly.'

'I was planning on making a big reveal of this,' I admitted to Ruth. Her stunned expression was trained on me. 'I was intending on embarrassing you, making you feel small, like you did with Tilda all those years ago. But when you fainted just now, I couldn't do it.'

Ruth swallowed and dropped her eyes to her glass desk.

'I was all set on revealing who the real artist was in front of all of those people. I wanted to show everyone how talented Tilda was. I also wanted to make you realise how petty and jealous you are. But then … well…' I adjusted myself in the leather chair. 'We know how talented she was. I don't have to yell it from the rooftops.'

Guilt controlled Ruth's expression.

'My grandma wouldn't have wanted me to humiliate you like that. She wasn't malicious.'

Ruth looked like she wanted to slither under her desk and vanish. She toyed with her swan dress ring, twisting it over and over. She bored her attention into her own hands for what seemed like ten minutes before finally forcing herself to look up at me again. 'What that reporter said was true.' She licked her lips. 'I did try to pass off one of your grandma's paintings as my own. I don't know what I was thinking.'

I sat up straighter in my chair. 'What happened? Why did you do it?'

Ruth rubbed at her face. 'It was over forty years ago now. I wanted to win this prestigious artist award, but although my work was good, it wasn't a patch on your grandma's art.'

'So, you decided to steal one of Tilda's pieces?' asked Mitch beside me.

Ruth blanched. 'I'm so sorry. She'd painted the most beautiful impression of Rowan Bay harbour. It was the stillness and the atmosphere she'd created. I couldn't compete with that.'

I eyed her. 'What happened?'

Ruth kept putting her hands to rest on top of her desk and then removing them again. It was as if she didn't know what to do with herself. 'I submitted my application with a picture of your grandma's painting and I pretended I was the artist.'

Colour illuminated her cheeks. 'But what I didn't know was that one of the judges was the sister of one of your grandma's friends. She spotted the yellow butterfly insignia and she knew straight away I hadn't painted it.'

Mitch flicked me a charged look. 'What happened when Tilda discovered what you'd done?'

Ruth tried to keep her voice calm. 'She was furious, and rightly so. Of course, she was. Anyone would've been.'

'But?' I probed.

Ruth let out a painful sigh. 'But she said she wouldn't take things further if I promised to make a significant donation to a charity she supported, helping working-class children to enter the arts.' Ruth paused. 'My parents were very comfortable. They owned their own interior design business.' Guilt tore through her lined eyes. 'I was so jealous of Tilda. Of her talent, of her looks, of her as a person.'

I angled my head to one side. 'Jealous, also, because she was married to my grandfather?'

She stiffened and looked away. 'Yes.' Her words sounded like they were about to crumble, but she fought to keep it together. 'I loved my husband, but he wasn't in love with me. I deluded myself by thinking he was.' She swallowed. 'Jacob only married me for what he could get out of me. He knew my parents had money and he wanted a slice of the good life.' She tried to compose herself. 'Then Tilda and Howard moved to Rowan Bay, and I was smitten with this gorgeous, kind, funny man who loved to play rugby and go fishing down by the harbour.' Her smile wobbled. 'Howard had the most twinkly eyes I'd ever seen.' She shook her head. 'But your grandfather never gave me so much as a second glance. He was only ever in love with one woman and that was your grandma.' Her voice finally broke. 'I was eaten up with envy. It consumed me. This charismatic, lovely young woman had moved to the area and everyone admired her and her art. I couldn't deal with it. I became someone I didn't like, but it was as if I couldn't help myself.'

I glanced over at Mitch.

Ruth pushed a lock of hair back behind one ear. 'There was Tilda Michaels, this stunning young woman with the flame red curls and the artistic talent to match, married to a man I adored. She seemed to have everything.' Her fingers laced and unlaced themselves. 'And so, I decided that she wasn't going to get everything her own way.' Tears glistened in Ruth's eyes. 'I tried to make her feel unwelcome here, never included her in anything, drove her out of the local artists' society, I even tried to spread some gossip about her.' She blanched with embarrassment.

Mitch and I watched Ruth, the confessions tumbling out of her, then she suddenly shot up from behind her desk.

Without a word, she made straight towards her office door, opened it and stepped out towards the exhibition guests.

'Ruth?' I called after her, scraping my chair behind me. 'What are you doing?'

She didn't answer.

Mitch and I picked up speed and followed her back out into the gallery.

Ruth drew up. She stood there in her shiny, dark court shoes as my grandma's paintings shone down on her from the art gallery walls.

Outside, there was a flurry of snow spinning down from the black sky.

Ruth looked lost in her own thoughts. Then she thrust up one hand. 'Ladies and gentlemen, could I have your attention for a few moments, please?'

The talk and bubbles of laughter died down. Someone clicked off the music wafting from the sound system.

Reece spotted us and came dashing over and hissed. 'What's going on?'

Mitch slid one supportive arm around my waist. 'I think it might be confession time.'

Ruth waited until all sets of eyes were focused on her. Outside the gallery, the December snow continued to waltz down and settle over the roads and pavements.

I noticed her shoulders stiffen under her fitted suit jacket. She took in one long inhalation of air before she spoke. 'Mitch Carlisle didn't paint these beautiful pictures that are all around you.' She pushed out her jaw. 'It was a lady by the name of Tilda Michaels.'

The guests swapped frowns and confused looks.

'And the sad thing is, if I'd known at the time that Tilda had painted them, I would never have offered to exhibit them.' She paused. 'And that would have been a travesty.'

She composed herself and carried on. 'And the reason why I wouldn't have exhibited her paintings is because I was jealous of her. Both professionally and for personal reasons.' She flapped one hand in the air. I could see tears shimmering in her eyes. 'I was eaten up with envy, because Tilda was everything I wasn't.'

The guests exchanged more looks between each other as they listened avidly.

Ruth gestured at the watercolours on the walls, lit up by the spotlights. 'As you can see for yourselves, the late Tilda Michaels was such a unique and passionate artist. All her paintings show her talent and what a genuine person she was.' Ruth took a deep breath. 'I don't feel at all proud of the way I behaved towards Tilda. I did everything I could to make her feel unwelcome here in Rowan Bay. There was and is no excuse for it.' Ruth turned to me. Her face was etched with regret. 'I just hope that Rosie here, Tilda's granddaughter, can accept my heartfelt apology. I don't deserve it, but I'm begging for it.'

And with that, Ruth left the stunned crowd and headed straight back into her office and shut the door behind her.

The gallery was stunned into silence before bursts of chatter about what had just happened filled the air.

I waited a few seconds. 'I'd better go and see if she's okay.' Reece and Mitch lingered with the other guests.

I approached the office door and tapped on it. 'Ruth? It's Rosie.'

There was no answer.

'Ruth?'

Still nothing. I pushed my face closer to the closed door and tried the handle. It was locked. 'Ruth, please let me in. We need to talk. We should clear the air.' I let out a frustrated sigh. 'Do you know that today is her birthday? Thirteenth December.'

For a few moments there was nothing, and then I

thought I detected the faint sound of sniffling from the other side of the door.

Finally, there was the sound of the key in the lock and the door eased open.

I slid inside and closed the door behind me.

Ruth sat back down, hunched in her chair, her lit black and silver desk lamp casting shadows down the planes of her taught face.

'We all have to move on,' I commented, smoothing my dress as I sat opposite her. Pictures of Joe cartwheeled through my mind. 'We can't live in the past, however much we want to.'

Her attention drifted out of her office window, where we could see slivers of snow through the partially closed, wooden blinds. The amber street lamps lit up the snow, and it looked so festive.

'My grandma harboured a dream for years that she might one day have her work exhibited, but she kept it to herself, and if any of us asked her about it, she'd laugh it off and deny it.' I studied her. 'I only found out her true ambition after she passed away, when I stumbled across journals she'd kept.'

Ruth's haunted expression met my solemn one.

'This was the only way we could get her work in here, by pretending that Mitch had painted those pictures and not her.'

Ruth looked shamefaced.

'Grandma often mentioned what a gorgeous gallery this was and she'd name the artists who'd been fortunate enough to have their work exhibited here.' I leant forward. 'You obviously were deeply in love with my grandfather.'

She swallowed and looked away, back out at the snow swirling against the dark.

Pictures of Joe and the apartment in Hampstead, our married life together, us dancing to our first song at our wedding – 'Everywhere' by Fleetwood Mac – which we used to belt out in the car, him becoming hoarse shouting instructions to the TV for the football referee, Joe making me laugh with his impersonation of Owen Wilson; they were packed away now. They'd meant so much at the time, but they weren't treasured memories anymore. They were no longer real to me.

Mitch was.

I stood up and moved to leave Ruth's office.

I cranked open the office door.

Ruth rose up from her desk and walked slowly towards me. Her papery voice carried around her office. 'Thank you. I mean it.' She jammed her lips together to try and stop herself from crying. 'You're a credit to Tilda and Howard. They both would've been so proud of you.'

Then, to my surprise, she opened her arms and tentatively embraced me.

I gave a fleeting smile and departed her office.

Mitch spotted me and approached. He took me in his arms and delivered the most tender kiss on my mouth.

Reece squeezed my shoulder and as the snow continued to spin down from the sky, I knew that being with Mitch here in Rowan Bay was where I was meant to be all along.

Epilogue

December, twelve months later

I bristled with anticipation. Then I realised I was grinning.

With one excited, nervous finger, I pressed 'Send' and watched my new, feel-good romance, *The Lighthouse at Rowan Bay*, make its way to Mia.

Mitch has reignited in me my belief in love and romance. He'd made me realise, over the last few months, that I had missed being an author and how much it meant to me, that I wasn't Rosie Winters without it. With this had also come clarity. All that time, Joe had made me think that I had to have him in my life, in order to write. He'd gaslighted me, made me believe that he was the source of my ability.

Now, I knew differently.

You can imagine how delighted both Mia and Lola

were to hear that I'd decided to return to my romance writing. They both insisted they'd been sure I could never have given up on it – not really – but I think underneath it all, at the time they had been concerned I meant it. Which I did.

I've now got a brand-new, three-book deal from my publishers, so that will keep me out of mischief for a while!

Mitch and I, along with Kane and Bronte, are settled together and now all live in my grandparent's cottage. It's rather chaotic, with our two fur babies bounding about, but it's convenient for Mitch for his lighthouse duties; the views over the bay and the harbour are spectacular and very inspirational for my writing and I wouldn't have it any other way. We were two very broken people who found each other, and I'm so happy we did.

There are so many wonderful memories of my mum, dad and grandparents built into these walls, and we hope to be adding to them day by day.

I've converted Grandma's studio into my writing room, but I made sure it still retains traces of her. The ornamental butterflies remain on the shelf above the fireplace, and Mitch put up three of my personal favourite paintings of hers on the walls. I kept her old desk; Mitch and I cleaned it up and it still resides in its original place.

She'd be happy to know that her granddaughter is using it now for her own artistic endeavours!

The gorgeous, towering, strong and dependable lighthouse means even more to us now than it did before. It's as if it showed Mitch and me the way, not just the shipping vessels and boats which rely on it to reach home safely.

Mitch and Romilly's decree nisi was confirmed in June. Romilly is marrying her fiancé, Oscar, in the spring. It looks like moving on and making new lives is catching.

The apartment in Hampstead was sold in March and all the legal papers have now been filed away. Another chapter of my life has ended.

Reece comes to visit us regularly from Edinburgh and Mitch and I have visited him in the capital. We have a link now, an invisible bond that binds us together with my much-missed grandma, and I know that link will never break. The love we both had for her, and still have, remains real and alive.

Ruth still owns the Lumiere Gallery and has just launched her latest exhibition. It's by an up-and-coming young artist by the name of Noah Colton…

It transpired that Noah returned to painting after his accident at Mitch's former outdoor activity centre and was also undertaking an Open University art degree course too.

One night a few months back, Mitch was talking again about Noah and what happened, so I did a bit of detective work, reached out to Noah through the magic of social media and discovered that the young man had decided to take up art again.

I then contacted Ruth, explained the situation and things moved quickly from there.

This has all put Mitch's conscience a little more at ease.

Ruth is moving on with her life now and is doing

everything she can to accept herself for who she is, and that's all any of us can do. In fact, she and Reece seem to have become good friends, and he has been more than happy to help out at the gallery whenever he comes up for a few days.

Lola has been promoted to Editorial Director, which she is thrilled about, and as for Mia – well, she's fallen hard for one of her new authors, a dashing American crime writer. Her air miles to and from New York are piling up, but James is a lovely guy and I couldn't be happier for them.

I kept my word and I'm keeping in touch with Joe's parents. I know they feel somehow responsible for what happened, but Joe's decision to have an affair was his and his alone. Things will always be a bit odd between Nancy, Jeremy and I from now on. The dynamics have changed. But I've moved on and I've told them they have to as well.

But the best news of all is that Mitch and I are about to get married! Yes, even on my wedding day, I'm tying up some loose ends because I wanted to get my latest book fired off to Mia. I suppose it feels like another new chapter beginning.

We wanted a small, simple affair, but Reece and Ruth had other ideas…

It's the twenty-second of December, and Rowan Bay Church is decked out with garlands of holly, ivy, pine cones and berries.

Everyone is here to see Mitch and me start our married life together. Mia, Lola, Ruth and Reece of course, together with Barclay, Mags and all the other locals who have become such an important part of our lives – even Rhea Stafford!

After Mitch's daring rescue of Rhea she apologised to me for being so nosey during our fraught conversation in her corner shop when I first arrived in Rowan Bay, and I apologised too for being so prickly. She would always miss her Freddie, she told me, but that day when she'd fallen in the sea, brought clarity that she wanted to live her life for both her and her husband. Sometimes it takes a moment like that to make you realise what's important in life.

Everyone is wearing festive-coloured outfits. Mia and Lola look stunning as my two bridesmaids in their fitted, satin, knee-length cranberry boat neck dresses and matching bolero jackets.

I did invite Nancy and Jeremy, but they politely declined. As Joe's parents and after what he did, I would've been surprised if they had accepted. But they sent a lovely letter to Mitch and me, wishing us all the happiness for the future and hoping that I'd keep in touch with them.

Even Kane and Bronte look resplendent, trotting down the church aisle ahead of me, Kane sporting a red bow tie and Bronte a gorgeous big pink bow tied around her neck.

A series of laughs, gasps and comments reverberate around the church.

I breathe in and smooth down my ankle-length, high-necked ivory wedding dress. The air is frosty, but winter sunshine drizzles in through the stained-glass windows. I adjust my faux fur cape around my shoulders. I have a single, white tea rose clipped into my loose hair and the bouquet I'm clutching with happy but nervous fingers is a mixture of white lilies and white and cream roses.

On either side of me are Barclay and Reece. I couldn't decide which one of them I wanted to walk me down the aisle, so I decided to be greedy and have both of them! They are both channelling James Bond in their dark suits and sharp ties.

And waiting for me down at the altar is Mitch. He looks so, so handsome in a navy and beige checked three-piece suit with a tweed tie.

He mouths, 'You're beautiful,' and my heart zings as I clip towards him in my white, Victorian-style ankle boots.

The ceremony is over in a flash, confetti is thrown and when I toss my bouquet over my shoulder Mia elbows every other person out the way and catches it. She lets out a delighted 'Whoop!' which makes James laugh and wink at her enigmatically.

Then the photographs are taken.

Once that's done, I slip away for a few moments to place a couple of flowers from my bouquet on my grandparents' grave and spend a few quiet moments with them. I tell them how much I love them and that they're always with me. I also say to my grandma that I hope her exhibition did her proud and that Ruth is so sorry for the awful way she treated her.

I decide to keep a few flowers from my bouquet and press them so I can put them in a little frame at my parents' resting place in Ealing. I'll take Mitch there when we go for a visit after Christmas.

I've only just returned to the church when Reece and Ruth take hold of Mitch and me. We've no idea what's happening!

We find ourselves being led around the back of the church and past its glinting, jewel-like windows on a short but mysterious journey.

'Now close your eyes, both of you,' Reece instructs.

We do as we are told. 'Now, open your eyes, but keep them trained ahead,' said Ruth next, excitement rising in her voice.

Mitch and I gaze out at the shimmering horizon of the water and the frill of the cliffs.

'Okay,' says Reece. 'Now turn to your right.'

We do as we're told, and there stands the biggest, prettiest marquee I've ever seen, strung in rose-gold fairy lights.

The flaps to the marquee are open and we can see tables and chairs inside. There are gorgeous Christmassy centrepieces on each table made up of festive candles and holly and huge red ribbons are tied to the back of every chair in enormous bows. More lights are laced around the roof of the marquee and mobile heaters are stationed around to keep the wedding party cozy.

Mitch and I gawp at one another. It looks like something out of a fairytale.

'Do you like it?' asks Ruth.

'We wanted to surprise you both,' adds Reece with a bashful smile.

I'm finding it hard to talk. 'But we thought we were just having a quiet reception in the town hall.'

'Ha! As if,' chuckles Reece.

We hug them. 'It's beautiful,' I breathe, struggling for words.

Mitch gives Ruth a kiss on the cheek and Reece a slap on the back. 'No wonder you two have been acting strange lately.'

'No stranger than usual,' jokes Reece, offering Ruth a delighted smile.

We greet the guests as they meander in, marvelling at the Christmas-themed beauty of it. Even Kane and Bronte, who are noshing on some kibble Rhea has fed them, seem impressed by it all.

Then Mitch steers me out of the marquee. The bay is gliding and whispering below.

He smooths his tie down in the sea breeze. 'I got you this, Mrs Carlisle.'

I gaze down at the glittery, grey box wrapped in a silver ribbon which he has just plucked from his suit trouser pocket and has handed to me. 'But we've already given each other those gorgeous crystal whiskey glasses.' I grin. 'I think that was your idea of a warped joke. But I promise I won't end up in the same delicate state as last time.'

Mitch laughs, making his eyes crinkle in the December afternoon light. 'Don't make promises you can't keep.' He indicates to the box. 'Well, go on. Open it.'

'What is it?'

He rolls his eyes.

I gently tug the ribbon and slide off the box lid.

Nestled inside against electric blue velvet, is a delicate lighthouse pendant on a gold chain, an exact replica of the lighthouse in Rowan Bay.

One of my hands flies to my throat.

'I had it made for you,' explains Mitch, his voice hoarse with emotion. 'I like to think that the lighthouse brought us together. It showed us the way.'

I lift up my hair and Mitch fastens it around my neck. 'I love it,' I say, my hand stroking it as it rests against the lace of my dress.

And as we kiss, over and over, to the sounds of our guests cheering and clapping us from inside the marquee, I know I've fallen back in love all over again, not only with writing, but with life – thanks to this wonderful, amazing man.

I've also learnt that nothing stays the same and we're all much stronger than we think, no matter who we are, where we come from or what we believe.

Here's to love, life and the future.

Acknowledgments

Huge thanks as always to my amazing editor, Jennie Rothwell. She sprinkles her fairy dust over my writing and never fails to make magic! Thank you too, to Nicola Doherty, for her wonderful line editing skills, advice and gorgeous comments and to Federica Leonardis for her copywriting prowess. Grateful thanks to Caroline Scott-Bowden for her proofreading talents. It is all much appreciated.

Thanks also to all the team at One More Chapter and HarperCollins for being the best in the business.

Grateful thanks also to my wonderful agent, Selwa Anthony, and to Linda Anthony. I'm so lucky to have you!

Love also to my boys and to my fur baby, Cooper.

To all of you who buy and read my books – it means the world. Thank you.

And a special mention to gorgeous little Rosie Brindley-Heneghan, my namesake inspiration for author Rosie. This book is for you, from your Auntie Julie. Hope you enjoy reading it – when you're older!

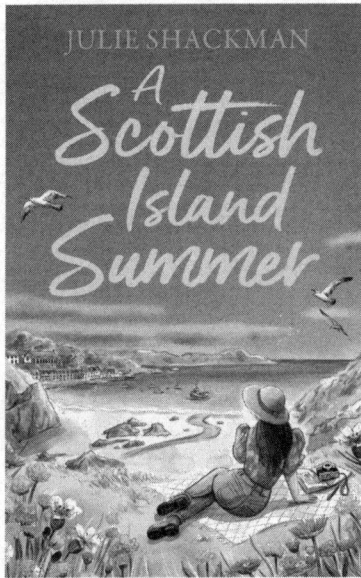

When city girl **Darcie Freeman** is sent to the Isle of Skye to conduct research for a travel guide, she's horrified. The prospect of having to travel to a remote island in the Scottish Highlands leaves her wondering what she'll do. Step in **Logan Burns**. Gorgeous and adventurous, he lives and breathes the island and is going to show Darcie everything she needs to know about Skye.

As Darcie swaps her designer shoes for her walking boots, will she learn there's more to life than the picture-perfect presence she shares on social media, or will it be the case that Skye is the limit…

Available now in paperback and ebook!

ONE MORE CHAPTER

YOUR NUMBER ONE STOP

FOR PAGETURNING BOOKS

The author and One More Chapter would like to thank everyone who contributed to the publication of this story...

Analytics
James Brackin
Abigail Fryer

Audio
Fionnuala Barrett
Ciara Briggs

Contracts
Laura Amos
Laura Evans

Design
Lucy Bennett
Fiona Greenway
Liane Payne
Dean Russell

Digital Sales
Laura Daley
Lydia Grainge
Hannah Lismore

eCommerce
Laura Carpenter
Madeline ODonovan
Charlotte Stevens
Christina Storey
Jo Surman
Rachel Ward

Editorial
Kara Daniel
Charlotte Ledger
Federica Leonardis
Ajebowale Roberts
Jennie Rothwell
Caroline Scott-Bowden
Sofia Salazar Studer
Helen Williams

Harper360
Jennifer Dee
Emily Gerbner
Ariana Juarez
Jean Marie Kelly
emma sullivan
Sophia Wilhelm

International Sales
Peter Borcsok
Ruth Burrow
Colleen Simpson
Ben Wright

Inventory
Sarah Callaghan
Kirsty Norman

Marketing & Publicity
Chloe Cummings
Grace Edwards

Operations
Melissa Okusanya
Hannah Stamp

Production
Denis Manson
Simon Moore
Francesca Tuzzeo

Rights
Helena Font Brillas
Ashton Mucha
Zoe Shine
Aisling Smyth
Lucy Vanderbilt

Trade Marketing
Ben Hurd
Eleanor Slater

The HarperCollins Distribution Team

The HarperCollins Finance & Royalties Team

The HarperCollins Legal Team

The HarperCollins Technology Team

UK Sales
Isabel Coburn
Jay Cochrane
Sabina Lewis
Holly Martin
Harriet Williams
Leah Woods

And every other essential link in the chain from delivery drivers to booksellers to librarians and beyond!